The Watchmaker

'Reverse Polish'

Chris Bailey

2017

THE WATCHMAKER
'REVERSE POLISH'

First published in Great Britain in 2017

Genre: Thriller, Mystery, Conspiracy, Suspense, Crime, Murder, Adventure

Acknowledgements:

I would like to dedicate this book to my Mum,
my Dad, my two boys
John and Oliver, and to Denise, my wife.
Oh, yes, and Olly the dog ☺

Chapter 1

William Harland paused momentarily as he read the last few words of the story that had kept his attention for the last hour, broken by occasional sips from a larger than average glass of port. It was September 1891, and unseasonably cool and wet. A crackle of hot wood pierced the almost-silence that was shrouded by the constant peel of rain outside on the cobbled street below. Harland looked up, and his mouth opened almost smiling as he began to speak.

"Victoria my darling, you really must read..." His voice tailed off almost as he began, as he realised the seat opposite was empty.

For one blessed moment he had forgotten that Victoria, his wife of seven years, was dead, and had been for this past year or more. Indeed, it was soon to be the anniversary of her death, a fact that he had been trying to avoid acknowledging in his own mind.

Harland's smile turned to a sort of twisted scowl, somewhere between anger and despair. "Villains." he spoke out loud, "Vermin!" He swiped his arm across the small side table, knocking his port glass into the fireplace, where it splintered into a hundred pieces.

He sat and stared at the reflections of firelight in the broken glass for more than a few minutes, by which time he had recovered some composure. For that hour, as he read 'Scandal in Bohemia' in his favourite

Strand Magazine, he had seemed to have been back in this very same drawing room with his beloved Victoria, enjoying an evening of reading by the fire together, as they had done so many times before. Her favourite book still sat on the matching side table by her chair on the opposite side of the fire, where they would often sit like two bookends in the evenings. It had not been moved, save for dusting, since that day – the day she was taken from him. Her handkerchief, monogrammed 'V.J.' for Victoria Jane, laid folded alongside. Harland had not come to terms with the death of his wife. The fact that those responsible might never be identified or punished meant that he would never be able to forget what they did – or blame himself less for not being there that night.

Harland walked across his carpeted drawing room, and picked up yesterday's Times newspaper. Returning to the fireplace, he carefully gathered up the pieces of broken glass onto the pages. Perhaps not that carefully however – a single drop of blood pattered on the paper like a rain-drop, as Harland suddenly felt the sting of a razor sharp slither of glass pierce his skin. It might easily have been surmised that this was a pure chance event, perhaps even an inevitable consequence of Harland's outburst, yet there is much in life that cannot be explained by mere randomness of events, which some would call fate, and others Karma.

Harland studied the column of text upon which the blood spots had came to rest, and then proceed to tear off the section, placing it folded in half upon the mantle beside a black-framed picture of his Victoria.

Harland then put on his heavy overcoat, and took a hat from the stand next to the old grandfather clock in the hall. He stepped out into the rain, closing the door behind him as the clock began to chime midnight.

Chapter 2

It was a few days later, when William found himself reflecting upon those events, as he sat in his workshop polishing a recently re-assembled silver pocket-watch brought in for cleaning and repair a few days earlier. Outside the familiar sound of a barrel organ drifted in through the top window light. The cacophony of chimes from the numerous clocks on display in the shop had just petered out, and William knew that his valued client Sir Bertram Overard would be calling to collect the now pristine watch which he had just placed back in its velvet lined and leather-bound travelling case.

The shop bell rang out, and Harland's assistant, Frederick, could be heard offering subservient greetings to the caller. Harland quickly stepped through and joined the group.

"Sir Bertram, good-day to you. I have your timepiece ready, it is in perfect order."

"Thank you Mr Harland, I am sure it is indeed, after your careful attention. Tell me sir, how do you fare?"

"I fare as well as I can sir." Harland answered.

There was a momentary awkward silence. In truth, his enquiry was not mere social politeness. Sir Bertram was minded of the recent tragedy, but this was an unspoken concern and it seemed insensitive to refer to it directly, yet to ignore the circumstances would be too cold a demeanour for Sir Bertram's generous nature.

"And your work Sir?, these magnificent clocks ... and this curiosity of yours. When will it be complete?" Sir Bertram waved his hand toward the large contraption in the corner of the shop, displayed within a glass paned cabinet.

"I fear Sir Bertram, this may never be operated as originally intended. It is a work of complexity which I have yet to fathom fully. They used to say that Babbage was mad – but everything of this mere fragment, salvaged from his great endeavour, speaks of a genius who was simply born before his time." Harland's spirits seemed to lift momentarily, almost becoming excitable. "If only I could see a full drawing of the machine ... but it is feared they are lost for ever."

"Indeed, it is beyond my reach to fathom," Sir Bertram added, "the machinations of the political world are puzzling enough for me. But, as an ornament, it is a thing of wonder – have faith - you may yet succeed."

Overard inspected the pocket watch, now presented to him on the counter, in its open travel case. He closed it, and picked it up from the counter.

"I am most glad you could repair this, it was handed down from my grandfather. There was a recollection that he bought it whilst on one of his diplomatic trips to Sweden. I believe it is quite an antiquity – no doubt old age was to blame for its demise."

Harland nodded. "That's quite probable Sir Bertram,

it is in fact a Lindquist Fusee, about 130 years old, made in the city of Stockholm I believe. No doubt it was already quite old when your grandfather obtained it. There is an unfathomably small winding chain within. I have repaired a broken link, and cleaned and lubricated all parts most carefully."

Sir Bertram looked pleased to hear his family story confirmed. "My watch looks quite excellent. Please, send on your invoices and I will pay them without hesitation. Now, I will bid you good day – I have a vote to attend at noon in The Commons, and a rather important one at that."

Sir Bertram left the shop, followed by his wife, who said little but often nodded out of politeness during her husband's conversations. Harland could hear them talking outside the shop, however, as they waited for their carriage driver to open the doors.

"He is such a charming fellow, yet he seems crestfallen – not the man he was when last we called upon his premises," said Mrs Overard.

"And should he be in high spirits my dear? After that abominable outrage! His wife taken from him in such a way. Damn the murderers, and hang them if they are ever caught. Somehow I doubt they will be, though it pains me to say it."

Harland was used to such overheard narratives. His Wife's murder had been the talk of London for many weeks after the event, and still after a year it was whispered around the doors of Martcombe Road, where many craftsmen and high-class traders had their shops, and of which Harland's *Horological Emporium* was known as one of the most magnificent. Harland himself was not spared the suspicion of idle and malicious gossip. Even the ensuing police investigation had sought to point the finger at him. Only the fact that he had been in York on business had ruled him out of any enquiries, but much time had been wasted before pursuing the true perpetrators.

In the shop, Harland carefully completed an entry in his invoice ledger for the watch, then returned to his workshop, and sat once again at his desk. He then set about checking the several gazettes and periodicals he had instructed Frederick to collect earlier in the morning. He followed his weekly routine religiously – checking the copy in each advertisement he had placed for the Horological Emporium, and then compile a list of his competitors advertisements for future reference. Occasionally he would cut out and retain an advert if significant, and place it in the cigar box upon his desk. He had followed this routine ever since his apprentice days under Jeremiah Varey, and he had enjoyed the perk of being able to read all of the publications avidly after work, as each new batch was procured. Harland was therefore extremely well read and prodigiously versed in matters of the day, and had amassed an encyclopaedic knowledge of watch and clock makers across the London boroughs, their specialisms and peculiarities, and the numerous miscellany in which they traded. Harland wrapped the new magazines in brown paper, ready to take home in the evening. Then he looked to his cigar box. Soon he was deep in thought as he pondered the ragged newspaper cutting held in his hand, and the small red blood stain that seemed so serendipitously placed as to mock the idea of happenstance.

Chapter 3

"Mister Speaker, if I may ... if I ... oh very well, I will give way to the honourable member this once." A cacophony of jeers, balderdash, and general muttering subsided to a murmur, as the Minister for Defence and Procurement sat down and Sir Bertram Overard cleared his throat, order paper in hand, and began to speak from the third row of the government benches in the House of Commons. An expectant silence fell over the chamber, only broken by the creak of leather upholstery on the benches arranged to either side.

"Mister Speaker, can the right honourable member really be saying that Her Majesty's Royal Naval Forces are not in need of a serious and urgent renewal of their capabilities – a fact that can be seen with our own eyes – and indeed observed also through more conspicuous others." This remark was perceived as rather sarcastic and it was drew a flush of laughs from the Members of Parliament sitting at the debate. Overard paused to allow their reaction to underline his barbed comment.

"Through such eyes we have seen that our continental cousins are hard at work building some of the best ships the British Navy can design!"

This last remark caused an uproar of both laughter and derision from the opposing benches. The German Navy's rumoured new Fifth Fleet was of course the main topic of conversation at Westminster, and as everyone knew, the mystery surrounding the Kaiser Willhelm's rapidly improved naval engineering over the past three years was no longer an enigma, but now known to be a result of one of the most audacious spying episodes of recent memory. The fact that the perpetrator of this subterfuge had managed to escape not once, but twice, from the grasp of the authorities, and had now disappeared without trace, was as much a cause of embarrassment as the theft itself: of numerous key naval inventions over a near ten year period. However, the fact that in spite of this debacle the British Government was determined to abandon the Naval Defence act of 1889, and curtail spending on new naval technology for the foreseeable future, was an anathema to Sir Bertram. To him, and to many others, this was a worse act of treason than the prostitution of the navy's best intellectual assets to the German state for financial gain by 'persons unknown'.

It was for this reason that Sir Bertram Overard stood on his feet attacking his own party, and his own government's cabinet ministers, over the whole damned affair. It would do his popularity among those benches little good, but he already had more enemies than friends there – loneliness is often the cost of principles and patriotism, as he was fond of saying.

"For the benefit of the less informed members of this house, let me highlight the German Navy's mercurial growth. Indeed, in the last two years alone, we have witnessed the bringing into service of the *Frithjof* and the *Beowulf*, the *Heimdal* and the *Hildebrand*, the

Kurfürst Friedrich Wilhelm, the *Brandenburg*, the *Weissenburg*, the *Wörth*, the *Kaiserin Augusta*, the *Bussard, Falke, Seeadler, Cormoran*, and the *Condor*, the *Meteor* and the *Comet*, and indeed various other vessels. We see all of this investment in naval power for a country that has barely a fraction of the coastline of Great Britain, and only a shadow of our overseas territories. One wonders if there are enough ports in Germany to fit them all in. Though, I suspect the intention is to find ports in other places, with or without the welcome of those states. One thing we can be sure of, if we decide to pursue this bill's disastrous emasculation of our sea prowess, Kaiser Wilhelm will not follow our lead into disarmament but simply seek to multiply his advantage further."

Sir Bertram sat down, having delivered his broadside with all cannons, and listened intently to the stock answer he well expected to hear, in spite of his intervention. The answer was of little purpose, for he asked the question only to remind the house of the context of the Naval Spending Review Bill on which the house was about to vote. There was feint hope of swaying the bill, but this was a last throw of the dice in a long fought rear-guard action, which had started over two years ago. The response was predictably defensive.

"The honourable member may well wish to air his anti-German sentiments in this house once more, but I have to remind him again that there is simply no direct evidence of German involvement in the affair to which he alludes. Let us not forget that our own gracious majesty Queen Victoria is indeed a close relation of Kaiser Wilhelm, it would hardly be appropriate for us to declare hostilities – even if only as a war of words, upon our dear friends in continental Europe. The bill is presented for the reform of naval spending, and I move that we commend it to the house with no further delay."

Eventually, after due process, the speaker called for a division, and members began moving to the lobbies to register their ayes or nays, with arguments breaking out in small groups as they shuffled forward.

Not much later, Sir Bertram stood in the main entrance hall of the parliament buildings, with several of his like-minded colleagues.

"So gentlemen – we have lost and they have their bill, the Naval forces will not be embellished by so much as a brass whistle, and all the while 'our cousin Wilhelm' builds a fleet to rival our best ships. It won't end well."

Overard tapped his cane on the tiled floor as if to underline his indignation. "But as we know gentleman, parliament is not really the place to find foresight – we must obtain that for ourselves – perhaps now is the time for us to consider moving our strategy forward, eh? Let us meet tonight for dinner, at my apartments, and then discuss our next move in a little more privacy."

Overard could not fail to observe the sneers from one or two of his fellow party members looking over at his small gathering. He may have lost one or two 'friends' today, but there was a longer game to be played, and the 'Britannia Club' was about to deal a new pack of cards upon the table.

Chapter 4

A leather-gloved hand reached for the bell-pull of 173 Merrington Place, Piccadilly, as the clatter of hooves and the sound of carriage wheels faded slowly out of earshot. Presently, a portly and grey-haired servant opened the door and greeted the visitors.

"Good Evening. Please come this way." he said impassively, to the lady and gentleman stood at the door. He then led the way to the drawing room, after allowing them to deposit their over-cloaks with the waiting maid. She stroked the wonderfully soft and voluminous mink collar of the lady's coat with a little envy as she disappeared into a side-cloak-room to hang it carefully on a silk-lined hanger.

Upon entering the drawing room, the grey-haired butler announced the new arrivals to the already present guests.

"Ladies and Gentleman, Mr and Mrs Belford Smythe."

Sir Bertram welcomed them warmly. "Belford, marvellous to see you, and Margaret too of course," added Sir Bertram, "I have an excellent vintage white port – you must try it before dinner."

The maid, who had previously attended to the coats, appeared with a small serving platter bearing a small glass of sherry and a slightly larger glass of white port, and offered the two drinks to the newly arrived guests.

Sir Bertram's wife, Amelia, introduced Margaret Smythe to the other ladies present, whilst Sir Bertram and Belford Smythe conferred on the quality of the port. She introduced in turn Mrs Stafford, Mrs Fowlhurst, and finally Lady Ainscough. Their conversations turned to fashion, and the theatre, suitable conversation for respectable ladies. Sir Bertram, and his male guests, talked about current politics, though they did not touch upon the subject that they would duly turn to after dinner.

At eight, the muffled chime of the grandfather clock, situated in the hallway just outside the reception room, curtailed Mrs Fowlhurst's enthusiastic review of André Messager's 'La Basoche', which she recounted she had attended at the recently opened Royal English Opera House near Shaftesbury Avenue.

Momentarily, Masterson, who was Sir Bertram's Butler, announced dinner, and Sir Bertram escorted Lady Ainscough to the dining room followed by his wife and Lord Ainscough, and then the others in turn.

The table, set for five courses, was a magnificent mahogany dining table with rosewood inlay showing hunting scenes. The polished wood reflected the gleaming silverware, fine porcelain, and delicate crystal-ware, that had been set out upon it with regimental precision. Serving began with beef consommé, and proceeded through several appetisers, before the presentation of the main course of roast pheasant and venison.

The men led the conversation, and Sir Bertram

played the good host, posing questions to each of his fellows upon topics he knew were close to their hearts.

"So Jerome, dear fellow, how plays the market?"

The well-known city financier, and philanthropist, stroked his short beard as if it were capable of indirectly stimulating his mental faculties to answer Sir Bertram's enquiry.

"Well, it seems everyone is mighty fretful over events in the Argentine these days, but I have to admit that my market instincts are elsewhere. I have doubts about the longevity of the market for American railway bonds, indeed I have only yesterday sent telegrams to my American stock and bonds agent in New-York – I have instructed him to liquidate all my holdings in discreet parcels over the next few months."

He put down his glass. "There are persistent rumours that the railway freight business has over-reached itself – too many tracks - not enough trains – I'd advise you to do the same as I if you hold any stocks on that side of the Atlantic ... mark my words, there are dangers there for those without foresight. Railways are yesterday's future. I rather have a fancy for putting my money into those new motorised-carriages, if I can find the right proposition."

"But what of all the talk of a new trans-continental link between the Pacific and Atlantic trade?" countered Belford Smythe. "Wasn't the great prize to be the joining of the Pacific and Atlantic by a road of steel?"

Jerome Asner smiled, almost as if he knew more

than he should, "it is only a matter of time before the Panama land-bridge is breached – sooner or later it will happen, and then shipping and naval concerns will be the key to linking the pacific trade to European ports – halving the shipping times from occidental shores, some say. Naval power would then have the pre-eminent role in the balance of world powers. The strongest navy could control world trade at the point of a gun, should they desire to do so. There is still an appetite for investing in new schemes, though perhaps not in the Parisian Bourse!"

This last remark caused a ripple of laugher, though possibly in bad taste – after all, the infamous failure of the French attempt to join the Chagres River Valley to the Rio Grande, via the Culebra Pass, ended a decade earlier with more than 20,000 men dead through disease and other misadventures. Yet the attraction of controlling what might perhaps be one of the most important waterways in international shipping, was still simply too much to resist for both governments and private speculators alike.

The dinner conversations moved from one topic to another over the next hour. The newspaper business, political scandals, and the complications of international shipping, were intermixed with talk of family estates and invitations to country retreats.

Presently, the gentle half-hour Winchester-chime of the large gilded timepiece, on the side table of the dining room, reminded Sir Bertram of the need to move on from dining. The true purpose of tonight's social event being recalled to mind, he checked his newly cleaned pocket watch, out of habit more than from need to establish that the time of 9.30 pm was indeed correct.

"Gentleman, perhaps it is time for brandy and cigars." Sir Bertram announced.

Customarily his wife took her cue to invite the ladies to retire to the drawing room for a glass of sherry 'leaving the men to talk politics' as she would always say with a smile – though the ladies often talked of their own politics, played out in the social circles of polite London company.

Masterson withdrew, leaving Sir Bertram to hand out cigars to the gentlemen encircling the table, each of them having been served already with a dangerously large glass of brandy. The Britannia Club was now in session. A large humidor had already been placed upon the table, containing a selection of fine Cuban cigars. Sir Bertram placed upon the table his favourite curiosity – a small finely engraved cylinder no bigger than a cotton reel.

Fowlhurst smiled. "You still have that fascinating cigar cutter, I see."

He then proceeded to pick up the device. Having used it before, Fowlhurst knew that this was a rather unique clockwork contraption. Twisting the two ends of the cylinder in opposing directions, would wind up the device. Once released, it would then begin to cut the closed head from a cigar, as soon as it was pushed into the hole at the end. The device seemed to tick as the blades inside clicked repeatedly, closing in on the cigar with each step, until its head was severed and popped out of the other end of the cylinder. "Modern invention – one cannot help wonder if it will be the undoing of us one of these days."

The cutter was passed around, followed by a silver cigar table lighter, and cigars lit around the table in turn, like signal beacons along a distant coastline. Marcus Ainscough swirled the spirit in his glass, allowing it to absorb some warmth from the palm of his hand for a little while, to release the subtle aromas. Then, he stirred the atmosphere of silent enjoyment, his pronouncement seemingly cutting through the blue tinged veil of cigar smoke accumulating around the table.

"So – our fears are now reality, gentlemen. The Naval Bill will be passed without hindrance in the upper house. It is as good as law already. We have fought well, but I think we all know that our tactics were simply to delay, and to prepare."

Cecil Fowlhurst nodded. "Indeed, time is a commodity we must spend carefully now. Leaking the details of the Portsea espionage case forced the cabinet to delay their plans to present their damned bill by four months, but its given the London press a bitter reputation in Whitehall. Just as well we ensured the story found its way to the Times as well as my own London Daily Enquirer, we've managed to avoid the worst of the backlash this time."

Ainscough followed on. "And I hear that my old

friend Admiral Colomb has been busy again. He was rather excited when I met him in the Gainsborough club earlier this week. He has delivered a manuscript to you, Cecil, has he not?"

"Indeed," Fowlhurst replied, "his latest writings are a perfect foil to the current circumstances. '*The Great War of 1892'* he calls it. A novel which explores the consequences of a superior German navy in the hands of a belligerent and expansionist government, bent on turning the European order upside-down.' I could almost have written the plot myself. We start serialising it in several of our newspapers in less than a month. It is sure to be a talking point among the politically aware classes, which is precisely what we desire."

Sir Bertram reflected for a moment. "So gentlemen, we have played one round of cards to some advantage, though not winning the hand. Now we must deal a new deck in this game of ours." He paused to puff his cigar, quite possibly for dramatic effect. "I fear Great Britain may rely too much on the Triple Entente for reassurance, just as our rivals cling to the skirts of their own German Triple Alliance. With Bismarck we had an understanding of the need to steady the balance of power. But I fear now, that as he has retired to the wings of the Reichstag, we will see Germany determined to have the best of *British* naval technology in its new fleet as well as its own. They seem to have succeeded on this occasion. The question now, must be what can we obtain to counter-balance these newly resurgent naval ambitions?"

John Stafford was next to speak. "As you know I have a wide reputation in the engineering field, and many friends. With Sir Bertram's help, we had located and encouraged several contacts within the German naval procurement offices, and we have intermittently enjoyed access to documents at a high level. Once or twice a week our friends in Osnabruck find themselves working late in the drawing office, copying plans for storage in the naval archive vault, or for despatch to Berlin. This ensures that plans of the highest importance are kept safe in event of some mishap. It is therefore quite possible for a plan to be not only duplicated but indeed to be triplicated, during these late-nights in the drawing offices. Naturally we keep these additional copies safe too, but not for the benefit of the German Navy! We now have a number of such blueprints secreted in several locations in Germany. The most interesting of these documents are to be escorted to England in the next week or two, under cover of a shipment of 1876 Miterlrhein Riesling. I thought it might be a sweet irony to toast their arrival with a German vintage."

Sir Bertram urged Stafford on. "And what do we have in store for our future scrutiny?"

"Most of the copies passing through the drawing offices are of fairly standard technology. However these particular plans have been selected for shipment precisely because we have no idea from initial inspection as to what they relate too."

Around the table, the friends sipped their drinks and listened intently as Stafford continued. "What we do know is that some of them contain unusual and highly complex mechanisms. They undoubtedly require a very specific expertise to understand fully. We shall see more when they arrive at my offices in Limehouse later this month. So, let us convene then, and see what sort of pheasant we have bagged."

"Very well, gentleman," Sir Bertram said, "perhaps now that we have settled the business of the evening, we should return to our ladies and avail ourselves of another glass of my vintage white port?"

Chapter 5

William Harland's apartments were modest by the standards of many of the clientele he dealt with at the Horological Emporium. However it sported numerous rooms by comparison to many smaller apartments in the area. Victoria had insisted upon a larger apartment, with enough room for a young family to grow. Her dearest wish was to have a large family, and indeed Victoria had once been with child during their marriage, but the pregnancy became complicated, and she miscarried. It had then seemed that she was destined not to fall pregnant again.

William had gradually taken over the unused nursery, turning it into a workshop for his experimentations. As an apprentice, he had served at the very same shop which he now owned. William was never a student content to simply learn the established mechanics of watch and clock making, and put them into textbook practice. Of course he did as much when required, and with enough skill and attention to detail to earn him the respect of Jeremiah Varey, the now retired previous owner of the Horological Emporium, and William's master and tutor in the skills of watchmaking. William Harland was a young apprentice then, and started 'cutting his teeth' some twenty years ago - quite literally if one knows of matters pertaining to the machining of such cogs and gears as are found inside a typical timepiece. He started with cleaning and servicing of large clock mechanisms. Often these would be old but serviceable pieces bought from dealers and, once refurbished and mounted in a case in keeping of current fashion, such pieces could turn a good profit. He moved on to finer repairs and gradually moved down in scale to smaller clocks, and eventually to pocket watches of increasingly valuable and intricate nature.

However, as diligent as he was, William was not content to learn and then practice his skills by the book. He had a mind for mechanics, and to the annoyance of Jeremiah, had a habit of inventing new ways to build ever more accurate and compact pocket watch mechanisms, rather than following the practiced designs handed down through the Varey Family. Jeremiah soon came to respect William Harland's skill though, and eventually they became partners, until Jeremiah's retirement due to failing eyesight at the age of 78.

Since those happy days, William had worked hard to secure the Horological Emporium's reputation as one of the best watchmakers in London. Nevertheless, William was not content. His curiosity had led him down several paths that had provided him with much distraction – often working late into the night at home in his growing workshop. One of these fascinations was the idea of a 'thinking machine' – an exaggeration perhaps, but it was hard to deny that the Babbage 'difference engine' was something well beyond a simple mechanical novelty. Babbage had spectacularly failed in his endeavour. But, as William Harland had come to appreciate, this was predominantly a result of the lack of refinement in manufacturing parts to devilishly fine tolerances, rather than a failure of vision or design. The Babbage machines had long since been broken up and parts scattered as items of whimsy or curiosity among the more enlightened gentleman of the City. William had made it his pastime to track down and obtain whatever parts he could, and he had collected numerous parts and partial blueprints to date. The largest section of the machine in his possession was now proudly on display, as a talking point in his shop. The longer his customers spent there, the more likely they were to make a purchase, and the machine often drew attention.

His other pastime, perhaps some might say casual obsession, was the continuation of his unorthodox work as an apprentice, this being the refinement and reduction of timepieces and other mechanisms to their logical limit. For several years William had worked on ever more elaborate designs for pocket watches with all manner of extra capabilities – moon dials, low and high tide indicators, even experimental winding mechanisms that used movement of the watch within the owners pocket to maintain operation. However, William's true revelation had come to him one day whilst watching a child in Hyde Park, playing with a Russian doll. He had realised that the machine tools he used, and which he often adapted to achieve higher degrees of sophistication, were the final obstacle to his pursuit of ever more complexity. Just as Babbage's difference engine could not operate reliably with components that were manufacturable in its time, William's experimental timepieces would always be limited by the precision of his machining tools. But then he made a breakthrough: On that summers day in Hyde Park, walking with Victoria and taking the morning air, he had found himself sitting on a bench when a young girl skipped over to Victoria, eager to show her the Russian doll 'daddy had brought back from Prussia'. William realised in an instant of inspiration that if his machine tool could not reach higher tolerances, then the solution was to use the tool at its limits, to build a smaller and thus more accurate machine tool. Then, to use that tool itself, to make a smaller and even more precise tooling mechanism. It had taken several years of experimentation to perfect his unique methodology. Initially he had tried to move too quickly to smaller machines, reducing the scale of each generation of tool by too far a stretch. Eventually, the ability to reduce the machine tool's scale by a factor of two at each generation was found to be the best approach. William then set about making the most precise implementation at each new generation that he could – failing as many times as he succeeded at each step, Finally he succeeded in reducing the standard watchmakers tooling machines in entirety, halving and then halving again. Now he had the ability to produce mechanisms with such refinement that the smallest components were no more than a pin-head to the naked eye. Only under a powerful glass optic, could such specks be clearly resolved as cogwheels, with neatly cut teeth, axial pins, and polished surfaces. So small were these minutiae that William was obliged to invent and construct equally refined and miniaturised devices for moving and placing these components, using a complex set of winding handles and levers to reduce the smallest movements of his fingers to yet smaller manipulations. Even the best gas lighting he could obtain had proved to be a hurdle to be overcome. Fortunately, William had acquired some newly devised electrical lighting apparatus. With the aid of a stack of voltaic plates, he could call upon a bright light of superb clarity to aid him in his work, night or day. But his intellectual fascination with the limits of technology had long since given way to a new obsession, driven out of grief for his Victoria, and her unborn child — for she had at last fallen pregnant again only a few months before the time of her murder.

William sat in his experimental workshop and pondered the contents of a cigar box on the table. He had taken out a newspaper clipping, with a dried smear of blood, faded from the fresh bright red to a ruddy brown somewhat reminiscent of the penny postage stamps that also lay in the cigar box unused.

He dripped sealing wax onto the folded letter, which he had just finished writing some minutes earlier, and then pressed his seal into the setting wax. He would deliver this by hand to the London Times Newspaper Office on his daily walk to the Horological Emporium, upon the morning. He placed it next to the cigar box, within which now lay a piece of blued notepaper with a handwritten poem, in his own handwriting. It was part of Victoria's eulogy.

The clock ticks.
Dawn and dusk become one,
Days become weeks, weeks become months.
And still I wait.
Flowers bloom. Petals fall.
A white cloak covers all.
Soon meltwaters run.
Winter's heart pierced by the sun.
And still I wait.
Time may pass, and ease the pain,
But tell me, when shall I see thee again?.
When the clock ticks no more,
When Death knocks upon my door,
Then shall I see thee again.

The paper was water-stained, having caught a tear more than once from his streaked face, how often he had read this and wondered how he could live a good and long life without his beloved Victoria. Without his small obsessions, he may well have become ragged and unkempt, descending into malaise and self-pity. For a short while he had done so, but somehow he had borne his grief and convinced himself that there must be some purpose to his life.

Harland had indeed found a new purpose to his being, a reason to go on, and a purpose to drive him onward. As the grandfather clock in the hallway chimed the hour, he was already finishing the small glass of whisky, which had accompanied him in his study these past two hours. He often anticipated such things, perhaps his ear was particularly well attuned to the small changes in the sounds of a clock's mechanism that preceded the engagement of the chime mechanism, or else he had acquired a 'minds-eye' sense of time that surpassed most individuals. He collected his cloak and preceded down the stairs into the dim street-light, and the enveloping fog of a cold autumn night.

Chapter 6

At almost the same moment that William Harland stepped out into the dimly streets of London, another wheel was turning many miles away. It was just over an hour after midnight in Hamburg. Jacob Maierhofer skirted quickly through a maze of dark alleyways towards Berth C18. The SS Fathom was due to depart at high tide, 01:45 am, and it was necessary to ensure that the delivery was made to the captain himself, before departure. Maierhofer knew he should have completed this task three hours ago, and would have done so and been home in bed now, if not for a certainty that he had been followed since leaving his lodgings in Hohenfelde district earlier that night. Several hours in a *bierkellar* flirting with one or another of the loose women who spend their time there, and their patrons money, late into the evening, had seemingly thrown his shadow off the scent.

As he made his way across town, he lamented a missed opportunity. The working girls in the bierkellar were not lacking in forwardness, and Maierhofer had not one but two girls vying for his business that night. Although he enjoyed the way the two girls competed to be the most lascivious, he couldn't help feeling like he was still being watched, even though he caught sight of nobody stealing more than a casual glance... most likely they were more interested in the two ladies and their frivolity, or perhaps their over-exposed flesh. Their bawdiness had provided him with a useful opportunity. He slipped up the balcony stairs into one of several backrooms, where Karla and Juliane started to undress.

"So lets see what's in your pocket then..." Karla joked. She was giving a subtle reminder that they expected to be paid before and not afterwards.

Maierhofer pulled out several banknotes and slipped them into her basque. "I'm sorry ladies but not tonight, I need to get out of here without taking the stairs. If anyone asks, I paid you two to have a good time up here with me for the rest of the hour."

Juliane looked disappointed.

"Not another bad gambling debt! You men need to give up the cards and stick to women," she smiled as she chastised him playfully, "here... you can climb out of the first window, and onto the coal house roof, you are not the first to leave this way, it is quite safe."

"But are you sure?" Karla pleaded. "Won't you stay for a little while before you scurry away 'Klein Maus'?"

Maierhofer was already pushing open the window, and didn't answer to her enticement.

"Don't worry, we will stay in here for an hour so your friends think you are busy, but here is a taste of what you are missing..."

Juliane French-kissed him, making his pulse race, and reluctantly he disentangled himself and climbed through the window to make his escape.

"So back to the drunks downstairs then!" Juliane

31

sighed.

"Oh no you don't." said Karla. "The customer has paid two of us for a good time, I suggest we keep our side of the bargain..." Karla stroked Juliane's hair, and slipped her tongue into Juliane's mouth as they kissed.

Outside, Maierhofer made his way over the back wall of the Bier-kellar's rear yard and into a dark alley-way into the night. Slipping into a backroom, then climbing out of a rear window had seemed like a perfect cover. But now, after walking for perhaps twenty minutes, his heart was pounding again, for a different reason. Once again, he felt sure he was not alone on his journey.

Maierhofer, a tall and wiry figure with sharp features, knew these back alleys well, and he skitted from one side street to another, to try to remain a step ahead. He felt instinctively certain that his shadow was now only one turn behind, and invisibly stalking its prey like a night-hawk. Suddenly, flitting out of a narrow access between the buckled brick walls of two warehouses, he stumbled as a darkly lit figure knocked against him, spinning both of them into the dim gaslight of a nearby streetlamp.

"Dumkopf – whats your business?" shouted the man. Unshaven, and smelling of drink, the man waved his bottle, then staggered back against the wall where he had been leaning earlier. Maierhofer, who didn't pause to excuse himself, recovered his footing and slipped into yet another dark *hintergasse*.

Moments later, a blade plunged into flesh, and a

sickening cry called out, then faded, as life spilled out of a mortally wounded body. Two shadows then crawled over the lifeless soul like carrion-crows.

"There's nothing here – no papers." said the first of the men.

The second figure stepped backward, and kicked the leaking bottle of kirsch halfway down the alley in anger.

"Gott Damm – we will get it for this – we've lost that shit for sure this time. This stewed carcass isn't his! Let's go back to the tenement and wait. If he comes back we'll have his skin if not the merchandise."

~

Not long after these events, Maierhofer looked out over the harbour area from the prow of SS Fathom, which was now slowly receding from the faint city glow: perhaps his last view of Hamburg. He had made his delivery, but it was too dangerous to stay in Hamburg now. He fancied he had heard the sound of a man's throat being cut as he ran down that last alleyway, and wasn't about to risk his own by going back ashore now.

Even without the threat of cold steel, Hamburg was becoming a city for which Maierhofer no longer felt any affection. He had returned to look after his father in his last few months of fading health. That was two years ago, his father had indeed passed away after an uncomfortable decline, but then there was also a dalliance with Magda, from the bakery, though that did not last long. And now, with Hamburg in the grip of a cholera outbreak, anyone who had a reasonably lined pocket, and no responsibilities, would be forgiven for jumping on the first ship available.

One day he could return, of course. But for what? He had nothing much to come back for, except unpaid debts and the possibility that his pursuers might still come across him by chance and recognise him. Being a Jew in Germany these days, even a non-practicing one, was not so easy. His father's generation were too stubborn to see it, but he noticed the prejudice, and it was growing.

No, his time in Germany was over for now and perhaps for good. London was a better prospect, and he would be well paid for his delivery after all. London was a city of opportunities for those with cash in hand, and he had distant cousins there, so it all made sense. So, it was decided. For now, he would blend in as a member of the crew at the captain's suggestion, far fewer questions that way. And what else was there to do at sea for the next ten days anyway?

Chapter 7

As the Hansom cab bumbled along the uneven streets of Charing Cross, William Harland thumbed through the small clutch of correspondence that had been set in motion by his original letter to *'reply box number 38'*, at the London Times newspaper offices. It was that which had brought him on this current journey through Piccadilly on this rather cold morning. Outside, the horse's breath billowed steamily like a railway engine, drifting past the half-open glass window of the cab. He had arranged each of the letters in chronological order, starting with a letter dated 17th September 1891.

Dear Mr Harland,

Thank you for your correspondence in the matter as advertised in the London Times Newspaper. I have been instructed to respond to state that we are most certain that you might be of service, and we shall correspond with you again within two weeks, whence Mrs Amshaw will return to London from her family in Berkshire

Yours most Sincerely, Douglas Barringer,
17th September 1891

It was now October the fourth, a Sunday. The streets were busy in spite of the cold chill in the air, with churchgoers returning from Sunday service.

Harland folded his papers carefully, then slipped

35

them into his overcoat pocket. He would soon arrive at Mrs Amshaw's residence, as requested in the final letter he had brought with him. The carriage driver called a halt to his horses, and slid open the hatch, announcing arrival in a guttural accent.

Harland paid the carriage driver, and soon found himself immediately outside the Amshaw residence. It appeared at first sight to be a large regency townhouse of three floors, with the advantage of a cellar and attic window-light's, both showing signs of being in use, perhaps as servants quarters. But, in reality, the frontage was a more modern addition, grandly extending upon a much older building. This was a residence which could be afforded only by the better off members of London society, but not quite in the echelon of the more 'upper class' types who often frequented his shop.

The door was answered by a maid. She must have been expecting him to arrive, and had observed his approach, since he had not yet rang the bell-pull.

"Would you be Mr Harland sir?" she asked in a soft lilting Irish accent.

"I am indeed, here is my card."

The maid checked his particulars and invited Harland to enter the hallway, taking his long winter overcoat and hat. Momentarily, a tall gentleman appeared from the morning room doorway.

"Good morning Mr Harland, I am Douglas - Douglas Barringer. Please come through to the morning room, Mrs Amshaw is ready to see you."

They exchanged cards and proceeded through to the adjacent rooms. Mrs Amshaw was standing in the morning room, dressed in a long dark-violet dress. She offered her hand to Harland in greeting. She wore delicate black lace gloves, and a finely netted veil of black lace over her face. This was mourning attire, though not in keeping with the full protocol of mourning that usually expected black crape for a full year after a spouse's death. Nonetheless, the dress was plain and finished with carved black buttons, matching the Whitby-Jet brooch and mourning jewellery, which she wore to affirm here state of recent bereavement.

"Mr Harland - I am most grateful for your attendance. Please sit and take tea with Mr Barringer and myself."

Mrs Amshaw proceeded to pour the tea herself, the servants having withdrawn. "Mr Barringer, would you mind explaining the circumstances of our concerns to Mr Harland?" Mrs Amshaw spoke as she finished stirring her tea in a fine bone-china cup that was almost translucent in the morning sunlight. Barringer took up his cup, but before drinking from it, he began his commentary.

"Mr Harland, as you know I am Mrs Amshaw's family solicitor, and advisor. It was I who placed the advert in the London Times newspaper several months ago. As I made you aware, we have had numerous respondents, but none of a suitable character or expertise for the problem we have to assign ourselves too."

Barringer sipped his tea, and then put down the cup. "Let me get to the nub of the matter. Four months ago, Mrs Amshaw's late husband disturbed an intruder in this very house, in the depths of the night, and in the resulting commotion, he was murdered. The household staff were roused by the noise and disturbance, and found him laid dying in the very same hallway from which you entered a few moments ago."

Harland nodded in a show of empathy.

"I am deeply sorry for your loss Mrs Amshaw, I myself have lost my wife only this year or so past, and I must say that the circumstances were equally tragic and disturbing."

"Yes," Mr Barringer continued, "we are aware of your dreadful bereavement, if you will forgive me, it was necessary to make enquires as to your background before this meeting. Let me continue – The following morning in the full light of day, it became clear that certain items had been removed from Dr Amshaw's study. This was as might be expected for a robbery of course, but these were somewhat unusual items, and I believe that your expertise will be invaluable in assisting us. The truth is we have consulted various professional investigators – Mosers, Chevasse, Chamberlains... but their expertise does not stretch to a useful understanding of Dr Amshaw's collection."

"Thank you Douglas." said Mrs Amshaw. Her bottom lip trembled slightly with emotion as she spoke. "We would of course like to recover that which was stolen, but perhaps more importantly if we may discover what happened to these items after their theft, then it may shed light on the identity of those involved in this disgraceful incident. As you can imagine it is still hard for me to recount these events in such a matter of fact way, however I can answer your questions, and provide what detail I can of these matters, if it will assist you in helping us. Of course you will be paid well, and if you succeed I will be indebted to you – I am not without influence, one day perhaps I can repay you for your assistance. Perhaps we should adjourn to my Husband's study, and we can shed further light on the matter."

The group moved back toward the hallway – which Harland now viewed somewhat differently. He found himself looking to the floor subconsciously, as if expecting to see some signs of Dr Amshaw's demise – a blood stain, or some other remnant of a deathly struggle perhaps. However, all seemed normal. As is so often the case, the normality of a scene masks the truth of some outrage or tragedy to which it has previously borne witness. William started to think back to his seat by the fire at home and Victoria's comfortable chair, which he also felt often to be waiting for her to return.

Momentarily, Mrs Amshaw took out and then turned a key in the lock of the door they had come to. She kept this in a small lace pouch with her scented handkerchief. The door quietly creaked open. Upon

Entering, Harland observed that this was a study of a gentleman of science. It was extensively oak panelled, with floor-to-ceiling bookcases, and a large window at the end offering an abundance of natural light. However, what seemed far more interesting were the curiosities on display on a large leather-topped desk under the same window.

There were a number of glass cases, containing what appeared to the layman to be clockwork mechanisms and small mechanical pieces. The largest case was empty, and the frame showed damage near the lock. It must surely have been forced open.

"As you can see Mr Harland, my husband collected curiosities of the mechanical kind, automata, and calculating devices. Of course I understand nothing of these, but my husband had a great interest and collected many pieces which he meticulously dismantled, cleaned, and reassembled. More than once we have been late for the theatre, because I found him in here still at work when he should be dressing."

Harland had suspected as much when he entered the room. He recognised the signs – scuffing and scratching of the leather desktop, something he was familiar with in his own study for exactly the same reasons. Also, a desk mat with an inset of fine blotting paper was marked with grease traces. Any gentleman using his study for correspondence would surely not find that acceptable – but for those devotees of horology it was often the norm.

"There are certainly some interesting pieces here Mrs

Amshaw, indeed I am sure that one piece is a section of a *Fowler ternary calculator*, and there is a reproduction of a small part of a Babbage machine here too – it is a copy but interesting nonetheless. Perhaps you might recall did your husband have more of this device?"

"Although I am far from an appreciator of such things Mr Harland, I do not believe he did, though he often talked about some folio of papers, and his frustration at having only part of the set of drawings. However, the device he had in the large case here was his constant obsession of late, and it has been stolen. He referred to it as 'the Polish Machine'."

"If you will forgive me Mrs Amshaw, what exactly would you like me to do to assist you?" Harland asked. "I can certainly tell you much about these devices, but to what end?"

Douglas Barringer took up the response to Harland's enquiry. "Mr Harland, I think perhaps you might have surmised that we do not simply want to locate some stolen collectors pieces in order to restore this menagerie. It is people we wish to collect. The person, or persons, responsible for removing this piece from its display case, this 'Polish machine', would undoubtedly be responsible for Dr Amshaw's murder. Recovering this device, or at least finding out where it has been on its way elsewhere – that may well shed light upon the identity of these braggarts, and perhaps even bring them to justice."

Barringer continued, "Mr Harland, I will not pretend

that this endeavour is an entirely safe and sedentary pursuit. Whoever did this will not wish to be apprehended, but your knowledge of such devices is the lynchpin. The police have been of no use. After all, how can they find something they have never seen and do not understand, and what chance have they of making investigations in such a vein without alerting those responsible, or their associates? I believe that you are among the very few in London who could make such discreet enquiries - after all you have a legitimate interest in all such mechanisms, and could feign interest in all sorts of things without raising suspicions."

"Perhaps we are asking too much, Douglas." Mrs Amshaw interrupted. "I have no desire to see any more harm come from these machines than has already been done."

"Madam, I see perhaps there are dangers," Harland began, "however Mr Barringer is quite correct – I could make enquiries, purport to be seeking unusual mechanical curiosities for clients, and thereby veil my pursuit of information. I am sure I could do so without too much being suspected - it is, after all, something I already engage in both as an idle pursuit, and as a professional interest of course. Indeed, I feel this is something I *must* do! In some way, if we were to reveal the truth about your Husband's assailants, I might find some comfort in my own grief for my darling Victoria."

Mrs Amshaw touched her hand on William's own

hand in an assuring way and nodded her empathy. She could not help noticing that his hand was a little bruised, but naturally she did not comment upon it – to do so would be indiscreet.

Douglas Barringer paused for thought, and then made a suggestion as to a way of proceeding. "Might you agree that we should busy ourselves initially in cataloguing and documenting everything of relevance in this study? Perhaps within the cabinets of documents we will find clues as to this 'Polish enigma' we have been set upon solving."

"Indeed," Harland replied. "Perhaps we can begin during this coming week, shall we consult our diaries?"

Mrs Amshaw made her withdrawal, and left Barringer and Harland to discuss their arrangements.

Chapter 8

Six miles across the capital, Maierhofer had located 'three colts' – or *Three Colts Street*, to be precise, and had then found himself at the Stafford Maritime Engineering offices, Limehouse. He was now situated in the outer office of the company's chief clerk, who viewed him, with his unkempt facial hair and musty-looking coat, somewhat suspiciously. Presently, the thin figure of John Stafford appeared. The clerk stood as Stafford entered the room.

"I'm sorry to disturb you sir, this... gentleman claims he has business with you, I sent the office boy out into the engineering yards to fetch you, he refuses to leave, I ..."

Stafford interrupted – "I have been expecting our friend."

Stafford's clerk had seemed a little doubtful of the caller, after all he was unshaven, and not dressed in a professional attire – his thick felt overcoat looking damp and well worn, and with a scruffy looking hat that he couldn't help surmising might hide an even less appealing head of hair underneath.

"Please come this way Stafford said."

Unusually, he intimated to his chief clerk not to follow. Stafford was normally diligent, perhaps obsessive, in his meetings being minuted in shorthand on every occasion. But not in this instance, it would seem.

In Stafford's office, a well-made fire burned warmly, and Maierhofer drew to it like a moth to a candle. He had spent a long morning traveling across London, taking an indirect route to avoid the possibility of being followed, as he was still understandably nervous after the incident in Hamburg two weeks ago. He recounted his story to his host, and explained how the SS Fathom had departed from Hamburg and called at several ports en-route to the Thames Docks.

"As you instructed sir, I placed the papers in the packing cases of the Riesling wine – I made sure the cargo number was as you stated it would be, of course. No one saw me do it. I trust no-one unless I have to."

"The captain was most accommodating, he even paid me for my work on-board during the trip. However, that is not a great compensation. I can't return to Hamburg unless it is to attend my own funeral."

Perhaps this was his way of saying he would like a little more payment for his trouble. The deal was he would deliver the plans to the ship and he was paid half in advance on the night when the plans were handed over, and the rest to be collected from the captain of SS Fathom on his return to Hamburg. Himself being part of the shipment was not part of the plan."

Stafford was reassuring. "Don't worry Mr Maierhofer – you have done well, possibly avoided some complications, and by the sound of things, you have risked a lot for your pay. I will compensate you well for your trouble, but consider it a retainer – I think I will yet have need of your skills again here in London."

"My secretary will issue you with ten shillings right away, get yourself some lodgings and some local attire. Come back tomorrow so we can go through everything that happened in detail, and we will arrange for you to draw a weekly salary."

Stafford sat in thought for a few minutes after Maierhofer left. The transfer of the blueprints had been successful – but not without a significant degree of luck by the sound of it. Could they risk transporting another batch of papers any time soon? Perhaps that was not wise for now. But, clearly, someone knew far too much about the activities in Hamburg. Perhaps they knew more, maybe even about the late nights at the drawing office in Osnabruck? But if that was the case then why had they not arrested the two infiltrators?

Telegrams had been received from an office in a small town near Osnabruck as usual. Each week one would arrive as a way of confirming all was well without raising suspicions. He read back through a small notebook, in which copies of these messages were noted. The most recent messages all ended with 'Uncle Gustav is as well as could be expected'. Reassuringly, this was the correct message in a pre-arranged set of apparently innocent correspondence.

"At least the 'Riesling' consignment was now in London." thought Stafford. Indeed, his latest purchase was already being transported to his town house.

Perhaps it was time to call upon his associates to join him for a wine tasting? He called in his secretary and dictated several invitations to be hand delivered that same afternoon.

Chapter 9

Once again, the Britannia Club, Sir Bertram Overard's small band of compatriots, found themselves assembled to consider the business of their unofficial 'shadow defence cabinet'. Sir Bertram had known each of his colleagues for many years, a few from his days as a Harrow boy, and the others from his business and political dealings.

One common denominator was shared by Lord Marcus Ainscough, Belford Smythe, Cecil Fowlhurst, and Jerome Asner, and that was the belief in the growing threat of German expansionism. They shared the desire to see Great Britain maintain its position as a counter-balance to German ambitions. This was the view also of John Stafford, their host on this occasion. The apparent failure of the British establishment to grasp this most critical issue was their constant concern and impetus.

"Well then gentlemen," Stafford began, "thank you for joining me this evening – I am sure that my invitation to 'uncork' the Miterlrhein Riesling was understood – We have all of the accompanying 'paperwork', which I am sure you will wish to look at. Incidentally, I had to purchase rather a large quantity of the Riesling in order to make the shipment appear to be of no particular importance. I still have 60 cases awaiting delivery from the bonded warehouse, I trust you will be happy to share these - at my expense of course – my cellar is already full now!"

"Bravo, Stafford!, we can drink to your generosity on evenings to come." jested Overard. "Now tell us what you have discovered."

Stafford proceeded to unroll a set of blueprints across the large rosewood inlaid dining table, using various pieces of tableware to weigh down the corners.

"Gentlemen, here we have four separate parcels of documents, and there is a story to tell about how they came to be in our possession. But first let us take a look at what we have gained for our troubles."

The friends spent the next hour browsing back and forth between the blueprints and discussing what they had acquired. John Stafford had the advantage here – his shipping business and his maritime shipbuilding interests meant he had an excellent understanding of shipyard engineering. He acted as the commentator as each of the plans was studied.

"We have something of interest here – look at the shape of the stern section – this has clearly been designed to allow self-propelled torpedoes to be ejected underwater from the rear of the vessel. It is not a new idea – there have been many such trials since the Whitehead Torpedoes became widely available, but it is notable that this was redrawn with amendments only 4 months ago – which suggests current development."

Stafford continued. "The other plans aren't so interesting – an improved drive shaft for high speed propellers, and a novel riveting pattern – all worth looking into nonetheless. However, here we have something quite unusual, and which I believe may have made our efforts to date worthwhile. I have to confess, though, that it is a mystery to me, and to my best engineers, as to what its purpose may be."

Sir Bertram and the others watched as Stafford brought out the final set of plans from a green leather storage tube which they had assumed to be empty - the plans all being thought to be upon the table. He then spread them out like the others.

"Quite remarkable," said Jerome Asner, "it is certainly a complex piece of work, and I say that in spite of it being beyond my limited knowledge of engineering."

Stafford went over the features of the plans as far as he could divine any sense of the complex system laid out before them.

"There is no doubt that this is something unusual, and if we do not understand what it is then we are at a serious disadvantage. We could of course build the thing. But, if we do not know what it does, or the purpose of its existence, then that may be something of a challenge."

Cecil Fowlhurst moved forward and browsed back and forth through the plans.

"My friends... what *I* find interesting is not the design itself, but the fact that this is not a German invention. See here gentlemen – the Osnabruck copyist has done a good job in reproducing everything in the plan as an exact copy as you would expect. Have you not noticed that all of the labelling on the diagram is not actually German, but most likely Polish? Moreover, the name at the bottom of the plan is 'KJ Zamolyski'. Whatever it is, it seems that the German Navy has 'acquired' this invention from another of its friendly European neighbours, in much the same way as they have plundered the best inventions of the naval engineers of our admiralty."

Asner exhaled cigar smoke in a typically dramatic cue for him to speak next. "Well, we all know they have made it their business to know what everyone else is doing. More pity on us for not doing the same thing. But what does it mean to us Cecil? Is this part of some sort of new secret weapon?"

"I have to say I don't know the answer to that, but I have no doubt it is of great importance to someone – people who are willing to kill to stop people like us getting our hands on these plans. There is one more thing I think we should note gentlemen, look at the numbering of the sheets..."

Cecil flipped through the plans, and enunciated them in turn, "one – two – three – five." One of the sheets is missing - and that means that without the mysterious missing sheet number four, nobody has a full design and I suspect that no-one is able to complete the mechanics of whatever it is we are looking at. I am certain that our copyists in Osnabruck would not have missed a sheet from a set... especially with such an unusual design, and it is hard to see why the fourth sheet should not be kept with its friends. Therefore we can only hope that the Germans do not possess a full set of plans either."

"And what shall we do now we have these plans?" Sir Bertram asked, though fully intending to answer his own question:

"I suggest we need to find this sheet number four. But I suspect that will be dangerous... asking the wrong questions in the wrong places will expose our intent to those who may be watching. Meanwhile, we should also start to have this device built as far as we are able to complete it."

"I'm afraid that my engineers aren't able to help out here." said Stafford, lamentably.

"This is small scale machinery, my engineers are used to dealing with components fifty times the size – heavy drive units, synchronising gears – nothing of this precision. We need someone with the specialised skills and knowledge that we ourselves do not have."

"Someone like a watchmaker perhaps?" Sir Bertram observed. "If you will allow me – I suspect I have a solution to that problem – the very same man who created that remarkable cigar cutter of mine that you have so admired."

"Very well," Stafford agreed, "if you think this man of yours is the fellow, then I trust your judgement, as we all do. But gentleman, I must say I am somewhat concerned about the events in Hamburg which my man Maierhofer related to me after he delivered these plans."

Stafford paused to sip his brandy, and then continued. "Someone certainly knew that our man had something of value - something worth following him halfway across the city to get their hands on. They would have killed him, and indeed, it appears they came close to doing so. According to a newspaper cutting, of which I have here a transcription from the Hamburg Taggespiegel, a drunkard was killed at the docks exactly where Maierhofer had been that same night. My Hamburg office telegraphed this after I asked them to report anything suspicious at the docks. Maierhofer told me he was pursued, and I suspect this unfortunate fellow was mistaken for our man by whoever was hunting down their quarry."

"No doubt these assailants are mere thugs in the employ of others, but it is likely they were able to report as to the area where Maierhofer's trail was lost. Their masters have surely had the ingenuity to check the departure logs for nearby berths on the night of their butchery. I expect they now know that the Fathom was the only vessel departing at that hour from there, who operates that ship, and where it was headed. If they want what we have badly enough then we must assume they have already set themselves upon the task of pursuing it to London and are intent on doing further malevolence."

"So you foresee dangers here then?" Sir Bertram asked Stafford.

"There could be. I think your man, this 'watchmaker', might do well to know less than we do already. I will

53

have the plans copied, but without the Polish annotations, and identifications – we will 'sanitise' these plans so that they convey only the technical detail of this mysterious machinery, but nothing of its origins."

The others nodded in appreciation of this suggestion.

"Your man will not be able to let slip anything which he does not himself know. Even so, I am minded to take further precautions." Stafford did not expand upon this last point but, in his momentary silence, he was making a mental note to put in place some additional 'insurance'.

Chapter 10

Swirls of mist and fog hung heavily in the air. It was a cold and damp night, lampposts glistening with condensation, and the usual bustle of the city muffled by the still, heavy, air. A smell of dank humidity pervaded the streets, mixing with the chimney smoke of countless coal and wood fires. The air even tasted of it. Gas lights cast feint shafts of light onto the cobbles, cutting through the veil of smog, but in doing so created dark voids, which could hide a multitude of misdemeanours or one or two more serious crimes.

Mary Biddle stepped briskly, making her way home to the single room that was home to herself and her three children, her buttoned boots scuttling across the cobbles. What had happened to her man, Alfred, was a mystery. After three months at sea, his ship came home but not Alfred. The crew knew nothing – or knew too much? Either way they had nothing to tell. When the money ran out she had to move into a dilapidated lodging house, one room, one fireplace, three straw mattresses, and filthy back yard toilet shared with six other families. Yet, she still had to feed her children somehow. She was lucky, aged 25 she still had unusually good looks, and could pick her clients, and appeal to the city gentlemen. At least that way she only needed to work the streets two nights a week, and do laundry in the daytimes. Better than frequenting filthy drinking dens where less fortunate girls got blind-drunk on cheap gin to make their own regulars look, and smell, a little more bearable.

The smog was very thick this evening. In these less well-lit streets, where the gaslights were fewer and dimmer than the main thoroughfares, her journey home was largely a matter of skirting by familiar shop fronts and other landmarks. She had done this often on past nights like this one, not unlike the early navigators of the seas who stayed close to the coastline to find their way. Suddenly, she found herself face-to-face, under the gaslight of a streetlamp, with a man who seemed to come out of no-where. His face was pockmarked, his teeth rotten, even in this half-light that much was apparent.

"Oh my life! you gave me such a turn mister!" Mary blurted out, as she tried to side-step the man and continue on her way. But he stepped back, and blocked her path. He grinned – rotten teeth and all.

"A decent girl shouldn't be out on a night like this should she," he said, "but you are not a decent girl are you, Mary Biddle?"

"I don't think I know you sir." said Mary, thrown by the fact that the man knew her name.

"I've seen you around. Saw what you get up to with those fancy nobs up the embankment."

He smelled of various unsavoury odours, not the least of which was the stench of stale beer, but that could not mask the more pungent smell of the gutter that hung about him.

"I know you Mary Biddle, - seen what you do up the back alleys – I've watched you when you think you're out of sight – on your knees for those well-to-do plummy-mouthed fuckers. Everyone knows you're a filthy dolly-mop."

"I'm going home, let me past." Mary said. She tried to sound firm and show she wasn't scared, but she was, and her voice unintentionally betrayed it.

"I'm not good enough to pass for a toffer, is that it? Can't talk all fine and proper. Haven't got a sovereign in my pocket to pay you for my pleasures eh?"

Suddenly his hand was at her throat. She didn't see it coming, and couldn't stop him pushing her into a darkened doorway. She could barely speak.

"Please, just do what you want and then let me go home to my children."

Mary Biddle was resigned to having to prostitute herself one more time tonight – like it or not. But instead, the man turned his face away and spat to the side. "I don't want you, you filthy whore, but I'll take your purse. I fancy its a good weight." With one hand still on her throat, he used his other to search for her money pouch, ripping open her coat buttons.

Mary pleaded, "Please, don't, I have children to feed, we haven't eaten for two days. Let me go home to my daughters."

The man ignored her. Soon he found what he was looking for, a heavy purse, warm from her body, and pushed it into his overcoat pocket.

Mary began to speak again "Now let me go home…"

But even as she pleaded, she stopped dead in mid sentence, as she saw the glint of a cut-throat razor in the man's hand, drawn from the same pocket into which he had just stuffed her purse.

"Can't have you blabbing to the peelers can we dearie. I'm not hanging for your sort."

"Jesus, please... what will become of my girls, just let me go, I won't tell anyone I swear mister." Mary's head spun with a surge of fear as she struggled desperately to loosen herself from his grasp.

"Don't you worry about them girls Mrs Biddle, I'll be payin em a visit. Their long lost uncle Joe will look after them, if you know what I means. One for the street and one for myself should do nicely. What's a ten year old worth to one of your fancy men then? Or maybe she's for my own."

He began to grin as if he was about to laugh, but suddenly he tensed up like a board, his body bolting upright from his previous hunched posture. His hand loosened around Mary's throat, his eyes widened, a strange look on his face, his hands shaking. Then, slowly, he slumped and slipped down at her feet, falling into the gaslight as he rolled onto his side. There, Mary could now see a long thin piece of bloodied metal, half buried in the back of his skull. He was stunned - eyes staring without seeing – not quite dead, but all life frozen, like an insect trapped in amber. Coming to her senses, unable to utter a word, she stumbled, and then ran into the night, dissolving into the smog that swirled into her wake.

After a few moments, slow steady footsteps announced the approach of another figure toward the now lifeless body of Joseph Stoke. With a boot on his bloodied head, the metal implement jerked free with a twist, and a spurt of blood. It was wiped clean on the arm of the coat of the now dead man. His blood pooled around his head, filling the gaps around each of the cobbles like small rivulets, a hint of steam rising from the hot effluence of his perforated skull. The same footsteps now receded from the scene, and Joseph Stoke lay alone and dead, the smog and chill embracing his corpse, undiscovered through the remainder of the night.

Chapter 11

Harland sat with a strong pot of morning tea, reading through the notes which he and Douglas Barringer had made earlier in the week, from their first cataloguing of the late Dr Amshaw's collection of mechanical curiosities. The plan had been to determine which pieces had been stolen on the night that left Mrs Amshaw widowed, and eventually to sell the collection. However, there was a further intention to this work — to trace the whereabouts of the missing pieces and, in doing so, obtain information about those responsible for the thefts. The very same people were of course the murderers of Mr's Amshaw's husband, and this was her only hope of justice.

Harland's crosschecking of each item of his own notes, against the meticulous journals kept by Dr Amshaw, had highlighted the existence of some remarkably detailed sketches. Several items had been identified to be missing, in addition to the 'Polish machine', which had so obviously been removed from its display case in Dr Amshaw's study.

Harland's concentration was broken by the sound of clocks chiming the half hour past eight in the main shop, which floated through into his back-room workshop and office. As if in perfect synchronisation, the shop door opened and in came Frederick — who was always punctual in his arrival, and cheerful in his disposition.

"Good morning Master Harland, there is a fair frost this morning, I'm glad of my scarf on a day such as this."

"Indeed," said Harland, "winter is coming upon us quickly this year. I should think to order an extra load of coal for the workshop – anthracite if we can get it. There's a good brew in the pot. Sit and have a cup, and warm your fingers before starting on that pair of carriage-clocks of Mr Broadstairs."

Frederick was a little surprised. "You want *me* to work on the champlevé carriage-clocks?"

"Yes," replied Harland, "I think you have spent enough time refurbishing our second-hand stock, and I am a little pre-occupied with some other matters. You are skilful enough – I trust you to do the job well. The larger one is to be restored and returned to Mr Broadstairs, the smaller piece is to be restored and sold as payment for the work."

Frederick was very pleased. Having worked as an apprentice for Master Harland, he knew one day he might be trusted to move on to cleaning and refurbishing the more valuable clocks, some of which were bought up from house clearers and dealers and then re-cased in modern styles. But working on a client's family heirloom was quite another matter – no room for mishaps there.

"I won't let you down Mr Harland." said Frederick. "Would this paperwork you are studying be to do with our Christmas window display?"

Harland set down his cup. "Goodness, I had forgotten it was so close to Christmas. We must not disappoint the children, or our customers. I shall have to give that some thought too."

The Horological Emporium, William Harland's renowned watch and clock shop, was well known throughout London for its Christmas window displays. Ever since William served as an apprentice under Jeremiah Varey, he had invented increasingly complex and entertaining automatons for this purpose. In some ways, this had been a saviour for the Varey family business, passed down through three generations. New production methods had gradually eroded the demand for high quality hand-made craftsmanship. But the Christmas windows soon became a word-of-mouth advertisement for Varey's Horological Emporium, and brought much new custom from well-heeled clients seeking some impressive time-piece in the latest style for their drawing rooms, or an impressive seasonal gift for a loved one.

Harland's skill at devising automated figurines, was in the best traditions of the craftsmen of Versailles. Past Christmas scenes had included Saint Nicholas, dressed in his traditional green fur-lined robe, handing out presents to poor orphans, fairy tale stories, and even a 'William Tell' scene in which an archer fired an arrow every half-hour through the day, splitting a fresh crab-apple on the head of a boy on each occasion. This tradition continued when Jeremiah retired and sold his share of the shop to Harland, who by then was an equal partner.

Victoria Jane would always help at the shop at Christmas, gift-wrapping items for customers in her home-crafted marbled papers and dyed silk ribbons, and handing out sweets to the poorer children who would come by to see the window display throughout the day.

It was hard for William to forget that he too had once been a 'street-urchin', for want of a better title. Orphaned, barely able to remember his father, or his mother, and dodging the workhouse, he had lived on the streets until eight years old. Had Jeremiah Varey not found him half frozen in the shop doorway one morning, he may well have died like so many others. Varey took him in, gave him a small store room as a lodging, a new set of clothes, and paid him a small wage as a 'night watcher" for the shop, and later as a runner – collecting and returning items to customers. William could read well in consideration of his circumstances, and he passed his nights by the workshop fire, reading everything he could find by candlelight. He was always well aware of the topics of the current interest, having read what he could of the papers each night. He particularly liked the short stories that were often serialised in the papers of the day, and reports of new and wonderful inventions. However, it was Varey's large collection of technical volumes, with their intricate diagrams, that became his constant fascination on those long evenings.

Then, to Jeremiah's great surprise, one Christmas

Eve, William presented him with a small clock-work train-engine, which he had secretly made in the workshop from discarded parts during his long evenings. It was then that Jeremiah realised that the apprentice he had been looking for was right under his nose all along. With schooling paid for by Jeremiah, Harland soon became passable as a young gentleman, and was an eager scholar during the day. His evenings were spent studying and copying simple clock mechanisms, under Jeremiah's tutelage, and in time he became a full apprentice. He was often invited to come round to Jeremiah's house after Sunday church service and then take dinner with the family.

With a new peel of clock chimes, announcing nine o'clock, Harland suddenly realised that he had spent the past half-hour reminiscing about his boyhood, triggered by the talk of Christmas window displays. His tea was now cold, and Frederick was busy front-of-shop winding the timepieces one by one. Remembering his priorities, he returned to the bookwork pertaining to the Amshaw collection. Since Victoria's death, he had not worked on any new curiosities, but now he had in the back of his mind the idea that he might dust off the 'William Tell' automaton for this year's Christmas window.

After a few hours work, the cross-referencing appeared to be complete. Dr Amshaw's collection was quite impressive. Thirty-seven mechanisms of various designs, calculating machines, curiosities, several automata dating back to the previous century, and a number of clocks and pocket watches. Harland had made careful notes, and was now able to summarise his conclusions in a letter to Douglas Barringer:

Dear Mr Barringer

I have now concluded my initial assessment of the late Dr Amshaw's collection. Dr Amshaw has kept a most diligent record of his acquisitions. As a result of our recent endeavours to catalogue everything remaining of his collection, I have been able to compile a list of the items now being found to be absent, which we must presume to be items stolen by the disgraceful interlopers of whom we wish to obtain further information.

You are aware of course that the device Dr Amshaw referred to as the 'polish machine' was removed on the night in question. I have also noted the following items as being unaccounted for in our inventory:-

i ~ Gold Pocket Watch, maker- John Bushman dated to 1702, with enamel portrait

ii~ Two matched Silver Fusee time-pieces, Boltman and son, 1822

I have also noticed that one leather-bound journal is missing from the set of five within which Dr Amshaw kept drawings of each of his collectables. I cannot find any reference to the 'polish machine in the other four volumes, yet he must surely have recorded it in detail as one of his most prized pieces. We might conclude that the missing volume is the one which contains such notes as he may have made.

I would observe that this is a rather odd situation. Having taken the time to remove a large and heavy device from its case, other items were left undisturbed. It seems that these additional items are of far less value than several other pieces within the collection that could have been taken. I cannot help but surmise that these items were taken in order to give the impression of a random theft. Yet, when one considers the missing journal, it seems that there was only one reason for their actions, and this is undoubtedly the acquisition of the mysterious polish machine. I regret that I have not yet found any drawings that might be linked to this device within the cache of loose papers, which you provided, so we have little idea what the device looks like.

Now that I have some information about the missing items, I shall begin to make some discreet enquiries, and report upon my progress.

Yours Faithfully, William Harland.

Harland sealed the letter with wax, and after giving a few instructions to Frederick, he set off to walk to the postal-office himself, since he was planning to use the new express messenger service, and needed to pay over the counter. Nonetheless, he welcomed a walk in the crisp but fresh air. As he walked down the street, he was still thinking about what to do about the Christmas window. But even if he had been paying more attention, he would not have noticed that he was now being followed at a considerable distance by an unknown observer.

His errand to the postal office was uneventful, in spite of the additional shadow in his wake. Whoever it was, they seemed content to observe – for now at least.

As Harland returned to the shop, he arrived at the same moment as Joe Parkin, a boy of nine, whom he had employed two years before. He had done this primarily to help keep him from ending up on the streets of London, as Harland himself had endured before Jeremiah Varey's charitable example was set for him to follow.

Joe would round up the local papers and advertisers each day, and bring them to the shop. Harland had always sought to stay abreast of matters of the day – it helped him to engage with his customers and at the same time, keep up with current fads and fashions whilst keeping an eye on his competitors through their various advertisements and announcements.

He handed Joe a sixpence, and took the clutch of papers.

"Look here in *The Herald,* Master Harland, some mutcher's gone and done another murder, so he has." Parkin waved his finger at the front-page story on the topmost paper, replete with a sketch of 'the actual killing', which owed much more to artistic licence than any of the facts that were recounted in the accompanying report.

"The world is full of rogues and thieves young Joe, you'd best keep your eyes about you and stay away from trouble."

Harland headed into the back office with the papers, after checking with Frederick that everything had been kept in order whilst he was absent. He then proceeded to read the front page of the Herald with studious interest...

HAS THE SLAUGHTERMAN
KILLED AGAIN?

IS LONDON'S POLICE SERVICE NO CLEARER AS TO THE IDENTITY OR MOTIVE OF LONDON'S LATEST STREET KILLER? MANY WILL BE ASKING THIS QUESTION TODAY AFTER A FIFTH MURDER IN NO MORE THAN SIX MONTHS, BEARING ALL THE SAME HALLMARKS THAT MUST SURELY LINK THEM TO THE ONE AND SAME KILLER NOW POPULARLY CALLED THE SLAUGHTERMAN. THE VICTIM, IDENTIFIED BY WITNESSES AS JOSEPH STOKE, AND WELL KNOWN TO HIS OWN KIND AS A VILLAIN AND VIOLENT MAN, WAS FOUND EARLY THIS MORNING IN THE DOORWAY OF A PAWNBROKER'S ESTABLISHMENT IN ASCOMBE LANE.

OUR ENQUIRIES WITH CONTACTS WITHIN THE POLICE SERVICE HAVE CONFIRMED THAT THE SORELY INFLICTED INJURY TO STOKE'S HEAD IS OF THE VERY SAME NATURE AS THOSE OF FOUR PREVIOUS KILLINGS. RECALLING THE OCCASION OF THE SECOND KILLING, OUR READERS MAY REMEMBER THAT THE HERALD REPORTED THAT A METAL ROD-LIKE PIECE WAS FOUND NEAR THE SCENE OF THAT PARTICULAR MURDER, WHICH MANY HAVE CONCLUDED IS NOT DISSIMILAR TO THE PNEUMATIC BOLT USED IN SOME SLAUGHTERHOUSES FOR THE INCAPACITATION OF SUCH CATTLE AND SHEEP AS WILL BE TAKEN FOR BUTCHERY.

THE MOTIVES OF THESE KILLINGS REMAIN A MYSTERY, AND APPEAR TO ALL EXAMINATION TO BE RANDOM AND HAVING NO PARTICULAR PATTERN IN CHOICE OR LOCATION OF THEIR INCIDENCE. MOTIVES OF ROBBERY MUST SURELY BE DISCOUNTED, AS SEVERAL VICTIMS WERE FOUND TO HAVE UNTOUCHED VALUABLES UPON THEIR CORPSES.

Harland shook his head, "Complete nonsense," he thought to himself, "but it serves a purpose." Harland then sat back at his desk and began to make a list, selected from his large leather-bound directory of dealers of horological items, gathered from many years under Varey, and latterly by his own effort. This was far better than any of the modern tradesman's directories, incessantly hawked around to the businessmen of London by agents of their publishers. Harland's directory contained not only reputable dealers, clockmakers, and watch repairers, but also the details of many house-clearers, curiosity shops, and even scrap merchants. The less reputable of these were marked with a red cross to show they were best avoided, often receivers of dubious goods who did not ask questions. More than once Varey had found himself in possession of a timepiece that had undoubtedly been stolen, passing up a chain from some receiver for a handful of shillings to increasingly reputable tradesmen, and increasing handsome profits. Varey was honest in his dealings, and always handed over such items to the Police once he was sure they were items that had been reported stolen. This was another reason for Harland's constant reading of the daily journals – being forewarned of recent thefts helped him to avoid losing money unnecessarily.

However, on this occasion Harland paid particular interest to the red-crossed entries in his directory. The Amshaw incident was no ordinary case of thievery and murder. He had thought this over carefully. There were at least two men involved – the Polish mechanism was obviously large and heavy – that much was obvious from the size of the case it was kept in. Having being disturbed, and then gravely assaulting Dr Amshaw, they proceeded to carry away this large object, and also one particular journal which they must have selected before being discovered. They then made an expedient departure, as the rest of the household was rousing itself. And yet, they still had time to take several valuable watches? This was either through avarice or to falsely set the scene as a petty robbery. Whatever the case, they would be unlikely to keep several stolen gentleman's watches for long. Perhaps these watches would turn up? If they did, then Harland was determined to try to find them.

Chapter 12

Harland had begun to make subtle enquiries, working through his list. And, on this particular morning, not more than two days later, he was preparing to leave his shop in Frederick's hands once again, thus freeing himself for a morning of investigation. However, Harland's intentions were diverted by an unexpected visitor.

"Mr Harland, there's a gentleman at the counter wishes to speak with you."

"Thank you Frederick, would you mind putting today's journals on top of the shelf above the stove for me – they are a little damp from that wretched sleet this morning." said Harland, as he straightened his tie and buttoned his jacket on his way to the front of shop.

"Good morning Sir, I am William Harland, owner of this establishment. May I be of assistance?"

"And I am Samuel Masterson, Butler to Sir Bertram Overard, a distinguished client of yours, I understand." Masterson presented his card.

"Indeed, I know Sir Bertram Overard very well, and his custom is most appreciated. How can I be of assistance? I hope there was no problem with his Lyndquist Pocket Watch? I am sure that it was repaired to the highest standard. I did the repair myself."

71

"I understand he was most pleased with your work Mr Harland, indeed it is upon another matter that I call. Sir Bertram has a rather sentimentally valuable grandfather clock in his study, which it appears has ceased to operate. He would be most grateful if you would call today to appraise the cause of its failing, and if at all possible, effect a repair.

Harland was somewhat preoccupied with his enquires regarding the stolen Amshaw pocket watches. In truth, he would rather have made the suggestion of sending Frederick to call on his behalf. However, Sir Bertram was a valued client, and had always had kind words to offer since the death of his beloved Victoria Jane. No, on this occasion he felt that his own attention was merited out of courtesy.

"Very well, I can call this morning. If that is your carriage waiting outside, then I would be happy to come now, if it is convenient?"

Masterson nodded, "Yes, that is Sir Bertram's own household carriage, we can return to Merrington Place as soon as you wish."

"Then allow me five minutes to collect my tools and instruments and I shall join you."

Harland instructed Frederick in his duties, and then gathered his best set of tools from the back workshop, and joined Masterson in the waiting carriage.

The journey was not long – twenty minutes by Harland's own timepiece. However, Masterson was not talkative, so Harland had spent the journey in thought. He recalled the last two days, which he had spent enquiring with the first of his list of calls he planned to make, in the hope of happening upon information about the Amshaw incident.

Several of his visits had been uneventful. Harland's first calls had been to the numerous scrap dealers, based in an area well known for its scrap merchants. Some of these turned out to be of no interest, mainly dealing in old cook-pots, ironmongery, and broken industrial machine castings. Old Jeremiah's list of contacts was evidently rather dated, and many of the smaller scrap dealers had moved away from smaller quantities of brass, bronze, and other more valuable metals, and capitalised upon the flood of scrap iron and steel now being thrown aside by the industrial revolution in full flow. However, there were still a few dealers specialising in brass work, and these offered better pickings. Barens and Son, was a scruffy establishment, one of several built into the arches under the railway viaducts that ran alongside the busy street. Lit by a couple of smoky oil lamps, it was hard to see anything of real interest. Scrap was sorted into large piles – gas-lighting fittings, handles, cogs, and mechanisms. Nothing of interest, though Harland had asked a few subtle questions nonetheless.

"I'm looking for spare parts for repairs, they need to be as-new condition – do you have anything recently arrived?"

Old Barens was not helpful, though his ill health was the main reason for his manner, and not a fault of his own making. Having lost a leg in the Crimean

73

campaign, he had been cast aside by society. Had he been an officer he would have been treated better, perhaps even revered as a returning hero. But, as a veteran of the lower classes, he had nothing to expect save for a wooden leg and a difficult life scraping a meagre living. He left Harland to rummage through the pile of miscellany for himself.

Harland picked something out at random, "Is this Polish?" Harland asked innocently.

"Polish?" Barens snapped, "What's that you're on about, it could be from Timbuktu as far as I know." Barens muttered on to himself, "I'll give im Polish..." Harland hadn't paid much heed to this. The old soldier had a habit of muttering to himself, in-between puffs on his clay pipe, and these monologues often made little sense to the casual listener.

Harland's other forays were all similar in outcome. There was nothing to be found that was worthy of more than being melted down for cheap scrap. More importantly, none of Harland's 'innocent' comments raised any kind of response that would make him think them notable enough to require any reading between the lines. Harland reconsidered each item on the list he had ticked off in his small notebook, as they journeyed on. There were still the more upmarket establishments to visit – antiquarians and house clearers mostly. He was considering visiting some of them this same morning, before having been called upon by Masterson to attend to Sir Bertram's grandfather clock. But then Harland suddenly recalled anew his trip to Barens and Son. Somehow he'd missed something. It now seemed so obvious...

As he scraped though the scrap pile, he had vaguely overhead Barens muttering as his son came along with a mug of tea for his old father.

"Here's a drop of rosy for yer, father."

Barens took the cup – his hand shaking with infirmity. "Is it Polish he sez ... bloody Polish..."

The Son had been stoked up by this, and his hackles were raised.

"Is it that kraut geezer again – I'll slap him one if it is, let me sort im out some brass if that's what he's after." Whereupon, the son had reached for a long brass stair-carpet rod, which his father kept nearby his sitting place, to stoke up a small brazier he sat next too for warmth during the winter days.

Barens stayed the rod before it got any further. "No, he's a Londoner alright, don't bother im." said Barens, who then began to cough heavily – and didn't stop. Indeed, after a minute or so, he looked like he was ready to spit up blood. Harland, by this time, concluding that he would not get any more conversation out of Barens, or his son, had taken his leave. He had forgotten what he had half-overheard in this commotion, until recalling it just now, as he rode to Sir Bertram's house.

Had someone else been around to the same scrap dealers asking about Polish machinery? And, if so, then when? Whoever it was, Baren's son had called him a Kraut, and he did not seem much pleased to have thought him calling again. This *was* something, undoubtedly, but *what*?

A few moments later, the carriage bucked harshly to one side, and came to a halt, rocking as it settled back on its springs to a normal angle. Masterson stepped out of the carriage and berated the driver. "Watch the kerb-stones you arse! You had better get that scuff sanded and painted before Sir Bertram needs a carriage again today, or I'll have it out of your wages."

Masterson remembered he had company, and tempered his chastisement. "Water the horses and then get yourself fed – we will need you again shortly."

Masterson then invited Harland to enter through the tradesman's entrance, making a point of scrubbing his shoe-soles on the coir mat, as if to emphasise that he expected the same of Harland. Inside he took William's overcoat and ensconced him in a waiting room situated to the far end of the main house.

Presently, Masterson returned. "Sir Bertram entreats you to come to his study to observe the miscreant timepiece, please follow me." Masterson was given to over-embellishing the plain and simple, a point that was more obvious having witnessed his rather lower turn of phrase with the errant carriage driver a little earlier.

Overard was in his usual welcoming mood. "Mister Harland, how good it is to see you – please come in and let us talk."

"It is my pleasure to call to your service, Sir Overard."

"Don't stand on ceremony Mr Harland, everyone calls me Sir Bertram. Masterson, fetch the 1875 amontillado and two glasses if you please."

Masterson shuffled uncomfortably. In truth, he would wish to have said "two glasses sir – are you sure?" Nonetheless, he had the sense to keep that to himself, and withdrew to his task somewhat in distaste – serving drinks to a tradesman?

"Now then, Mr Harland, my grandfather clock is misbehaving. Naturally you are the first person to come to mind for such a valuable piece – it was a wedding present to myself and Mrs Overard, from a former Dutch ambassador, and I wouldn't trust it to an amateur clock-smith."

Masterson returned and filled the two glasses with the drinks as requested. He then stood hesitantly to one side, not quite sure if it were better to stay or to go.

Sir Bertram realised that his man needed a prompt. "Thank you Masterson, you may leave us – I assure you Mr Harland is an excellent fellow – he is not about to rob my cigar case."

After Masterson withdrew, Sir Bertram was reassuringly welcoming. He asked with genuine concern how William had been since his wife's passing, and thanked him once again for the repair to his Lindquist pocket watch.

"Well perhaps we can see the problem with the old man here then..." Sir Bertram said, gesturing toward the grandfather clock.

Harland set to work, and quickly discounted the obvious: "The winding mechanism is working perfectly, I can tell by the sound of the ratchet as I turn the key. The hands appear to have plenty of free-play, they aren't restricted nor detached from the mechanism."

Harland was about to consider removing the faceplate, but took a quick look up inside the case to see what he could of the internal mechanism. With a small mirror, from his workbag, he directed sunlight up into the case to illuminate the interior.

"How odd... one moment..." Harland reached an arm up into the mechanism, now working blind. But, with many years of experience, he knew instinctively where his hand was in relation to each of the intricate parts. He withdrew his hand and presented an object to Sir Bertram. The clock stuttered and then almost immediately began to operate again in its distinctive and reassuring measure.

"I believe this is the problem, though I must admit I am at a loss to explain how the off-cut end of a cigar would come to be wedged in the escapement..."

"Extraordinary." said Sir Bertram, though his surprise was not entirely convincing.

"I cant help but notice that the cigar has been cut by one of my circular cutters, Sir Bertram. It leaves a mild but distinctive conical profile on each cigar it cuts."

"Well Harland, you have demonstrated your prowess once again, no wonder you are known as one of the best watchmakers in London. Let us celebrate with a little more amontillado, eh?"

Of course, there was no credible explanation for a cigar off-cut to have ended up in the mechanism of a grandfather clock. Sir Bertram maintained his air of innocent surprise in the matter, though it was he himself that had flicked it up inside the case, and, after quite a few attempts, found it lodged in such a way that the clock eventually came to a halt. Once this pretext for requesting William Harland to call upon him had then been set, he then needed only to despatch his long-suffering butler, Masterson, to the task of requesting Mr Harland's assistance.

The real purpose of Sir Bertram's ploy, was to bring to Harland's attention the unusual blueprints that the Britannia Club had smuggled out of Germany, hidden in a consignment of Riesling from Hamburg, a few weeks earlier.

"Tell me Mr Harland, what do you make of this curiosity? I obtained these not too long ago from a fellow I know at the Branton Gentlemen's Club."

Sir Bertram rolled out a set of blueprints. They appeared crisp and barely touched, having been copied carefully from the originals only days earlier by John Stafford's Chief Engineer at his Lime-house offices.

"This is quite an outstanding thing Sir Bertram. Whatever it is, it is undoubtedly of great complexity – I must presume it has been refined over many years of work by an accomplished clock-maker. The sheets have been kept well too … they look as good as new."

"A clock-maker you say, but not an engineer?" asked Sir Bertram, sounding a little surprised.

"Well, indeed there are aspects to this design that would suggest an engineers hand, but I also see subtleties that only a watchmaker would consider worthwhile. It could even be influenced by Babbage in places – I see patterns that remind me of his early drawings - I was fortunate to seen them in a private collection some years ago."

"Can you hazard a guess as to its purpose Mr Harland?"

"That would be most difficult without further study. This has a complexity about it, which must suggest something rather unique. It is a mystery, yet in parts it seems to me so familiar that it tugs at something distant in my mind, which I cannot quite recall at this moment."

"Mr Harland, I cannot help thinking of the story you recounted to me of Mr Babbage, and his amazing automated calculator. The fact that his work was lost and scattered, like pieces of a child's puzzle throughout the collections of Europe. That is a great tragedy for our industrious Empire. And so I would like to set you to work on this mystery, find out whatever you can of it, and I would have you rebuild it as far as it is possible, if that serves to tell us what its purpose is. Spare no cost sir – I will not be rested until I know we have an answer to this conundrum and perhaps preserve a unique piece of ingenuity for future generations to appreciate."

"Sir Bertram, I am most honoured by your confidence in me. In all honesty, I cannot say I can guarantee to meet your generous expectations, but I will do every bit as much as I am capable of doing to solve this puzzle."

"Excellent! I knew you would not be able to resist the challenge Mr Harland. I would like you to report to me each week to update me on your progress if you will? Even if you have no progress to report, I shall be vexed with myself if I should not be able to continue to discuss this device with you on future occasions. Here is a letter of engagement for your services."

Harland took the unfolded letter offered by Sir Bertram, and looked it over. "But this... well it is a sum I would not dream of asking for a months work let alone a weekly retainer."

Sir Bertram smiled reassuringly, "As I say, no expense is to be spared, and please do not hesitate to invoice any further expense that may arise."

The fact that Sir Bertram already had a contract of work to hand certainly did little to reinforce the 'incidental' circumstances of Harland's visit, but Harland was happy to leave his client's quirks to himself. This was a supreme challenge, and the sort of thing that brought back the enthusiasm of his youth as an apprentice to Jeremiah Varey. As Harland left the Overard residence, with a leather-bound folio tube, he was still a little dazed. Having been called upon to remove a cigar butt from a grandfather clock, he was now retained to undertake a work that he could rarely have dreamt of, and for a fee that would make him blush.

He approached the carriage, with newly re-polished wheel-rim, and directed the driver to return him to the Horological Emporium. On arrival he gave the driver a generous tip and retreated into his shop, unaware once again of the shadowy observer who had followed his carriage all the way to the Overard residence, and then all the way back again.

Harland saw sense in placing the leather tube straight into his secure room, where he kept all of the valuable items and materials overnight after closing. This was the small box-room he once called home – when Varey had taken him in off the street. Now the room had been fitted out with a steel door, and locks built by Harland himself, unlike any standard design in common use, and thus likely to defeat most practiced locksmiths of the criminal persuasion. The doorway was itself hidden behind a set of shelves, which were populated with various reference books, old clocks, and miscellany. Harland kept many secrets in this room, and not just those relating to his client's property.

Chapter 13

The next week or so was a busy time for Harland — divided between studying the plans provided by Sir Bertram, and the enquiries he was making on behalf of Widow Amshaw. Somehow he had managed to fit in time to set up the Christmas window display — the 'William Tell' automaton was already drawing crowds who would wait excitedly for the half-hourly event, when the automaton archer would fire a real metal arrow at the crab-apple placed on the metal boy's head, accompanied by a music box rendition of Rossini's overture.

Frederick had been a great help, taking on extra responsibility at the front of shop, and he was becoming quite accomplished as a salesman. Harland would undoubtedly give him a large bonus this year, especially as his retainer with Sir Bertram had been such a handsome and unexpected surprise.

Harland had also spent long evenings at the shop studying his treasured small section of a Babbage prototype, alongside Sir Bertram's plans. There was certainly an element of borrowed thinking in the plans provided by Sir Bertram, aspects of the Babbage style of construction were obvious, but there were other elements in the design that did not yet make sense. Nonetheless, Harland had cut and machined most of the components and would begin building a copy from the plans very soon.

Harland's daytime hours had been spent elsewhere – completing his enquiries regarding the Amshaw thefts. He had already spoken to all of the jewellers and antique dealers on his list, with no hint of the missing pocket watches. He had however made a point of asking innocently about Polish 'automata'. At each visit to a dealer, he would ask the same question "I've heard that there has been increased interest in curios from the continent – several customers have asked me about Polish novelties." In most cases, this raised no eyebrows. However, on two occasions the response of the dealer was very similar to the one he gained from Pitchman, the Jeweller.

"Perhaps you are right, we had a gentleman making such enquiries a few months ago, a foreign sounding chap, he wanted to know if there were any collectors who may have such items and might be persuaded to part with them." Harland had then asked the same question on each occasion, "And would this be a Frenchman with a brown moustache – he may be a friend of mine." Both times, he was told, "No, this fellow sounded German or something similar, he was clean shaved, and had black hair, his friend also somewhat similar."

Harland had been piecing these parts together in his head for the past few days, as he dismantled and rebuilt the Christmas window display. Did Barens say there had been a German asking about Polish mechanisms? He seemed to remember something of it

– though he ought to go back to find out more about this. Certainly, two men, possibly German, had been making enquiries about the city for some months, and accumulating much information about collectors in the metropolis. But was that enough to suggest that they were engaged in malevolence? Could they perhaps even be the ones responsible for the Amshaw thefts, and the murder of Dr Amshaw himself?

Harland had concluded that a further trip to the Barens scrap sheds might help to settle this, and he was now walking through the fairly filthy streets leading down to the riverside arches, where the scrap dealer's yards were congregated. In the far distance, the skeleton of the as yet unfinished 'Tower Bridge' straddled the river. It was a sunny day, and in spite of the cold, the streets were full of children chasing and playing, wives were gossiping on doorsteps, and a few sweeping their carpets out into the streets to get the houses ready for the Christmas festivities. Through the open doors, Harland could see a few of the houses had homemade paper-chains of newspaper hanging in their hallways, made by their children no doubt. Everything seemed homely, though this was a run-down and decaying cluster of streets. It reminded Harland of his lost childhood. He could barely remember life before his years of living on the streets. But, even in poverty, he and the other homeless pals he had kept with, would find a way to get some coal and a few other bits and pieces for Christmas day – through thrift, and occasionally a little theft, if the truth be told. A few chestnuts to roast, and perhaps enough other scraps to keep them from hunger for a change. Even if they had to spend that day like every other, in a derelict brick building by a railway junction, it still served as a roof over their heads and was their home, such as it was.

As Harland came to the turn at the end of the street, he heard a hubbub of distant commotion – shouts which he couldn't quite make out, and then as he drew closer there was a pall of smoke hanging in the relatively still air, and an unmistakable smell of burning. When he finally reached the arches, and Barens scrap sheds, he was shocked to see that the smoke was coming from within the same establishment that he had intended to call upon.

"What's happening here?" Harland asked a burly looking woman resting her washing parcel on her hip.

"The place is afire sir, they say there was a shouting match inside then the place went up all smoke and the like."

As Harland pushed through the crowd, a few men were carrying buckets of water to the doorway and throwing them in. It seemed that the worst of the flames were doused but that only made the smoke thicker. Then Harland noticed that the brass stair rod by old Barens seat was missing.

"Where is the old man and his son – not inside surely?" Harland spoke loudly to get a response from the men closest to the door.

"Can't say mister, the flames were all up the front

doorway here – no-one could get in or out – if old Barens is in there he'll be done in by smoke, what with that chest of his."

The conversation was cut short by the arrival of several constables, who pushed the crowds back. This was followed by a lot of disorganised chatter and people milling around the doorway with more buckets, until the smoke eventually died down. A constable went in and came back after a minute, coughing, and with a handkerchief to his mouth to keep out some of the smoke that was still filling most of the inside of the building.

"There's murder here – the old fellers dead – could be the smoke, but the younger one has got a cut throat – no mistakin that … get word to the yard to send down more men."

The crowd, on overhearing this unofficial and undoubtedly tactless proclamation, reacted with a mixture of murmuring, and gasps, and a few of the women started wailing.

Harland could see there was nothing he could do here now – if he stayed too long he would only draw attention to himself, and he did not want to have to explain to the police that he was here only a few days ago – they would only start asking all sorts of questions he did not have time for. In any case, he had good reason not to trust the competence of the police in such matters. Harland started to muddle back though the crowds and began to walk back toward the tenement streets, a little shocked, and wondering just what was going on? Dr Amshaw murdered in his own home by persons as yet unknown. Persons, who ignored valuable items, and yet carted away a large and heavy mechanism, in spite of the house being roused by a fateful commotion moments before. The curious foreigners about town asking about Polish machines, and now murder at Barens scrap sheds... where there was likely nothing of value, certainly nothing worth killing for. Barens son had been ready for a fight when he thought Harland was someone else, a 'Kraut' in his own words, had they returned and got embroiled in an argument that went too far?

Walking back through the adjacent run-down terraces, Harland kept going over these thoughts in his mind. There did not seem to be much hope of finding out anything else here now that Barens and his son were dead. He was preoccupied and a little dazed after witnessing the fire, smoke still making his eyes feel sore, so much so that he almost walked right into a small group arguing outside a house. It had now started to rain lightly, and the late afternoon sunshine had given way to the beginnings of dusk. Most of the children had melted away, and the gossips had gone inside to gather in their washing or wandered down to the arches to see the aftermath of the commotion. However, here were two boys being sorely dealt with by what Harland presumed to be their mother, on the steps outside their house.

"You little Dipper – I'll put your fingers through the mangle if you do this again." The mother had the older boy by the hair, "ma don't – I swear I'll ditch it and no-ones to know." Harland almost made to ignore this cameo of slum life. He had seen it enough times before, after all, when he was a boy out on the streets it was every day life. But then Harland caught a glimpse of something and he glanced back. A watch, which the boy had dipped from the pocket of some unfortunate. It looked familiar...

"And who's business is it of yours eh?" the mother turned her anger on Harland, who she saw was now looking at the watch.

"My boys no thief – who sez he is?"

"Madam, don't be concerned, I am not the police, and nor do I have any interest in doing their business for them. If you will allow me – I would take a look at this watch and perhaps take it off your hands, there may be a reward for you in finding this - *lost property* - shall we call it?" The woman bid the boy to give the watch up to Harland, but eyed him suspiciously all the while. Two scruffy looking smaller children peered through the dirty front window at the same time. He looked at it closely – there was now no doubt it was one of the two watches stolen from Dr Amshaw – it was engraved with an inscription just as documented in Dr Amshaw's journals, and inside, a picture of a younger Mrs Amshaw hand-painted within the inside of the lid was unmistakable.

"Madam, I will reward you for the find, but I will double that sum if your boy can tell me where he 'found' the piece – and be frank – I am not a magistrate – I only seek to know what the boy can tell me for my own business."

The boy spoke up without being prompted. "I *found* it in the fellers pocket, back up at the scrap yards mister. There was a jolly on at the Barens yard, two fellers were slanging it out with the old codger, then his son came out, next thing I knows they was rolling around up against the crates where I was sitting, nearly knocked me off, they did."

"So I sees he's got his yack hanging off his chain and I dips it away before he noticed anything amiss for it."

"Then I hears the big feller shouting something I didn't hear right, something he was sayin to his mate – sounded foreign like - and I did a run for it. I thought they saw what I done, but I runs fast and no-ones followed."

Harland nodded, and then passed a gold sovereign to the woman.

"Bloody Saints, that's a pretty penny sir."

Harland slipped the watch into his pocket, "I'm giving you that on an understanding that you'll keep this lad's fingers out of the mangle, and perhaps out of peoples pockets too I'd say, for good measure. And I must suggest that you do not speak of this to anyone – I fear the man who lost this watch is not someone you would wish to meet again – the less said of it the better for you and I both."

"I don't know anything about no watch mister" said the woman loudly – as if to let it be known to all the eavesdroppers. She ushered her two wayward boys into the house, clipping the older boy round the ear as he went, and then slamming the door in Harland's face. Harland understood that this was a piece of theatre – anyone looking on would assume he had been sent packing without any assistance.

Harland continued walking back toward the riverside to pick up his usual route home. It was now turning toward evening. He had taken no lunch as yet, and his stomach ached, but he would need to get back to the shop to finish up. However, this watch, it was a piece of luck he had not expected. Whoever was involved with the altercation at Barens scrap sheds, must have also been at the Amshaw house on the night of the robbery and murder, or a close associate of those who were. It could not be a coincidence, could it? No, one of the miscreants, perhaps even the murderer himself, took this watch and kept it as his own, maybe even as a macabre souvenir of his violent adventure. He would have to visit the Widow Amshaw very soon to report this development, and yet it meant more questions than answers.

Chapter 14

Later that evening, the same night as the fire at Barens Yard, Harland had worked late in his workshop at *The Horological Emporium*. He had examined the newly retrieved watch closely. There was no doubt it was the same piece taken from Dr Amshaw's study, during the robbery in which the doctor had himself been murdered. Harland had already sent a telegram to Douglas Barringer, Widow Amshaw's trustee in dealing with his contract, to find out what else he could of the watch. He hoped for a reply from Barringer first thing in the morning.

Meanwhile, he had busied himself in further study of the problem set by his new benefactor, Sir Bertram. Having built several trial assemblies based upon the blueprints supplied by Sir Bertram. Harland had now built what he could of the mysterious mechanism. It now appeared to be fully operational, though it was far from clear what this device actually did. It was not a clock, or any kind of regular timekeeper, that much was certain. The whole device measured some 40 inches in length, and a foot in height and width. Perhaps it was too large to transport conveniently to Sir Bertram's residence? He would have to ponder that before the next report to Sir Bertram upon his progress. It was also apparent that an important section was missing. "The blue-prints must be incomplete." thought Harland. Nonetheless, he could see that the missing part appeared to receive a number of actuations from the surrounding parts of the machine, via levers and rods in the adjacent mechanisms.

It was now quite late, as had just been announced by a cacophony of chiming timepieces in the main shop, counting the twelve hours of midnight. Harland decided that he was too tired to continue fruitful work, and his stomach reminded him once again that he had yet to eat properly since lunchtime. He turned out the workshop gaslights, and his main work-lamp, having first locked away the plans and prototype device in his strong-room. Harland then put on his long-coat, locked the shop, and walked out of the doorway, pausing to admire the Christmas window display. It was only then that he realised that it was almost Christmas. *'Two more shopping days'* read the hand-written card, which was newly replaced on display by Frederick at the end of each day.

Harland began to walk homeward, thinking of Christmas past. Such happy years he had spent with Victoria, who always held the spirit of Christmas in her heart. He remembered how they would give out sweets and candies to the poor children, who flocked to the Christmas window automaton displays and music boxes devised by Harland himself each year. Only the pain of being childless had tempered the joy of the festive season for William and Victoria. But what was Christmas to him now? His wife was gone, his home empty of joy and happiness. He had barely noted the passing of the days toward Christmas day itself. Indeed, he should have remembered to gather some titbits and Christmas fayre for his table, take delivery of some extra logs for the fire, and obtain a choice bottle of port to salve his loneliness. There was still a day or so to purchase a few items he thought, though he did so with little enthusiasm at the thought of being alone on Christmas day once again.

Harland had been walking for ten minutes or more, through the near deserted streets, and had been too lost in his own thoughts to realise he had strayed into the run-down back streets that were best avoided. In daylight, or even early evening, he would feel comfortable walking these short-cuts and snickle-ways, and did so often. But these streets had a character that could change with the hours – much like the tragic Dr Jekyll he had enjoyed reading of, in a novella by the author Robert Louis Stevenson. By day, they would be bustling streets, with cheery characters who would bid good day, and a few of whom Harland would stop to chat to when the weather encouraged dallying. But, by night, they could become a dark and dank series of iniquitous rat-runs, harbouring the unsavoury and unkempt underclasses, the ladies of the night, the gin-sodden, and the knife-men.

Harland came to an abrupt halt, shaken from his ethereal memories and thoughts by two large men, blocking the alleyway down which he sought to proceed. The route was not completely dark. A few houses, with light straying from behind ramshackle shutters, added to the dim gaslight glow of a nearby street-lamp. Harland stepped back a pace, and the two men stepped forward. Harland had done this instinctively, as it brought their faces out of the shadow and into at least a little light. He could now see the faces of the two men. They were both ragged – unshaved, and one had what might be described as a beard, though it did little to disguise a long scar running down from his cheek and across his chin. The other had an uneasy smile, not flattered by three missing front teeth. They both stank of gin, and did not look like characters that one would wish to reason with.

"Gentlemen, forgive me, I did not see you in the darkness. Allow me to stand aside so that you can pass." said Harland, intimating that he would step into a doorway and make room for them to continue on their way.

The men did not move. Instead, the scar-faced one spoke gruffly. "What's a well dressed feller doing down here – looking for a touch of the mop... is that your game?"

Then the second man interjected, and displayed that he was clearly the lesser intelligent of the two.

"If he's after a wagtail then he must have some coin eh skinner, or maybe eez a soddin drake."

Scar-face erupted at this. "You flamin mug, have I not told yer about names? I'll shut that big mouth up for good next time, and now we'll have to shut this geezer up as well, for good measure."

Scar-face then turned his anger on Harland, pulling out a knife from his sleeve in the blink of an eye. "Turn out your pockets you frig, and maybe we'll let you go."

Harland's mind raced with conflicting thoughts... he could empty his pockets, and then make a run for it whilst the two fought over their shares, or perhaps they would take what he had and then set upon him regardless. But then as he fumbled in his greatcoat pockets, stalling for a moment to focus his mind, he suddenly rediscovered the Amshaw watch wrapped in his handkerchief. He had forgotten to put it back in the strong room before leaving the shop!

He could not allow them to take that... and they surely would if they went through his coat. Besides, handing over anything to these two villains went against his principles, even though he knew life on these streets was a hard living. If they had begged the price of a bottle of gin, he may well have given them a few shillings to tide them by. But these two were not petty thieves, they were seasoned and likely to be quite capable of killing to save their own skins.

Harland tried to slip the watch back without being noticed, but it was too late. The gleam of the metal had caught the dim shafts of light from a nearby window-shutter, and Scar-face had seen it!

"So you *are* a well-to-do then, by the looks of that jerry. Hand it over, and the ring." Scar-face prodded Harland's right hand, and the mourning ring he wore in memory of Victoria. He had commissioned it to be

96

made from her own wedding band, which was still on her finger when she died in his arms. Unusually it had not been stolen when she was attacked. He certainly was not prepared to give *that* up.

"No!" said Harland, instinctively protecting the one thing he would never give away, even to avoid bloodshed.

In a moment, the dynamics of the situation were transformed from standoff to conflagration. Scar-face was enraged. In an instant, he lashed out toward Harland's face with his blade, attempting to slash Harland across his eye-line. But Harland reacted quickly, pulling his head back to dodge the tip of the razor sharp metal, and blocking his assailant's forearm with his own. The leather of his heavy overcoat was cut through, such was the sharpness of the blade, but he himself was not cut – instead the sound of metal grating against metal signalled that the blade had encountered something unexpected. Harland grabbed the wrist of Scar-face with his hand, preventing further knife-work for now. But Scar-face then grabbed Harland by the throat with his own free hand, a hand with a steely grip.

They struggled together, but Harland could feel almost immediately that he was losing the battle for consciousness, it was then that he caught a glimpse of 'toothless' coming toward him with a broken bottle, and raised his free arm toward him. Harland began to pass out. Yet, in that same instant, toothless felt a hammer-blow of force to his face and staggered back, slumping against a wall, blood spurting from his nostrils, a metal rod embedded in his cheekbone, eyes wide, barely able to summon a gulp of air, as he slid down the wall now supporting his failing strength. Within seconds Scar-face loosened his grip on Harland, choking on his own blood – confused – his throat cut ear to ear, he fell onto his knees right where he stood, coughing blood out of the six-inch gape opened across his neck, mouthing something breathless and inaudible before he too slumped onto the foul and dirty patina of the back street gutter. People were now rousing from their fireplaces... window shutters creaking open one by one... just enough for searching eyes to peer out anonymously at the commotion. But, silently, Harland's seemingly lifeless body was drawn away into the dark shadows, and then lost in the dark cloak of the night.

Chapter 15

Harland woke with a start. It seemed to him, through a fog of semi consciousness, almost as if he had been awoken by a door slamming in the distance. He recognised his surroundings, his own day room at his home, and found himself laying upon the chaise-longue by the bay-fronted window, curtains still open. In his blurry awakening, he thought he saw a figure down in the street, briskly walking away from his house frontage and into the half-light of the night.

He immediately felt his throat throb, and putting his hand to his neck felt painful to the touch. The smell of ammonia lingered in his nostrils, and he noticed upon the side table a bottle of sal-volatile smelling salts. Not only that, but the pocket watch he had risked so much to protect was laid there too, along with something else... something wrapped in a bloodied handkerchief.

Harland felt steadier now, his vitality returning, though his head and throat throbbed as each pulse of his heart grew more robust. He came to his feet and poured a large brandy, and sat for a few moments to salve his throat with its medicinal vigour.

"What on earth has occurred here?" Harland thought to himself, trying to reconstruct events from a dull mist of recollections. The dark alleyway, the confrontation, his throat being gripped like a vice, and then darkness. But how on earth did he awake here in his apartment, with his intended journey completed without consciousness?

"This makes no sense to me, yet it seems I am indebted to a stranger..."

Harland swallowed another mouthful of brandy, and then returned his attention to the side table. The watch was intact. That was a relief considering its cost in human blood was rising considerably. But what on earth was this claret-stained mess sitting alongside? He stared at a rolled up handkerchief, steeped with half-dried blood.

Harland carefully placed the bundled item upon a newspaper, and then, taking one still clean corner of the cloth, he unfurled the wrapping like a flag. Out rolled a metal rod, about five or six inches long, blood still covering its bright metal surface, but not so much as to disguise its unusual appearance. He noticed the squared profile of its cross-section, and the narrowly tapering point, needle-like but now slightly blunt from an impact of some force.

Harland washed the rod clean, and threw the handkerchief and some of the newspaper sheets into the fire grate, lighting some kindling to keep the small fire burning long enough to consume the dampened cloth and reduce the papers to ash. How it came to be on his table he did not know, but he would leave no trace of where it had been. He slid it into a drawer in his study, jangling against some other metal items as it rolled out of his hand. Harland was weary and ached everywhere from the earlier violent end to his evening.

He retired to bed with his half-finished brandy and fell into a fitful sleep.

~

Harland awoke early the next morning. His night had not been comfortable. His throat now felt a little less pained, but his mind was more so. Moments of more peaceful sleep had been punctuated by turmoil. Random thoughts swirled in his dreams, recollections mixed together, repeating through the night. But, always, the cadence of his visions would reach the same discordant climax... his beloved Victoria, choking at the hands of a foul and evil man, unable to cry out, her eyes flickering into unconsciousness, Harland somehow immovable... frozen and unable to intervene. And then, in an instant, he found himself transposed as the one being choked with foul hands, hands belonging to Scar-Face, tightening around his neck. And then finally, Victoria was the one being choked again. As the life ebbed from her, she pulled at the assailant's clothing, and a button ripped free, clattering onto the tiled hallway floor. Finally, tossing violently in his bed, Harland came to. In a half awakened state, he sat up, wringing with perspiration, his breath steaming with the cold air in the room. No fire had been lit that night and the air was sharp and frigid.

Harland raised himself from the edge of the bed, walked to the window, and drew back the thick curtains. He peered through the intricate feather-work traceries of ice on the inside of the panes, lit like a lantern by the early hints of a rose-tinted dawn sky. He looked out across his narrow vista of the city of London and spoke to his own thoughts.

"Where is justice? Where is right known from wrong in this vile city? Must each man seek that for himself?"

Chapter 16

Sir Bertram Overard began each day with a rigid regimen. The eve of Christmas was no different. Indeed, only Christmas Day itself was of enough importance to yield to any variation. But today was Christmas Eve, and Sir Bertram had already been roused by Masterson, who brought hot tea to his bedside before opening the windows wide. This was the daily morning routine, regardless of the season or nature of the day. Next, he would bathe in a hot copper tub, and finally he would appear at precisely 8.30 am to take breakfast with his wife.

Breakfast in the Overard household was always comprehensive: kedgeree, cold cuts of meat, a lavish cheese-board accompanied by freshly baked bread from his own kitchens, a selection of preserves, tea, and two blends of coffee. Sir Bertram preferred a strong Parisian blend, whilst his wife preferred something milder and less giddying.

However, Sir Bertram had only progressed so far as to settle into his ornate copper roll-top tub, and had begun to work through his morning postal deliveries whilst half-submerged in the steaming, salted, and perfumed waters. Masterson would always sort these into three batches, each bound with a ribbon. Any letter bearing a Westminster postmark, or indeed a hand-stamp from either houses of parliament, formed one parcel. This was always bound by a red ribbon. Other letters, usually of a personal nature, would be bound with blue ribbon. Finally, a green ribbon bound up the usual small cache of telegrams Sir Bertram received at his residence each day, delivered both by the General Post Office and often by daily despatch runners from Westminster. Sir Bertram could then deal with each batch in the order he preferred.

Sir Bertram could see that there were numerous cards of seasonal greetings in amongst the blue-ribbon parcel, and decided to keep these aside, to open at breakfast with his wife. He worked through the red-ribbon batch - letters from constituents to be passed to his parliamentary secretary, notices regarding forthcoming debates in the house, and a miscellany of correspondence between himself and honourable members. These days, the tone of these latter items was more often abrasive than supportive.

"Darrington!" Sir Bertram exclaimed. "The man's a complete ass." Sir Bertram would often speak his mind whilst reading these letters, something Masterson had endeavoured to learn to discretely ignore. Those particular letters would usually end up being scattered around the bathroom floor by the time Sir Bertram roused from the water to dress for breakfast, and Masterson was used to the task of having to dry out wet footprints from these on blotting paper more often than not.

Masterson hovered by the door for a moment, and then retreated, realising this was just another of Sir

Bertram's outbursts, and not a call for his assistance.

Finally, Sir Bertram moved on to the green-ribbon cache of telegrams. Late greetings of the season from a cousin in New York, a confirmation from an old friend that he would join Sir Bertram at his Highland estate for New Year celebrations, and then a telegram from Germany – Telegrafenamt, Zimmer Strasse, OSNABRUCK *(Zimmer Street Telegraph Office, Osnabruck).*

UNCLE GUSTAV PASSED AWAY LAST NIGHT STOP
HIS BROTHER IS NOT AT HOME STOP

Sir Bertram practically stood up bolt upright in the bathing tub, sending streams of water in every direction. "God's eyes!"

"Masterson!"

Masterson arrived almost immediately, fearing some mishap. He was slightly surprised to find Sir Bertram, dripping wet and naked, waving a telegram in his hand. He decided not speaking was best on this occasion, rather than making one of his occasional wry observations.

"Masterson..."

"Yes Sir, may I assist?"

"Take this telegram immediately, locate my Britannia Club members list, and have this telegram sent to each of them. Do so immediately, leave your other duties aside."

"I shall send Jacobs to the Telegraph office immediately sir."

"No! I need you to do this yourself... despatch each telegraph by your own hand, and add a further line to read as follows..."

URGENT
STOP
PLEASE ATTEND SUPPER THIS EVENING AT
MERRINGTON PLACE EIGHT PM
STOP

Masterson nodded as he noted down the additional line of the message. "Very well Sir, I will leave immediately for the telegraph office."

Sir Bertram dried and dressed himself. He picked up the blue-ribboned parcel of letters, and adjourned to the breakfast room, feeling deeply unsettled.

Sir Bertram presently arrived in the breakfast room, a large oak panelled room with huge windows. A well-established fire crackled in the fireplace. Masterson was absent and in his haste had not had time to instruct the junior boy, Jacobs, to take his place to serve breakfast.

Sir Bertram's wife, Amelia, had already served herself up a plate of kedgeree and devilled kidneys and was actually enjoying the solitude of breakfast without either her husband or the hovering attention of Masterson.

Amelia looked up from her breakfast plate, expecting to see Masterson coming back to explain his absence.

"Oh it is you Bertie. You do look rather ruffled dear - whatever is the matter. Did you not sleep well again?"

"My dear, I'm a little troubled today with bad news."

"What of it? is it Westminster business?"

"I wish it were as simple as that. I'm afraid there have been some developments regarding our Osnabruck activities."

Amelia frowned. She was well aware of Sir Bertram's Britannia Club activities. Sir Bertram was wise enough not to keep secrets from Amelia. In any case, she had a way of subtle interrogation that had helped Sir Bertram's political strategies on numerous occasions. Her intuition, for those who had a similar outlook as Sir Bertram, had helped him to make connections that he himself would have missed, several of which were invaluable to the Britannia Club's purposes.

"Amelia, I'm afraid that Uncle Gustav has come unstuck. I have called up the Britannia Club 'brigade' for supper tonight. I know it is all rather inconvenient with it being Christmas Eve, but we must discuss these developments at once."

"I understand my dear. I hope you haven't forgotten that we have allowed the servants time off this evening for Christmas midnight mass, though I suspect a few of our boys might find themselves in a local tavern before hand. I will ask the kitchen staff to prepare some cold plates for your gentlemen before they take their leave."

"Excellent my dear, though I'm not sure our appetites will be altogether as keen as they ought to be this evening, once we have discussed these developments."

"Well, let us not dwell on that now, I see we have a brace of greetings cards, shall we open them together and enjoy the calm before the storm Bertie?"

Sir Bertram finished breakfasting in his wife's company, but spent the rest of the day in a restless state. The telegram from Germany was a serious matter, and not just for 'Uncle Gustav'. He was well aware that this news could have repercussions that reach much closer to home. He spent the afternoon pacing the polished cedarwood floor of his study, ignoring the parliamentary paperwork that usually took up much more of his time than he desired, even on Christmas Eve. Finally, after managing a late afternoon meditation by a warm fire, assisted by a small brandy, Sir Bertram set about changing into his evening suit and preparing for the evening ahead.

Chapter 17

Meanwhile, in Bremen, at the same as Sir Bertram attended to arranging his evening affairs, darker matters were unfolding.

A coarse leather-gloved hand rapped on the unlit door of the disused *Faerber warehouse*, answering quickly to the voice behind its large expanse.

"It is Geltz, we are expected. Come on, open the door, we are turning to ice out here." Each word spoken by Geltz turned into a vent of steam in the cold air. The dim light from nearby buildings could barely penetrate the flurrying snowfall, which had laid out a white carpet, eight inches deep, in the street where the two had just walked. Their footprints were already starting to lose their shape, as new snow-flakes accumulated over their outlines, even as they stood by the doorway for just a short while.

The door grated and clanked, as several heavy bolts were drawn back, and the door itself snatched loose from an encasement of refrozen ice-melt around the door frame. Two figures stepped inside, feeling a wave of warmth penetrating their half-frozen noses and chilled fingers. Geltz wasted no time moving to the brazier to get some further relief, and poured an excessive measure of gluhwein into a large wooden cup. His hands stung with the heat from the fire as it penetrated his icy fingers.

"Get yourself some of this Eichel."

Geltz's compatriot said nothing, but pulled off his gloves, and poured another cup of the drink.

The door keeper, Brandt, spoke gruffly. "He is here, but he has told me to keep you down here until you are called. He also said I should keep you sober, so you had better steady your arm before you pour any more of that grog."

"Well at least we can get warm," said Eichel, "I've never seen such a cold winter these past few weeks."

"I'm glad to be in here with all this firewood, that is for sure." Brandt waved his arm toward a huge pile of broken packing cases at the other end of the large room they were standing in."

"Well, I'd rather be freezing here in Bremen than come down with cholera in Hamburg." Eichel almost stopped himself saying this, and he knew Getlz's scowl spoke of the fact that he had a big mouth. The 'Boss' did not like loose tongues, even among his own henchmen. Each business has its own place, and each man should keep to his own concerns. Brandt was well aware of this, and said nothing.

The three settled down near the brazier to wait, sharing some bread and cheese and talking of small things for a while. Then, a heavy-footed and somewhat large-built character came stomping down the wooden stair, stopping halfway down the flight.

"Geltz, the Boss wants to see you now, bring your dachshund with you." Eichel looked pained at this, but said nothing, and was probably well advised to do so.

110

Chapter 18

Sir Bertram chewed the butt of his cigar, already feeling a little apprehensive about the discussion yet to be had with the compatriots sat around the table with him. The Britannia Club was in session, and their business was not seasonal jollity.

"Gentlemen, thank-you for coming along tonight. I'm sorry you had to leave your families, tonight of all nights, to come along, but I am sure you will agree we have some worrisome news to digest. By the way, Cecil is in Edinburgh and could not make it back for our business – there's a swathe of snowfall across the north and into the highlands, the locomotives are head-to-tail in Edinburgh station with no-where to go."

Around the table were most of the regular 'club' members, among them John Stafford, Jerome Asner, and Lord Marcus Ainscough. Several silver platters were set upon the table, with sliced cold meats, bread, fruit, and pickles. A case of cigars sat at one end of the table, and the room was already thick with smoke.

"Well Bertram, I for one don't have to worry about tying up ribbons – or those damned pine-needles!" Jerome Asner made slight humour of his Jewishness, to lighten the mood a little, but he knew as well as Overard that this wasn't a good day.

"So, Bertram, tell us the facts as you know them and

then lets hear this other news that John is fretting about."

Sir Bertram sipped his brandy and fidgeted with the telegram card he had received earlier in the day. This was the very same card that had set in motion this whole gathering. He placed it flat onto the table, as if he was at the dispatch box at Westminster and about to address the house.

"As you know, we have received bad news." Sir Bertram paused, then picked up the telegram slip, and read it out aloud.

"UNCLE GUSTAV PASSED AWAY LAST NIGHT."

He read slowly, as if he were reading a newspaper headline.

"As we all should know, this is part of the coded telegram system we have been using since establishing our small outpost in Osnabruck two years ago."

"This hardly disguises its true meaning – Bernhardt Becker is dead. We must assume that this was deliberate. Especially as we also know that Schmidt is no longer in town - HIS BROTHER IS NOT AT HOME."

"Quite so," added Stafford, "we have to hope he was able to slip away unseen, and that he can remain out of reach of further risk to himself."

"That is my hope too," said Sir Bertram, "he has taken risks for us, and we should do all we can to retrieve him from this situation. I have already alerted our contact in Delmenhorst. If he arrives there, at our safe-house, then we can get him quietly out of the country. Let us hope the bad weather on the continent and seasonal distractions might allow him some advantage."

There was a silent pause, for what seemed like several minutes, whilst each of those around the table soberly considered their responsibility for what had transpired.

Jerome Asner put down his glass. "Since Becker is presumed dead, we have to assume that his killers know enough about what he was doing to make it worth spilling his blood, or breaking his neck. We may wonder... was it the German authorities, the military, or someone else? To my mind, this doesn't seem like an act of apparatus of the state. No doubt, they would not hesitate to kill for national interest, but here I say that national interest is precisely why they would not kill... Becker would be more valuable in a show trial. A foreign spy would be proof that Germany must build its defences, and so-on."

Stafford nodded in agreement, "Yes, that's an excellent observation, Jerome. That being so, we have to assume that this was the act of another interloper. One with interests similar to our own perhaps? But who are they? How far is their reach in all of this?"

Ainscough had not yet spoken, but straightened a little in his seat and cleared his throat. "We have irons in several fires, but we all know that the only really interesting thing that has come from these contacts is the Polish engineering drawings. And, I might add that they are the thing that we know the least about. I can't help feeling that, if we solve that conundrum, we will shed light on everything else that is afoot here."

Stafford took a sharp breath. "I certainly agree Marcus, but I'm afraid I have to add another matter into this maelstrom, and one that is likely as not to be related to your conundrum, as it happens."

Sir Bertram looked puzzled. "Then tell us dear Stafford, if it is of such importance then let us have it."

Stafford stood up from his chair, and paced a little as he recounted what he had to say, tapping his chin as if to stimulate his memory.

"I think you must remember our discussions after the delivery of Sir Bertram's Miterlrhein Riesling... the Polish papers were hidden in the shipping crates brought over from Hamburg by a former employee of our shipping office there. A very reliable fellow going by the name of Maierhofer."

Asner and Ainscough nodded, as Stafford continued to recall earlier events.

"After our 'wine tasting' I made arrangements to cover our backs and the back of your clock-smith, this fellow Harland, whom you have entrusted to examining the blueprints which we have had copied. When Maierhofer turned up at my offices in Limehouse, it was the same morning that our cargo-steamer the SS Fathom docked at our nearby berths. He explained how he had to save his skin by leaving Hamburg along with the 'wine shipment'. He very nearly had his throat cut doing our business. Naturally, I made sure that he could establish himself in London, since he had no hope of returning to Hamburg for the time being. I knew he could be useful to us at some point. I gave him some instructions... suggested he change his appearance before coming back to the offices, buy some new clothes and shoes, adopt a new identity, and then come and see me in a few days."

As Stafford continued, he replayed the earlier events in his 'minds eye', as if returning to his office on that particular morning...

It had begun with Maierhofer being ushered into John Stafford's large office and draughting room by the clerk, this time somewhat more deferential to Sir John's visitor, announcing his arrival.

"Mr Mayer. I believe he is expected sir."

"Come in, please have a seat." Stafford gestured, entreating *'Mayer'* to sit down. "So you have taken my advice on your arrival in London then?"

Mayer spoke with a softer Germanic accent than he had done upon his previous visit, appearing then as Jacob Maierhofer. A week in London, in his new lodgings, had allowed him to regain some of his proficiency with common English. He had picked much of it up working in the Hamburg shipping offices, where he regularly dealt with the English captains and crewmen of the Stafford Associated Shipping Company.

"I have made my self at home, and I think London must be home now, for 'Jack Mayer' as you no doubt know. So tell me what have you in mind for me?"

John Stafford sat down on the chair opposite, and poured fresh tea for each of them from a pot already waiting on a small side table.

"I need your services once again my friend. I know you have paid a price for the assistance you have rendered to me in Hamburg, I can only say I am sorry for causing you so much consternation."

Mayer nodded, "It is true I have had something of an unexpected journey, but I have one or two relatives here, and none left back there any more. My countrymen leave by the shipload every week these days, the great migration we call it, and from all over Europe too it seems. Besides, Hamburg is rife with the cholera, as well as the disease of anti-Semitism, and neither of these afflictions appeals to me, as a German or a Jew. So it seems I am at your service."

"Then let me explain," Stafford continued, " I will tell you as much as I think you will need to know to assist me. There is a man - a watchmaker - by the name of William Harland. Let us just say that we have some business with him, and I worry for his well-being. I need you to make sure he is not bothered by unexpected situations, and I would like to know where he goes, and whom he talks to as he busies himself with our affairs. He is undertaking some important work for us, you understand..."

"I do, Mr Stafford. Whatever it is, perhaps it is better I do not know. But you can rely upon my discretion and diligence."

Around the dining table at Merrington Place, the

assembled Britannia Club members were hanging on Stafford's next word as he paused in his verbal recollection of events.

"And so gentlemen, *my* Mr Mayer has been watching *your* Mr Harland's back for some time, and my precautions would appear to have been very prudent as there have been 'developments'."

Stafford then began to explain what had happened on the next occasion he had met Mayer face-to-face.

"Two days ago Mayer came to see me at Limehouse. I knew something was amiss as he usually sent written reports to my office each week, and was only to call in person on the first weekday of each month to collect salaries and expenses."

Sir Bertram interjected, "So what has happened? Has Harland been involved in some incident?"

"Indeed he has, but let me assure you straight away that he is safe... let me explain further what Mayer had to say."

Stafford's narration drifted back to his recent meeting ... Mayer was agitated, certainly not in a panic, but eager to talk to John Stafford, as he settled into a green leather chair in his office.

"Mr Stafford, I apologise for coming without sending notice, but you did say I should do so if something serious were to occur."

"That is the case. So, tell me what is your news."

"Mr Stafford, I have been keeping my close eye on your Mr Harland as usual. As you know, I have rented a small upstairs workshop that gives me a view of his

117

premises. By day, I can observe if he comes or goes. Of course, I make notes. And I know his habits in this respect. At night I can follow him to his house, and out again."

"Last night there was an incident, and I was forced to intervene. Earlier in the same day, Harland left his shop, and travelled over to an area known for traders of scrap and various 'bric-brac', as you English are calling it. I stayed at the far end of each street that he walked down, so that he was never aware of being followed. Then he got a little ahead of me, and when I caught up and turned the corner there was a great commotion. A place they call 'Barens Yard' was full ablaze, smoke everywhere and flames high over the doorway. Harland stayed for a while talking to people and watching. Then he came back along the same street I had followed him down earlier. He appeared to follow a boy, some way ahead of him, and called at his house. I couldn't see what business he had there, but then he moved on, and I resumed my following."

"And this commotion and fire... was Harland involved or injured?" Stafford had enquired.

"No, well not at that place, let me tell more: He returned to his shop and stayed their until very late in the evening. He then left, and I assumed he was heading home. It was very dark at this time, and I found it hard to follow him. But, as he neared his home, he took a few back alley-ways, and I found myself catching up again at a turn, only to be shocked once again by the situation."

Mayer shifted in his seat. "That alley was very dim, and I could not see so much, but I could see Harland stopped, and two men seeming to block his path. I edged closer with the darkness hiding me, and then I could hear that Harland was in trouble... raised voices and threats I heard. Then a struggle and fight broke out. One of these men had Harland by the throat, and had a large knife, the other held a broken bottle, I could see that he would soon use it without further hesitation"

"My God," said Stafford, "is Harland dead?"

"No, do not worry. You gave me a task to follow him and keep him away from harm, I was careless in my following perhaps, but not in the duty of keeping him safe. As they fought, I ran quietly toward the two. They had turned their backs to my approach, in the struggle, and the two men did not see me. When I approached, Harland seemed to be dropping at his knees, I could see he was having the life choked out of him. I am afraid to say that, at that point, I fell back on my instincts, and I sliced through the throat of the first... the one with his hands around Harland's neck. I was about to turn my blade on the second one when he was thrown back by some force to his head and he fell where he stood, just as Mr Harland passed out. As I went to his aid, I saw what had killed the second man. It was some kind of metal rod that had gone clean through his head and practically out the other side. I pulled it out and wrapped it in a handkerchief. Then I dragged Mr Harland into another alley to avoid attention. Many people were rousing from their doors, and I needed to get him away safely, without us being seen too clearly."

Stafford was shocked. "This is incredible... I can barely make sense of it. Of course, you have done a damned good job, do not worry about those two criminals, the police have little idea what goes on in the slums of London. I also have contacts in the press. We will make sure rumours circulate of the two men fighting each other over money, the police will lose interest soon enough, and the penny-gazettes will embellish the events to such an extent that they will have little resemblance to what actually happened."

"And what about this odd business... this metal bolt you mentioned? Have you brought it here?"

Again, Mayer looked agitated. "I'm sorry, Mr Stafford, I have made a mess again I think. After I dragged Harland away from the place of the fight, I got him to a safer area and waved down a cab. I said 'my master had too much to drink again!', and the cabman was all too happy to help – he said it happened nearly every night. At Harland's house, I gave the driver a big tip and carried Harland to his front room, and found some salts to bring him awake. I knew I had to leave quickly as Harland started to come round, so I slipped away, only to realise I had left that metal bolt, still wrapped in the handkerchief on his side table. I could not go back without Harland seeing me."

Stafford nodded "I see. Well, do not worry, you did

the right thing, you got Harland to safety, you made sure he was not badly hurt, and he knows nothing of you. I'm glad to add that you got away without gaining any scars of your own, that's more than enough. Though, I can't think what he will make of your left-behind ornament..."

Stafford sat back down at the table, where Sir Bertram and most of the Britannia Club members were listening attentively to his recollection. His mind returned to present company and there was much to discuss.

"We went over the whole thing again, and after Mayer Left, I was struck by something he said about this metal bolt... something familiar that I could not quite reach into my memory and grasp. I spent the afternoon searching through my newspaper archive, which our office keeps for various shipping and trade reasons. Then I found this..."

Stafford placed on the table a newspaper, pointing to an article, illustrated with a sketch of an odd metal spike. The accompanying headline was underlined with a red draughtsman's pencil...

"SLAUGHTERMAN KILLS AGAIN?"

Chapter 19

Eichel and Geltz stepped briskly up the cascade of wooden stairs, which linked the front area of the Faerber Warehouse to the first floor above. In front, leading the way, was the heavy-set figure that had called them up to see *'The Boss'*. At the head of the stairway, a door was half open and much brighter light spilled out from within. As they entered, the brightness forced their eyes to adjust.

One part of the room was well lit. A fireplace was well stacked with logs, and next to it a large desk, chairs, and other business-like trappings. With the addition of a Turkish rug laid on the floor between the desk and the fireplace, and several bright oil lamps set upon the desk, it was as if someone had scooped up a gentleman's study and dropped it in the middle of what was otherwise an empty and unwelcoming void of bare floorboards and dirty, roughly plastered walls.

The brightness of the lamps made the farther corners of the room darken by contrast. However, Geltz could make out figures in the dim light. The 'Boss' was there at the desk, but hard to see clearly with the lamps between him and themselves. As he raised himself from his chair, he became fully visible to Geltz and Eichel.

"So gentlemen, you have arrived – eventually – but I will overlook your lack of haste since the weather has been somewhat unkind to us these last few days. However, do not think I have forgotten about Hamburg - if you had slit the correct throat at the docks we would not be in the position we now find ourselves in... Do not make any more mistakes."

Geltz knew better than to make excuses, better to be deferent. "Herr Neumann, I tell you once more I am sorry for our failure, we will not be so easy to be made fools of next time." Eichel said nothing. He was the junior in this arrangement. Geltz did the talking and the thinking for both of them. So far, so good. Geltz had managed to keep both of them intact, in spite of their errors in Hamburg. They each still have five fingers on each hand, unlike some less fortunate employees of 'the Boss', who was fond of giving his charges permanent reminders of their mistakes, at least the lucky ones... the others did not fare so well.

How easy it would have been to slit the throat of their wiry dark-haired prey in Hamburg that night, if only they had not been thrown into disarray by a simple trick. Tailing their quarry across town, the plan was to find out where he intended to deliver his consignment, and to make sure he never got there. This meant following and not killing, at least in the first place. That was how they ended up in the bier-keller, distracted by loose women and jugs of beer when they should have been wondering what their man was doing upstairs with two of the girls. By the time they realised he had left through a back window, they had given themselves a lot of ground to make up.

More by luck than sense, they guessed he was headed for the docks – there was not much else around there, and by Geltz's reasoning they managed to get back on his trail and were virtually upon him as they reached the waterfronts. Had they not come across a drunk in the wrong place at the wrong time, and mistook him for their man, they would have been basking in glory, instead of wiping blood off their hands onto the overcoat of an innocent and wayward watchman steeped in kirsch. By the time they realised their mistake, their trail was lost. Three days spent back at the apartment, where their stalking began that night, yielded nothing. Their man had gone to ground, and Herr Neumann was ready to have them both skinned alive. Somehow Geltz had talked them both out of a tight corner. He had managed to blame the drunken night-watchman for intervening in a fight with their mark, and for allowing him the opportunity to flee in the commotion. Neumann bought the story that time. But Eichel was well aware that they had a close shave with Neumann's formidable intolerance for failure. There would be no second chances...

"So Gentlemen," Neumann began, "let me tell you precisely what you need to know, and I warn you not to ask about those things I choose to keep to myself."

Neumann paused theatrically, before continuing. "The rat you allowed to slip through your hands in Hamburg was simply a messenger boy. For whom? I do not know, but I expect that this problem may resolve itself rather soon if we lay our plans carefully."

Neumann looked over to a darker corner of the large attic store room, as if to point out what Geltz and Eichel appeared to have overlooked so far.

Two large thugs stood there, one being the large heavy-set man who had called them up the stairs, and in to see the boss. The other remained partly in the shadows. They framed a bloody scene like two bookends, one on either side of a sorry looking individual tied to a chair, head hung forward, and his hair tangled and bloody. He appeared to be alive, but certainly not fully coherent or even fully aware of their presence.

"My friend here will not be staying with us for much longer, such a shame. Let me explain... you see your rat was a regular visitor to Osnabruck, and we certainly knew his business whilst he was there. He took some papers from our friend here, and managed to make his way back to Hamburg on that same occasion where you were meant to follow him and find out where those papers ended up. Of course your shit-handed job has left us with a different problem to deal with."

Geltz said nothing, but he swallowed involuntarily in his discomfort as Neumann continued. He wasn't entirely confident he was off the hook yet. Perhaps this was Neumann's way of building up to a punch-line that would leave no one laughing.

"So, you see how it is now... because of you two idiots, I have had to talk to my friend here all day, and ask him where your rat was scurrying off to, and whom he has been talking to, and where our friend himself was going when we offered to take him for a nice little trip to Bremen."

The bloodied man in the chair raised his head a little and spat out a few words "zur hölle fahren" (go to hell). One of the thugs raised a fist but Neumann intervened.

"Leave him, he will be silent soon enough. There's enough blood to clean up already, and do not get any on my Turkish rug if you please."

Neumann continued. "So, our friend here has been passing papers to the rat that you could not catch. But whom has the rat been running too? That indeed is the question. Our friend has already told us that these papers are from the naval office, and I am certain that they are of great value to my contacts. Of course, I knew much of that already - from his accomplice - who is now kindly feeding the crows in Osnabruck. But it is always good to get two sources for a story, that way if they agree you can know the truth of it. Sometimes torture is flawed. When a man is in such pain, he will tell you what you whatever he thinks you want to hear, true or false. But two men rarely tell the same lie when their life depends upon it.

Geltz now spoke up, realising he wasn't imminently at risk of further punishment for now at least. "So what would you like us to do for you? Kill him? Get rid of the body? It seems a long journey from Hamburg just to dispose of some rubbish."

"Geltz, don't be so ridiculous! I have other plans for

126

you. Do you think I would drag you across country just for your butchery skills? No my friend, you will go to London. I shall travel there too, on the same ship. You will mix with the German and Polish immigrants in steerage class, and keep yourselves out of trouble, hiding in plain sight so to speak. I will instruct you further when I am ready to do so. Just as I have I said, I will tell you only what I want you to know, and you will not ask questions. Now, I want you to go back into town and get ready to sail out in two days. I will send someone to your lodgings with tickets for the Steamship Falke, and some English money. Do not spend it on drinking, or you will have more than a hangover when I get to London."

Neumann paused for a short while, as if somewhere else in his thoughts. "Now, since you have expressed an interest in assisting my friends, on your way in to town you can take a walk by the river and be so kind as to help cut a hole in the ice for our friend here to take his evening dip. It is rather sad, but I don't think he is a very good swimmer, certainly I have not encountered many men who could do so with his two arms already broken like that. Still, the river is frozen over, it would only prolong the agony if he were able to flap his arms about under the ice - don't you think?"

Neumann sat back down in his leather chair and picked up the clutch of papers he had been studying before Geltz and Eichel arrived. This was a signal that the meeting was over and they should take their leave.

Geltz and Eichel left, along with the thugs who

127

dragged their bloodied captive with them. Once he was alone, Neumann surveyed his papers one more time. His own hand-written notes on the whole affair, which he now had in his undertaking, were an eclectic swirl of thoughts, comments, facts, and questions. He read to himself again a few parts underlined with red ink by his own hand.

" They drew up plans, but they did not see all of it"
" Zamolyski – dead – 1876 "

"he built it then destroyed it - why?
"He was not paid ! "

"London – hammersmith – there he died"

"SS Fathom – Bremerhaven – Amsterdam – London."

Neumann felt instinctively that he was close to his prize now, but he also knew that he was not the only one getting closer. Did others share what he knew? No: "we have been careful – erased the trail as we have followed it.   There is still time..." he thought to himself. But this mess in Hamburg?, not so much a mess as a gift. Perhaps it was better this way? Now, the trail of this mysterious courier could be followed. This would not have been possible if he had found his journey cut short by a blade in the ribs.
Neumann recited something to himself. *"Was I deceived, or did a sable cloud turn forth her silver lining on the night?..."*

Chapter 20

Christmas Day in London was once again painted by a white veil of snowfall across the city. Windows were a canvas for delicate traceries of ice, creeping over the inside of the panes like the wings of faeries, whilst their outsides were framed by the curves of miniature snow drifts, settling upon their sills. The cold weather, which had spilled down from the fringes of the Siberian sub-artic, and swept across Europe, had now crept across the channel and thrown a frigid cloak across the southeast of England.

For most, this Christmas was much like any other. Children played with new toys, families joined together and talked of the events of the year. Many servants worked, but looked forward to Boxing Day, and their own celebrations. The virtuous attended Christmas church services. But this was not a day of unconditional joy for all in London.

Sir Bertram Overard grandly entertained a small circle of friends and family. But he was preoccupied with recent events, and the magnificent dining laid on by his staff was not as appetising to him as it should have been.

The Widow Amshaw spent her Christmas at home, her niece Gemma Amshaw by her side to comfort her on the day that all bereaved fear the most: Christmas without their absent loved one.

William Harland was no stranger to this fear. He sat alone in his chair, by a neglected fire, preoccupied with his own incalculable losses. He had awoken early this same morning, ate little by way of breakfast, and had then spent all morning by the fire's feeble embers. Though the fire was starved of fuel, he could not summon the vigour to go down to the coal store for another bucket of anthracite. How different it had been in times passed. Christmas was always the best of times. Victoria would be the life and soul of the Christmas spirit, the embodiment of a Dickensian vision of joyful giving. They would always invite friends to dinner, and take a brisk walk on Christmas morning. In times passed she had convinced William to buy up all the roast chestnuts from a street vendor, and hand them out to poorer souls, especially to the wide-eyed and underfed children, who would wander round the square, happily singing Christmas carols in spite of their poor fortune and bare feet. At this time of the year the shop was always stocked with barley twists and candy sticks too, and they would both enjoy giving out a handful of treats to the children who flocked to watch his automaton creations in the shop window of the famed Horological Emporium.

But, this year, he had barely remembered to set out the Christmas window, and was only latterly reminded by Frederick, his mindful shop assistant and apprentice. He was too preoccupied to think of giving out sweets. Today was the worst of days. He could not forget that Victoria was taken from him, and that he was not there to protect her. If only he had been home that night, and not away in the vales of York on a foray to seek rare timepieces.

Upon the mantelpiece, a clutch of envelopes sat unopened. Although greetings had arrived in the post most days in the week before Christmas, he had not opened them yet. Perhaps it was time to do so – after all Christmas would soon be over.

Harland summoned a little energy to replenish the fire with new coals, and then sat down with a glass of brandy to begin to open the envelopes. There were many gaily coloured cards, some hand tinted. However, as Harland had feared, this was a difficult task. Some cards included letters from good friends, echoing their sympathy for the difficulty of a time without Victoria at Christmas. One was from an old and distant friend of Victoria, in India, and still unaware of her death. He would have to write to her and break the news, as he had done so many times already this year. The last card was in a larger than average envelope of lilac paper. Inside the envelope was a bright red card, with a drawing of three children playing. A handwritten note was enclosed.

The handwriting was quite exceptional, and Harland noticed that the notepaper had a feint scent of sweet perfume.

Dear Mr Harland,

Please forgive me for not writing this in my own hand, I suffer from painful joints at this time of year, and I regret this has made its presence

131

felt once again. My niece, Gemma, has written this by my request.

You and I both know that this Christmas is a bittersweet time. I will keep Christmas in my heart of course, but you and I will both remember our lost loves, especially at this time. I wonder how many others must be alone with their loss on such a day?

We shall have a small gathering here on Boxing Day evening, from seven onward, and it would be a great pleasure to welcome you to spend some time with us and be our guest. This is not a time to spend alone."

Janice Amshaw.

Harland was surprised, and at the same time pricked with a little guilt for not having opened the cards earlier. The invitation was dated December 18th, nearly a week ago. Then again, with more time to think he may well have convinced himself of some reason not to attend, preferring melancholy reflection. But now it was too late _not_ to attend. Strictly speaking it was already ill-mannered to have neglected to reply. To simply not turn up now, after such a genuinely well-meant invitation, would be an even worse digression. As it stood, he had not replied either way. Therefore, he must feel obliged to attend.

Harland retired early to bed that Christmas evening, not wishing to stay awake only to think, and perhaps drink, too much. The next day, Boxing Day, was spent reluctantly readying himself for the Widow Amshaw's social event. By six o'clock that evening, Harland had sought to clean himself up, removing two days of unshaved stubble, and managed to dress well, thoroughly brushing down his best overcoat to a pristine condition. Harland took pride in his appearance, in public at least. His leather greatcoat was not appropriate for the occasion, and in any case had a slash across the forearm from his recent encounter in the back alleyway. Though recovered from his incapacitation, his still sore and bruised throat was hard to ignore. He was thankful that only the coat was sliced open and not his skin. With his shoes well polished, he tied a thin silk scarf around his collar with an oversized knot to hide his injury, it was somewhat the fashion of a dandy, but in keeping with the current style and not too out-of-place, if he kept his evening jacket on. This was fortunate, as luck would have it.

Harland set off to hail a cab, the coldness of the air biting at his ears and nose. After a brisk walk through the snow-laden side streets, he found a Hansom Cab waiting in a sparsely populated rank, many drivers still being at home on Boxing Day. For those who stayed at their duties, the reward was being able to charge double, and no doubt gain a generous seasonal tip, especially from those returning home after an indulgent evening.

Finally, climbing into a Hansom, Harland made himself comfortable, being thankful that it was a fully glazed cabriolet and not an open one. He gave the driver the address, and the cab pulled away.

Sitting in the cab, Harland slipped his chilled hands

into his pockets, unexpectedly finding that he had left, within the right side-pocket of his coat, a small object. It had been in his coat since he last had occasion to wear it. He retrieved it, and opened his hand to reveal the item. There in his palm, glinting by the illumination of the light of the street's gas-lamps, sat a small silver button. In an instant, Harland found his mind transported back to the day he had found it, now oblivious to the rocking of the carriage or his journey.

Chapter 21

William Harland's half-sleep was shaken from him by the heavy sound of an iron bolt being disengaged from a solid iron door. The hard wooden slats that comprised what would pass for a bed, if one were tired enough, left his sides sore and his joints stiff. This was not helped by the chill of the stone walls, or the floor he now sat upon.

A man entered the cell and began to speak.

"Mr Harland, I... "

But, as quickly as he started, he began to hesitate – as if not quite sure how to complete the sentence he had already started. He was dressed in an over-jacket, heavy shoes, waistcoat, dark-haired, carelessly shaved.

"Tell me Inspector Russell, have you come to hang me already? You seem to have convicted me after all..." Harland was intensely tired, yet adrenalin surged and drove his bitterness forward.

Russell barely made eye contact. "Well, Mr Harland: We have made our enquiries, and it seems that everything you have told us has been corroborated beyond doubt. Our police surgeon has made his report. Your wife must have laid there for nearly twelve hours before her final moments. And I can therefore rule you out of our investigations..."

Harland jumped to his feet, his anger barely restrained, preventing Russell from completing his expressions of regret.

"You stupid, arrogant, bastard." Harland uttered, pushing Russell away from the door as his junior sergeant stepped back, allowing Harland to step out of the cell into the corridor.

"I take it I'm free to go? I imagine you have no more idea who killed my wife now than you did when you walked into my hallway? And no doubt, less still a chance of catching up with them now even if you did."

Russell remained standing in the cell, and said nothing more as Harland walked away unhindered, and eventually found his way to the main entrance.

The brightness of full daylight momentarily disoriented Harland, as he stepped out of the police station and turned wearily towards Parliament Street. Only his deep anger sustained him as he sought to get home. He had barely eaten or slept for the three days of this ill-judged incarceration. His anger was not for himself, however. Rather, it was a sense of the urgency of the situation being thrown into disarray by the stupidity and misdirection of this idiot 'Inspector Russell'.

Having walked a good distance, without even realising where he had turned or which streets he had taken, Harland found himself walking towards his house, in the street where he had been handcuffed and bundled into a police carriage only three days before.

He was unshaved, his clothes scruffy, his weariness weighing upon his face like a death mask. He did not wonder, then, that curtains shifted and shaded figures spied upon him as he walked past the last few doors to finally come to his own front steps. Barely inside the door, Harland dropped at the bottom of the stairs and sat dizzied by the effort of his journey, lack of food, and his tattered emotions.

It must have been the case that he had drifted to sleep where he laid, across the bottom stairs. He was awoken by a soft purring, and the brush of a soft tail across his face. As Harland stirred to wakefulness, it seemed the daylight had dimmed - not dark, so not yet night, but the light shining through the coloured glass of the glazed arch above the door was duller and diminished now. The front door had not fully closed on his way in, and now he had a visitor, Heather, a neighbours cat. "Hello little one" he whispered as he took her up in his arms and stroked her gently. She nuzzled him as if he were her master, though in truth, like many cats, she was gregarious in her affections.

Harland did not get up. Instead, he remained sitting where he was, emotions and images circling in his head. Only a few days ago he had stood in that very same doorway, incredulous at the scene that greeted his homecoming. As he sat now, staring at nothing but the wall, Heather gave a little call, slipped down from his arms and skitted away through the door, off on another adventure. Then, as his eyes followed her, he noticed a glint of silver under the hall table. Someone had been in and cleaned away most of the blood. A good neighbour perhaps?   But this item had been missed by them, and the police. Harland reached under the table, and found the object. He studied it: A silver-grey button, with a wolfs-head, and a scrap of green fabric where it had been ripped away, perhaps from a waistcoat. There was no dust collected upon it, so it must have been newly fallen there under the table.

Should Harland have turned this clue over to the police investigators? Possibly... but for what purpose? Would they find the one to whom it belonged? Doubtful. Would they be able to prove anything of it even if they could? Unlikely. No, too much would be left to chance, disinterested investigations, and the caveat of 'reasonable doubt'. If this button held any hope of justice, then it would be Harland himself who must be its examiner and custodian for the moment.

But for now, all Harland could do was sit as the dusk gave way to the darkness of night, and sorrowfully reflect upon those past few days of pure hell. He began to wonder even if he knew who he was anymore.

William Harland had become a watchmaker of some repute, at least in London itself. Indeed, his talents for restoring timepieces of larger scale, mantle clocks, long-case escapements and the like were also appreciated by his well-heeled regular customers. To satisfy this market, Harland made regular forays to seek out and buy unusual and rare pieces for refurbishment. Glastonbury, York, and Winchester, were favoured haunts for his quests. It was on this occasion that William had returned from York, arriving in London by Train, and having supervised the unloading of various packing cases to be collected by his junior assistant Frederick and taken to the shop – the Horological Emporium.

On this occasion, only a few pieces of particular note were obtained, not a wasted journey by any means, but perhaps York was becoming too popular with visitors with an eye for a collectable piece – he may have to find a new hunting ground on his next trip to Yorkshire. Lincolnshire, perhaps? He had not explored much in the towns lying south of the great Humber Estuary, so perhaps he would do so on next year's trip.

After recruiting a station porter, by way of a generous tip, to keep a close eye on the cases until collection, he found a carriage and journeyed home feeling satisfied that he had enough items to keep him busy for a good few months in his workshop. Nothing had seemed amiss as he drew up to *Meridian House*, where he lived comfortably with his beloved Victoria. But appearances, as one might observe, can be sorely deceptive.

It was a cool afternoon, but brightened by full sunshine playing through the branches of the tree-lined avenue. Turning to climb the four marble steps leading to he front door, Harland half-noticed that the front curtains of the downstairs windows were not drawn open. This did not immediately register in his mind as a matter to be concerned about, rather it just seemed somewhat subconsciously a little unfamiliar or out of place.

Harland turned the handle. Though the door was not locked, it moved barely an inch before resisting. He could feel that the door was pushing against something. Had the cleaning maid visited today and left the hall carpet turned up by the door perhaps? Harland pushed a little harder, and the door gave way to a half opened position, accompanied by the sound of something rubbing along the lower door panel and slumping onto the floor. Then William Harland stumbled forward through the gap, one hand stopping his descent into a full fall to the floor.

Harland's hand felt wet, and slid over the tiles exposed at the side of the run of carpet that covered the hallway. As his eyes accommodated the darker interior, shaking off the bright sunlight outside, he saw his hand pressed into a sanguine pool of dark, red, and viscous liquid. It did not occur immediately to him that this was a pool of blood – "what on earth?" He spoke aloud to himself, still unaware of the devastating truth. Then he looked up from the floor and saw her – Victoria, pushed to one side of the door by the effort of his opening it, slumped against a hall table. From that moment, he was immersed in an emotional spiral of horror.

Victoria seemed motionless, bloodied, her dress practically saturated from head to foot with blood, and her body surrounded by an oozing pool that spread from one side of the hall to the other. Harland's voice was lost – he wanted to speak but he was incapable of forming a sound. Then her eyes flickered for a moment, meeting his for an instant, her right-hand barely moved as if straining to reach forward, and she whispered. "Will..." But, as quickly as the word had been spoken, her voice faded and her life slipped away.

Harland touched her face, as pale as bleached notepaper, her eyes still open, but her gaze emptied of all light. Everything that she was – everything that he loved and cherished had slipped away before his very eyes, in a moment that he was powerless to stop. He slid down beside her – held her in his arms, his face pressed into her hair, as tears flowed like streams in full flood from his eyes. And then he let out a sound that could be from a grave: a howl of pity and sorrow, neither a scream of fear or an outburst of anger. Rather, the sound of William Harland's life being shattered was like the cry of a cornered animal at the moment of knowing its own imminent death.

From that moment, time and place had no meaning – Harland was dizzied, dazed, flooded by adrenalin yet paralysed by an emotional storm that raged such that he felt as if he was drowning.

His cries were so out of place, and so primal that people stopped dead in the street as they walked. Neighbours came from their houses and looked at each other with a bemusement that masked their more serious unspoken concern. Something was terribly wrong.

Harland may have sat in the hallway for an hour, or it may have been only a few minutes – it was

141

impossible for him to tell. A small crowd had assembled at the foot of his marble steps, and one – Samuel Terridge, a neighbour, started up the steps at his wife's behest.

"Samuel, please see what is amiss. I cannot bear to hear that sound, *that* sobbing. God save us, whatever has happened?"

"I shall go and see, it will be nothing – I am sure we will all feel foolish for our concerns, perhaps everyone should go back to their affairs." Samuel half-heartedly urged the small crowd away with a polite wave of his hand, but in his heart he knew something was terribly wrong in the Harland household.

As he reached the door, he saw the bloodied mess. Victoria Harland lay dead in the arms of her Husband, William, both painted in blood like a scene from hell itself. He stumbled back to the steps.

"Mother of god..."

Terridge was momentarily lost for words, mouth open but not yet sure what to say next, and the crowd, which had not dispersed, fell silent.

"God help us, call for the constables, shout for them, run and find them, and bring them back here with haste – there's murder afoot..."

Then Terridge could speak no-more. His voice choked as he tried to give further account of what he had just seen, but even 10 years in the army and the slaughter of his fellows in the Crimea's Sevastopol campaign were no preparation for the sight he had witnessed. Yes, he had seen friends blown limb from limb by cannon, and bandaged those sliced to the bone at close quarters by cavalry-men's swords. But those were men of a martial breed, they all knew that war was brutal slaughter and they drank their fill of it for queen and country, when their duty had to be done. But not this – a young woman, subjected to such savagery – he could barely believe this was Victoria Harland, their good neighbour and friend, less still could he fathom that it seemed that William Harland had done such a horror to his own wife.

Outside the front door, Harland could hear the hubbub of voices and snatches of conversation, yet he seemed to be detached, as if floating somewhere nearby. Then the tone changed. There were a few shouts, and stern voices preceding the sound of feet on the outside steps. The door was pushed hard, but only yielding a little further than its previous half-open position. Two constables entered into the hallway and others stood outside the door.

One of the constables gripped Harland's shoulder. "I think you had better come along now sir, and not make a fight of it"

Harland was too far descended into shock and grief to appreciate the intimation – he allowed himself to be dragged away, and bundled outside. Meanwhile a more senior member of the party of policemen stepped past him and into the hallway.

"Gods mercy, he's done his wife up like Jack The Ripper. God only knows why, but if there is one thing that is certain, he shall hang for it."

143

He stepped forward and felt her face with the back of his hand. "Still warm – no doubt he killed her just this hour gone by."

And so in the space of a few seconds, Inspector Edward Russell summed up the crime scene, and formed the undeniable truth of the matter – an easy case – *'little else to do here except see him hang',* he thought.

Russell turned to another constable who had followed him into the hallway.

"Have the police surgeon come and supervise removal of the body – and establish cause of death – as if we need to ask ... and have the hallway guarded – no-one should enter or exit until the surgeon completes his business"

The constable nodded in agreement "very well sir."

And so it was that William Harland found himself thrown into a filthy cell, blood still drying onto his hands and clothes, even his face, with no further explanation. He had pounded on the wall of the police carriage in which he was locked whilst transported there. Once he had reached back to some sort of lucidity as to where he was and what had occurred, he demanded to know what was happening. He got no replies, but received two hard blows to the back of his neck from a truncheon on arrival at his destination, and then, half dazed, he was dragged to a cell and thrown in, falling into a corner that stank of stale urine.

However, it was no more than an hour before

144

Harland was stirred back to the present once again by the unlocking of the door, followed by the entry into the cell of Inspector Russell. He brought with him a stool, which he sat upon, staring face-to-face and eye-to-eye with Harland.

"Now then Mr Harland. I think it is best if we keep this simple – all you have to do is help me write out a little statement, and then sign it, and we can leave you be. Just tell us why you killed Victoria Harland, and how you did it, that's all a jury needs to hear from us – you will hang either way for murder, so why not make it easier on both of us."

Harland scowled – half anger, half confusion. "What are you saying? That I killed my Victoria? Am I not already beyond being broken, I need no more of this..."

Russell's initial air of superiority turned to irritation. "So you think you can deny it, do you? You can tell all the lies you like to me, but it is the twelve gentlemen of the jury you have to convince. Do you really think you could get away with that?"

Russell continued. "You were found wallowing in her blood, and her not even cold to the touch..." Russell's irate tone betrayed an undercurrent of impatience in his voice. He would not be made a fool of just because Harland could speak like a gentleman. He was still a killer and would pay for it.

Harland's eyes flashed with anger "God's eyes – are you so much of a fool that you make yourself out to be? You can have my statement if it means I can be left to my grieving."

A constable brought out a note-pad and pencil, ready to write whatever was said. Then Harland proceeded to tell everything that had occurred earlier that day – his arrival in London, the unloading of his purchases from his business forays in Yorkshire, his journey back to London and his return to Meridian House, the oddness of the closed curtains – the stuck door, and then the desolation beyond it.

Once Harland finished speaking, Inspector Russell stood up abruptly, the stool falling over behind him. "That's a fine tale, you know that we will check everything you say. And, when we have the facts, your lies will not loosen the rope round your neck one inch."

Russell spoke with an overbearing confidence, but somehow in his eyes there was a flicker of doubt. His bravado faltered, he made to speak further but then hesitated and said nothing.

"We shall make enquires then sir?" asked the constable taking the notes. "Shall I take details of his business appointments and his lodgings in York Sir?"

Russell turned away from Harland and left the cell. He spoke in a dismissive fashion as he walked away. "Make your enquires constable Chaldecott, and don't bother me with this matter again until you have all of the facts."

Constable Chaldecott took to his business, noting each detail carefully. Every trader Harland had met during his trip, their addresses, his business with them, items he recalled purchasing. He noted the lodging houses, the type of carriages Harland had hired on his business, his train journeys and timetables. Harland's pockets had been turned out and his leather-bound pocket journal, including receipts and other papers, were logged with great care. Whereas Inspector Russell relied upon his flawed intuition, Constable Chaldecott made use of his education. His ability to be meticulous with taking of notes, and his good memory for fine details, these had always stood him in good stead.

Constable Chaledecott too had begun to have doubts about Harland's apparent murderous intent, and also had long held misgivings about Russell's competence. Finally, all notes made, he left the cell. "I will have hot food brought to you, I'm afraid you may be here for a while."

The second constable locked the cell door. Chaldecott spoke tersely to him "Bring him food – and for gods sake give him a towel and warm water so he can clean that bloody mess of himself."

Chapter 22

Harland was jolted from his painful reminiscence by the shudder of his carriage over the cobblestones, as it began slowing down to a halt, finally entering Old Friary Lane. He had arrived at the location of the Amshaw residence.

The house appeared welcoming. Festive candle lights, set in each window, gave off an air of warmth even in the biting cold of the dark evening. A huge wreath was hung upon the door, and there was still a feint scent of Christmas greenery from it, in spite of the coldness of the air. There was little to suggest that this place, like Meridian House, had also borne witness to death and villainy in a not so distant past.

He pulled the handle of the bell-pull, to announce his arrival, and was shortly ushered in by the maid, who took his hat, coat, and gloves. Harland was glad to be able to feel the warmth of the house easing his chilled fingers, and the tips of his ears, back to some sort of normality.

The hall was broad and unusually long. Toward the end in which he stood upon arrival, the walls were smooth and straight, the doorframes were of a typically Victorian design. However, the far end of the hall was oak panelled, with what appeared to be a collection of much older doors. Harland remembered that one of these led to the late Dr Amshaw's study, and that those rooms were part of a much older section of the house.

Momentarily Widow Amshaw appeared, and following in her wake, she was accompanied by a beautiful young lady. "Mr Harland, I'm so glad you came, I would have quite understood had you chosen not to of course, but let us not dwell on our troubles tonight."

"You are very kind Mrs Amshaw, I'm very happy to have such good company at this festive time." Harland replied.

"Please do not feel the need for formality. I hope you will allow me to address you as William this evening, and you may call me Janice." Mrs Amshaw gave a warm smile, and turned to introduce the young lady by her side.

"I believe you have not been introduced, this is my Niece, Gemma Amshaw – a daughter of my late husband's brother. She has just returned from Paris, her mother and father are residing in India at the present time."

Harland took Gemma's lace-gloved hand and kissed it, "I am enchanted to make your acquaintance." He involuntarily inhaled the scent upon her gloves and as he straightened he could not avoid looking into her deep emerald eyes, her pupils seemed to expand as she looked back into his gaze.

Gemma broke what seemed to be a hypnotic silence.

"William, that is such a nice English name. I have spent this last year in Paris, it is a wonderful place, but it is so nice to be returned to London once again."

Harland could not help but be intoxicated by her beauty. Her long hair was like pure and brightly polished copper, with a natural translucence that played with the light through the curls of her flowing hair. Her skin was fair and smooth, covered by freckles, her eyes greener than any he had seen.

Widow Amshaw could see that something had passed between William and Gemma in that moment. Perhaps this was not the time to linger however, and she discreetly moved them along.

"Let us join the other guests, William, Gemma. I have been telling them of your wonderful Horological Emporium, but it seems that your Christmas window automatons are already the talk of the town. I feel I have been deprived, having not visited your shop to see them myself. I must do so before twelfth night."

Harland entered the drawing room a little apprehensively. Though he welcomed the warmth that permeated the room, resulting from the well-laid and rather huge fireplace, he was somewhat wary of another kind of warmth, one which he had encountered often this past year and more. Of course, this was well-intentioned. The unending tide of sympathy and kindness, brought to his shop counter and elsewhere, after the death of Victoria, was worthy of her memory. But, Harland had grown weary of repeating the same conversations over and over – constantly reminded of his pain and emptiness, and having to explain that the police had failed to make any progress. Indeed the authorities seemed to have given up on the whole affair.

As it transpired, Harland's fears were a little over-reached, there was no direct mention of his bereavement and no commiserations. Perhaps Widow Amshaw's own more recent loss had stifled the topic in the wider sense, or had William's recent sorrow become merely a historical fact?

William did his best to enter into the spirit of the evening. Polite conversations flowed freely, talk of politics and new inventions intermingled with talk of the theatre. Trips to The Highlands, and European summer sojourns were reminisced upon.

However, Harland had found himself unexpectedly distracted from the hubbub of conversation. More than a few times he found himself gazing across the busy room to one particular place. The startling red hair of Gemma could not be lost in the crowd here. She was certainly popular, with several young gentlemen proffering their attentions. As she rarely left her Aunt's side, these overtures were just a little awkward. In truth, Gemma was not overly impressed by them. Paris had been much more enlightening.

Widow Amshaw had a reputation for hosting the best of evenings – she had little need to worry about costs. A quartet had been arranged, and after a brief recess, they returned to their seats and adjusted their instruments. Earlier in the evening, they had played quietly, gentle Christmas ditties and the like, as the guests chatted. However, the mood now turned to dancing, as the musicians struck up, playing loudly and with a higher tempo. Ladies and gentlemen paired up with their partners and began to dance. William suddenly felt a little lost and alone. But, just as quickly as his discomfort surfaced, this was brushed aside by surprise as he felt the warmth of a lace-gloved hand finding his own half-opened palm.

"Come William, will you not dance with me now?"

It was Gemma. She had somehow circulated around the room without William noticing, like a red fox carefully stalking a fowl. Her eyes were wide, and they seemed almost deep enough to fall into. William did not have time to speak, as he was already being led to the floor without time to reply. Gemma was not going to wait for him to make an excuse not to join her.

So the evening proceeded, sweetmeats, savouries, and desserts being offered in profusion. Gemma returned to her Aunt's side after a while, but she had left her impression upon William, and it seemed that he had turned her head too.

Later in the evening, the conversations were somewhat more relaxed. The ladies sat in small groups, talking of the expectations of Parisian spring fashions, whilst an entourage of gentleman congregated in the second day room, enjoying cigars and brandy. Harland had not joined them. Instead, he found himself pondering the beautifully decorated Christmas tree in the hallway. Then, once again, Gemma appeared unexpectedly by his side.

"Mr Harland, I see you are admiring the tree – do

you approve?"

"Undoubtedly, miss Amshaw, its a magnificent display – did you help to decorate it?"

"I did, and please don't be so formal," she said with a smile, "Gemma is perfectly acceptable."

William did not resist. "Tell me then, Gemma, you must have spent much happier times here over the years?"

"Oh yes... I spent every summer here since my childhood – my cousin Charles also. He is in the Americas now, so far away... We had such fun playing hide and seek, and of course the priest's hole was a fascination to both of us."

"Priests hole? It is a term that sounds familiar..." William almost had in his mind the answer, but allowed Gemma to explain anyway.

"Well, this house is rather old. The rear of the property dates back to the Tudor period, and it was once part of a friary. The priest's hole is a small room, hidden behind wooden panels. It was a sort of secret sanctuary from dangerous times. Priests were persecuted if they did not follow the favoured doctrines of their times. Actually, my late Uncle's study occupies the room where it is hidden." Gemma's sparkle faltered for a moment, remembering that her Uncle's study had been a place of anguish for her Aunt these months past. Gemma recovered herself quickly however.

"Perhaps you would like to see it?"

"Indeed, it would be interesting, on my next visit

perhaps..." William did not wish to seem to impose, though he was certainly curious.

However, Gemma had made up her mind, and that was that. "Nonsense William, come, let me show you, it is of no trouble." Gemma slipped William out of the hallway with a certain accomplished discretion. As a young and eligible lady, it was not strictly proper to be wandering about the house alone with a young man.

They talked as they traversed the hallway for a moment or two, then moved on toward the back of the house. As they entered the late Dr Amshaw's study, it was already much quieter. The babble of guests chatting, and the musicians playing, were dulled to a soft hum.

William could not help sweeping his eyes around the room. He had been here several times of course. On the first occasion, his visit had been at the behest of Widow Amshaw and her assistant Douglas Barringer, regarding the advertisement they had placed in *The Times*. He had studied the room thoroughly, noting the valuable items in Dr Amshaw's collection that had apparently been ignored by the supposed thieves. Yet one item had drawn all of their attention... the now empty glazed hardwood case that had housed the Polish machine – a curiosity Dr Amshaw had acquired and apparently of some special fascination to him.

Gemma walked toward the oak-panelled wall, to the left of the large desk, and with the slightest touch and a click, her small lace-gloved hand slipped open a panel. As it pushed back seemingly a few inches into the wall, she was able to press a more substantial mechanism, and almost magically, a large six-panel section of the wooden panel-work opened up as a doorway. It was a masterful piece of carpentry. The joins had been invisible until that point.

Inside was dark, but Gemma took up and lit a candlestick from the table, and encouraged William to step inside.

In the confined space, William could not help but involuntarily inhale the scent of Gemma's perfume. Although the priests-hole appeared large, from the outside, once he walked in and Gemma followed, it seemed much smaller. Gemma pulled the panel-door closed with a click, and rested the candlestick upon a small stone plinth at the end of the small chamber.

Without any further pretence, Gemma slid herself up close to William, allowed her arms to rest upon his shoulders, and then kissed him, slowly and with great passion. Harland was lost for words.

"William, have I shocked you?" Gemma teased, with a slight light-hearted worldly lilt to her voice.

"Don't think badly of me, a year in Paris taught me more than impressionist painting. Forgive me, perhaps it was too forward of me?"

"I'm sorry, maybe I have spent far too long grieving. Perhaps I have forgotten what it is like to feel the warmth of another, and to dare to want it..."

Gemma suddenly felt a wave of momentary regret. "Oh no!. William... I see, now, I have intruded upon your loss. How stupid of me..." She looked away, feeling foolish.

"Don't be sorry. It is true, I have carried a heavy heart, and for far too long. But, I cannot deny that I felt something when our eyes first met. I just didn't think... well ..."

Gemma smiled, reassured. "You didn't think that a beautiful young woman would be so forthright in showing her feelings for an older gentleman?" Gemma held William's hand softly as she continued.

"I could sense you felt it improper to make your own advances. But I have seen how you look into my eyes from across the room, I can sense your gaze upon me, and it feels like sunbeams caressing my bare shoulders."

Gemma stroked William's cheek softly as she continued. "Perhaps we young ladies are not quite as prim and proper as you might imagine. Of course, I *was* something of an innocent when I arrived in Paris, but that city has a way of seducing even the coolest of hearts and the calmest of heads. I have learned all about men, and your eyes tell me everything I need to know... they way you look at me, and the way you make me feel."

William had recovered his composure, but he could feel his heart pounding, and he was transfixed by her gaze and her sudden air of assuredness. He felt that she was in control, and he did not wish to resist.

"And what do my eyes tell you?" he said softly, almost in a whisper."

"I sense that you look but you don't dare to touch... I

too have felt that way..." Gemma paused, as if she was not sure if she should continue, wondering how William might react if she bared her true self to him. But, somehow, this felt right.

"There was a time in Paris, when I first arrived, that I had that same feeling. There were a few of us ladies, lodged in a respectable boarding house, two of us to each small suite of rooms. Sarah Derrington shared rooms with me, we were meant to chaperone each other. But *she* had been to Paris before, and she needed no re-introduction to the intimacy of its delights. She would slip out at night more often than not. I was sworn to secrecy of course. Indeed, she tried her best to encourage me to discover Paris for my self. We went out now and then to places where young bachelors would be found, where artists and writers would sit drinking their absinthe and talking excitedly about the young ladies they would like to draw, what they should wear, or indeed if they should be clothed at all..."

Gemma paused for a moment, sizing up William's reaction. "Shall I tell you more William?"

William stroked her cheek with his hand. "Well you cannot start such an entrancing story without saying how it ends."

Gemma smiled, and then continued.

"Sarah did her best, but I was such an innocent. Dare I say, I was a rather straight-laced prudish sort in my nascent exposure to the amour of the gentlemen of Paris. She soon lost her enthusiasm for trying to lead

157

me astray, and I found myself alone most evenings, only dreaming of the things that free and youthful Parisians felt able to entertain themselves with..."

"Then one evening, I was sat in my window seat, looking across the city rooftops, and a multitude of windows lit up like sparkling jewels in a black velvet box. Across the street, I could see through a large window, and into a slightly lower room. It was well-lit, yet curtains were never drawn. That is when I first saw Coquette... or at least that is what I christened her, and she was no stranger to passion. That night, she was busying herself at her dressing table, applying her face powders, rouging her lips, tidying her hair, perfuming her bare shoulders. I did not imagine she had noticed me there watching her. I fancied I knew her. I realised later that she worked as a couturière in a fashionable dress shop I visited on occasions"

"She carried on her beautifications for a while, and then she got up, went to her door, and a young man entered her room. They kissed for a while, but before long, she began to undress, and soon they were both naked together. I felt somehow it was wrong of me to be so indiscreet. Should I be spying upon them like some sort of voyeur? But I could not draw myself away... there was something that prevented me from averting my gaze"

"This became a regular occurrence. Each night after Sarah went out with her latest young man, I watched those two, Coquette and her man, making love, their bodies together. I saw things I have never imagined possible of two lovers"

"Then one particular night as I watched, thinking once again that I was an unseen observer, I saw her look straight up at my window as they made love! It was so deliberate as to be clear she knew me to be watching. I closed the curtains in a panic - and felt ashamed."

William was entranced by the description, and in truth somewhat aroused by the story, he said nothing, he was not sure what he should say. Almost involuntarily, he caressed her soft naked shoulder. Gemma continued.

"The next night I resolved not to watch, but somehow I could not help but peek out of the curtains. The room was again well-lit, tidy, curtains open to the eyes of the night. But she was there alone that evening, and he was not with her. I have to confess I was a little disappointed.

So it was that I set myself to my reading, and a little time passed, perhaps more than I realised"

"Then, there was a knock upon my door. I thought perhaps that it was Sarah, returning and having forgotten her key. But, when I opened the door, there instead was a young man standing rather imposingly with a pink rose and a letter in a lilac envelope. He passed me the envelope without speaking, and I opened it and read the contents to myself."

"The first part was in french, it said *'Life has many rewards for those who seek them, but you cannot live life only through your own eyes and the deeds of others'*. The second part, in English said *'his name is Ettienne'* "

"Then I looked up at him and realised that he was the young man... the frequent visitor of Coquette, whom I had watched night after night, as he became one with his lover. He gave me the rose, and somehow, I am not even sure how, I found myself in his arms, and we were kissing each other passionately. We made love late into the night. I became Coquette, and in every way I had imagined myself, as I had watched her those past evenings "

"He never called again. After that night, Coquette's curtains were always drawn closed in the evenings. I think somehow she was telling me that I should live life not just watch it pass me by."

Gemma looked into William's eyes, wondering what his response would be as he spoke.

"And did you – live life - in Paris?" Harland asked the question, though he felt he knew the answer already.

"Oh yes." said Gemma, smiling. She was relieved to see that William had not been morally shaken by her revelations, indeed he was aroused and unusually short of words.

Gemma slipped her arms around Williams shoulders and they kissed once again, almost dizzying each other with the passion of the moment. Then they held each other close and said nothing for a few minutes. Both of them knew that there was now a connection between them that would not easily be forgotten.

"Shall we return to the party, before we are missed William?" Gemma was aware that she had stayed close to her Aunt most of the evening, but was now at risk of being noted to be absent.

"Indeed, we should do so." answered William. But, just as they made to emerge from the priest's hole, something unexpected occurred. As Gemma brought the candlestick toward the door to observe the door catch, and release it, Harland noticed something upon the shelf. It was a partly dismantled mechanism that appeared to be both complex and of exceptional craftsmanship, and somehow it seemed that there was something familiar about it.

"What is it William?"

"It is this mechanism ... I might be mistaken, but it looks like something I know, but from where I cannot recollect. It would be good to get a better look at it in the light. I find myself thinking it has something to do with the empty case on your late Uncle's desk, from which we believed a mechanism was stolen. That mechanism is surely entangled in his demise in some way as yet undiscovered."

"Then we must allow you to examine this contrivance, though I must hesitate: I would not wish to highlight the fact that we have spent some considerable time dallying in this secret room together unaccompanied. I don't wish to upset any sense of propriety that my Aunt may harbour, I am after all in her guardianship for the present time."

William smiled. "I understand, of course, and I

agree. Yet, it is of great importance that I take a closer look at this device. Would you be able to imagine a pretence in which I could do so without too many days passing?"

"I shall, and I'm sure I can construct a little coincidence to fulfil our expectations." Gemma reached to the collection of parts that had taken Harland's attention away from her, and took one smaller piece, slipping it into his jacket pocket.

"Take this for now, you may start your examinations, and we shall see what transpires in the course of a day or two."

Gemma stroked William's hand, and then opened the priest's hole door, blowing out the candle as they stepped out into the much brighter study. They were able to slip back into the congregation of guests without any notice being taken. Gemma returned to her Aunt's side in the main drawing room, where ladies were still talking excitedly about the latest fabrics arrived from India and the Orient. Meanwhile, William joined the gentlemen at their brandies and cigars. The conversations were engaging, yet neither William or Gemma could help thinking about the time they had just spent together. It would be hard to forget.

Chapter 23

Harland walked out into a flurry of snow, as he stepped out from the Amshaw residence into Old Friary Lane once again. Evidently, during the past few hours, when he had been nestled in the warmth and hospitality of the Amshaw household, and in more ways than one, the snow had been falling with great intent. There was a good six inches of fresh snowfall already settled upon the street, so that the edges of the pavements smoothed into the road in graceful curves, leaving one guessing exactly where the kerb-stones were.

Finding a cab was not so easy now – late at night and in poor weather. William set off to walk toward the busier thoroughfare, which he knew would offer better fortune. By luck, after only a few minutes walking, a passing cab arrived ahead and decanted its passengers - he was able to attract the driver's attention and was soon relieved to be sitting with a thick blanket over his legs.

The journey home was somewhat lengthy – the roads were no longer easy work for the driver, or the horses. The bitter cold ensured that even where cabs had driven not long before, the snow was still congregating, rather than being churned into less troublesome slush, as might happen on a milder night.

Eventually, after what must have been at least three

quarters of an hour, the driver pulled up his horses and opened the small hatch behind him to speak to his passenger.

"Sorry to say sir, but I cannot go further – the roads are getting quite troublesome, and I have to think of the horses too – they need to be home and bedded before we all freeze up."

Harland was not too concerned, however.

"No need to apologise, I am surprised we got this far, and I am certainly glad not to have been walking for the whole of the way on a night like this."

Giving the driver a handsome tip, Harland pulled his coat-collar up and began to walk the last portion of his route home, his thoughts flitting between Gemma, and the mysterious machine, part of which he occasionally handled in his pocket as he walked.

Lost in his thoughts, as he walked homeward, Harland found to his surprise, without even knowing how, that he was now standing motionless and alone in an empty street, with only the almost imperceptible sound of snow falling. Out of nowhere, thoughts of Victoria had flooded into his consciousness, like the wash from a passing boat on a river, and he had come to a standstill without even realising it. This was undoubtedly guilt. For a while, he had allowed himself to be embraced by the warmth of Gemma, and Victoria had slipped from his mind. How could he have kept her memory so close only to let it fall away so easily?

He began to feel a swell of self-loathing rising within

himself. Had he forgotten his purpose? The one thing that kept him from self-destruction in his darkest days – the belief that he could find the ones responsible – these destroyers of worlds – his world at least. Had he become distracted so easily? No, he must renew his determination, redouble his efforts, and leave no stone unturned until justice is served.

Harland was now very aware of himself. Standing perfectly still and alone in the light of a gas-lamp, snow flakes now falling again with vigour, and coming to rest on his coat sleeves. He made to start walking again. However, there was something not quite right – a feeling he could not pin down. He walked for a few minutes, and then there it was again – more instinct than fact – too subtle to observe yet definitely there. He was nearing his home now and passing near the Horological Emporium. On a better evening he would walk past to check the shop was all in order, but tonight his goal had been to get to a warm fire and then bed.

Harland was now highly alert, his senses primed. Something had him on edge. He thought, perhaps imagined, that he could hear foot-steps. Yet, the snow must surely muffle such a sound? Or perhaps the sound of snow being dragged over-foot with each step was not silent after all? He looked back several times but saw nothing. Yet he fancied he saw a swirl in the falling snowflakes, some way down the street. He had a sense almost as if someone had darted out of sight and left a turbulent wake as they moved. 'What is this?' he thought to himself.

It occurred to Harland that, if indeed he was being followed, then whoever it may be must certainly wish not to be seen, and that must mean that whoever it is must have some sinister intent. He had felt this instinct before. Several times in the past few weeks he had thought he was being watched, yet never had he seen any real evidence and had allowed it to slip from his mind each time. But now, he felt there *must* be something ...

Approaching the street where his shop was located, Harland realised he could answer to his curiosity – not so much to see where this strange presence was, but where it had been. Harland walked down the street, noticing that the snow here was smooth and untrodden. No discernible footprints were here, only those that he himself had left behind him.

He walked down the street, and once at the end of it he turned left. Straining his ears for any sound, he continued. Again, he came to a corner and turned left. Once more, he turned left at the approaching corner, and he found himself back at the start of the same street, facing toward his shop-front once again. Looking down at the footprints he had laid out only a couple of minutes before, he could see clearly where he himself had walked.

In reality, what Harland had done was to walk in a full square around a small block of buildings. Turning left, four times, had brought him back to the very same place where he had just been a few minutes ago.

He was, in effect, now following his own footprints. But alongside his own, a second pair of shoes had followed. This was exactly what he expected to see, if indeed he *was* being followed. His pulse raced at the realisation that he was not simply imagining the situation, and that he had set a trap not knowing if he was the hunter or the prey. Quickly, he darted into the doorway of his shop, having the presence of mind to walk in his own footprints and then contriving to hop into the doorway leaving no fresh trail. Slipping into the dark shadows, he had looked behind, and caught sight of nothing untoward. He anticipated that whoever was in his pursuit, they would not have realised that they too had been led in a circle. Harland reasoned that they would be following his trail in the snow, rather than his planned route home. With luck they may not realise these footprints were partly their own retraced steps, and would not expect what would come next.

Harland waited one minute, then two minutes, trying his best to avoid breathing out a tell-tale plume of steam from the doorway. Then, in the almost suffocating silence that comes to a world blanketed in new-fallen snow, he heard the footfall again, now much clearer. Indeed, it was the sound of snow shuffling off the feet of this unseen guest as they walked, and the creaking of snow compacting underfoot. The sound got closer, becoming a little faster than a gentle walking pace. Whoever it was, had seen the street ahead empty and they were now trying to catch up quietly to where they believed Harland had next turned.

Harland grasped the metal disc in his coat pocket – about 4 inches in diameter and solid brass, it was not insubstantial in weight. Then, in that same moment, he saw a shadow moving across the snow beyond the darkness of his doorway – and a figure walked straight past. In an instant, Harland stepped out of the doorway and brought down the disc against the back of the head of this mysterious stalker. He fell immediately to the ground – not fully unconscious but sorely dazed. Quickly Harland grabbed his victim's arms, secured them with his scarf, and dragged the still half-stunned figure into the doorway of his shop. He had made his trap well, the door had been quietly unlocked as he laid in wait, and now the hunter became the prey - 'the truth will out'. Harland whispered to himself.

Chapter 24

Gerhard Neumann sipped his coffee, and stared out over the grey vista – nothing but dull featureless sky, and a seascape of insipid blue-green tinted greyness. At least the sea itself was not rough by North-Sea standards. His coffee danced in his cup nonetheless – sometimes seeming to fall into a rhythm, only to be perturbed by some apparently random change in the ebb and flow of the swells through which the Steamship Falke was now pressing forward on this, the 27th December.

Neumann was content. He had embarked the evening before. Consequetly, although it was normal to board in the early part of the morning, he had been able to make himself comfortable in his cabin and sleep until breakfast, whilst most other passengers fought through the drifts of snow and the darkness of winter at 6am to make their boarding deadlines. No doubt a few had failed to make it, thought Neumann, *"Geltz had better not be one of them."*

So it was that Neumann was able to take breakfast after a relaxing slumber, find the best table, with the best view of the sea – even if it was one shade of grey upon another. He enjoyed the continental breakfasts on the Norddeutscher Lloyd Line, and the coffee was always hot and strong. As for Geltz, he would enquire discreetly via a steward, whom he had already paid off to do his bidding whilst on-board. Since Geltz and Eichel were travelling in steerage, there was no crisply pressed linen tablecloths, silverware, or bone china to drink their coffee from. As it happened, Geltz and Eichel were indeed on-board, waking early in the morning, each with a bad head and still drunk from the night before, in spite of their instructions to the contrary. Geltz was used to the sea, but Eichel was not – and he suffered for it, both as a result of the drink, and the constant swell as the ship cut through the waves.

Neumann said nothing as he sat taking breakfast. He acknowledged the breakfasting passengers with a nod as they came and went, common courtesy of course. But his inner mind was at work, grinding over the facts as he knew them, perhaps in hope of revealing some new insight he had so far missed.

"The machine was in five parts – we have four blue prints, and yet something is missing... and without it we have four fifths of nothing..."

Neumann was beginning to suspect that his search for this 'mysterious machine" was a wild goose chase. Was there ever a full set of plans for this device? But, if not, then how would it ever be complete?

"And yet, all roads seem to lead back to London. We have been close - perhaps closer than we realised? Somehow this must be the key. Things will become difficult if this time we do not succeed. We must! And this time there will be no amateurism. We must make our own luck if we are to succeed."

Neumann took another sip of his coffee, then caught the eye of a steward, and quietly made an enquiry of him. The steward nodded.

"I shall return in two minutes sir."

Meanwhile Neumann took two pieces of paper from his pocket. The first was ragged, and stained with dried blood.

"Our cousin will arrive as your guest in four days. He may not be alone."

The second item was a telegram form, not yet completed. But it had been addressed, 'S.B.O. Aldgate TGO, London.' Evidently, there had been an intention to send the scrawled message to the addressee. But who or what was S.B.O? The Aldgate TGO, Neumann had guessed to be London Algdate Telegraphic Office, something he had confirmed with a copy of Bradshaw, borrowed from the chief steward. But who is S.B.O.? And why no further address? Was S.B.O. a person, a place, or perhaps a business concern? That much remained opaque to Neumann for the time being.

At that moment, the steward returned.

"I can confirm that your telegram was sent via the Thunstrase telegraph office before we departed, as you requested. Here is the telegram slip for your records sir."

Neumann passed him a gratuity in return. "Thank you, here is something for your assistance, as we agreed."

Neumann knew one thing: the man from whom those blood-stained papers were taken, was now at the bottom of the river, perhaps now even floating in this same North Sea which he was now steaming across. He knew, therefore, that the unfortunate author of that telegram was never able to send his intended correspondence. However, Neumann had rectified this omission. He read back the telegram slip, which the steward had passed to him.

S.B.O. ALDGATE TGO, LONDON.
OUR COUSIN WILL ARRIVE AS YOUR GUEST IN TWO DAYS STOP HE IS TRAVELLING WITH A COMPANION STOP

"So, we shall see who awaits the arrival of our mutual cousin" Neumann thought, smiling sardonically to himself. *"Then we may measure how well luck can be made."*

Chapter 25

Harland sat and sipped coffee in the workshop of the Horological Emporium, his shop and constant inspirational muse in his creative endeavours.

The workshop, which was well lit, had at one end of the room a large cast iron range in which a fire burned lazily in the centre grate. Upon the stove, a pot of coffee bubbled as Harland paced around in front of the fireplace.

That morning, the early post had brought several pieces of correspondence, each deserving his full attention, and yet he already had another job that needed his devotion. He was beginning to think he had taken on too many responsibilities, but it was too late now to change that.

The first letter, sealed with a wax impression, was from Sir Bertram Overard, and postmarked 27th December. Unusually, it was handwritten by the man himself, rather than his usual dictated communications...

Dear Mr Harland,

I must request your attendance this evening, if at all possible. There are some concerns I must address to you. I have heard, from sources within my influence, that you have been sorely set upon in these past few days. I sincerely hope that you are well recovered.

I fear that your work for me, in examination of our 'curious machine', may have brought unintended interest from some, as yet unidentified, malevolent.

I wish to speak candidly with you to set my mind at rest.

Your faithful Servant,
Sir Bertram Overard.

Evidently, Sir Bertram had heard something of the recent altercation in the back street. This would already have seemed to be a distant memory, were it not for the remaining bruises around Harland's neck, that resulted in his unconscious state, and his rude awakening with smelling salts – sal-volatile. The mystery of how he inexplicably came to be returned to his home, only to be revived by a disappearing Samaritan, may now have been uncovered, but exactly how was Sir Bertram entangled in all of this? What should he make of it all? He would find out soon enough, when he called upon Sir Bertram.

The other correspondence was of a different complexion entirely. Whilst Sir Bertram's letter was written on stout paper, and the envelope franked with the House Of Commons own postal office dispatch mark, this second letter came in an prettily embossed envelope, and inside was a fold of silk threaded notepaper, in keeping with a lady's writings.

Harland read this also to himself, equally surprised to hear from Widow Amshaw on a personal matter.

My Dear William,

I do hope that you will allow me to entertain a less formal greeting than 'Mr Harland', I feel after all that we are well enough acquainted, and I pray you will agree to a little informality.

It was most enjoyable to meet you in social circles at my festive evening, and I do hope that it was to your liking. Indeed, I believe that perhaps it was, as I have spoken at length to my Niece Gemma. She has told me much about the time you spent together, talking, and dancing.

So I must say that I am not entirely surprised to receive your letter, in which you express your desire to be a suitor, and to court young Gemma's affections. You must understand that Gemma's mother and father are in India and will not return during this coming year. I am, therefore, entrusted to her guardianship in all matters.

I do approve, in principal, to your courtship, and I understand that Gemma wishes to take tea with you at our residence one afternoon this week.

I do hope we can agree a mutually convenient time, and I look forward to meeting you again.

Yours Faithfully
Janice Amshaw

Harland was indeed rather more surprised than Widow Amshaw, at her 'receipt of his letter' requesting permission to court Gemma. After all he had not written such a letter! It occurred to him that Gemma had set in motion this chain of events all by her self – she did say she would think of a pretext for him to visit the house once again, and to conveniently 'discover' the priests hole and its contents. Gemma must have written a letter purporting to be from William and expressing his desire to be a suitor! He almost allowed himself to smile at her ingenuity, but felt a pang of guilt – was it right to begin to think of love again so soon?

Chapter 26

Abbey Street was a fairly run-down area, situated around Bethnal Green. It was, in the view of the social champion Charles Booth, undoubtedly a slum - but not quite of the worst order. Nonetheless, there were some residences that were marginally less badly off than others, and for those who could afford to rent a lodging without sharing a single room with several other families, it was bearable. At least these tenements had glass in the windows, unlike some neighbouring streets where sackcloth and nails offered little resistance to the biting winds.

For the figure huddled around the fire-place, with blankets at his back to keep out the cold, this was not the best place to spend the winter. In truth, he could afford considerably better than this. But, what he could not afford, was to be too visible in his comings and goings for the time being. Here, an outward appearance of being of no account or worth could be maintained by his choice of lodgings, and he could at least afford a good supply of coal and decent food behind closed doors. A small beef roast sat in a roasting tin in the hearth, and he picked at it with enthusiasm, in spite of a badly bruised wrist and a still sore head. How he came by these, would need some careful explanation to those who paid his wages, and he reflected upon that whilst he drank from a stoneware bottle of ale, which had by now become lukewarm from the heat of the fire.

It might be remembered that Harland had suspected he was being followed, as he made his way home through the snow-bound streets, after adjourning from Widow Amshaw's festivities. The snow, being too deeply covered for carriages to make way easily, had forced him to walk the last half mile toward his home. As he walked, he had become aware of being followed and had laid his trap. He had led his pursuer astray and then events had culminated in the unseen stalker hurrying past the shop doorway in which Harland had deftly secreted himself, without leaving obvious prints in the snow. With a good deal of luck, he had timed his strike well, and the toothed metal disc retrieved from his pocket had found its target soundly, knocking his adversary nearly unconscious.

Consequently, Harland had that night found himself facing the unexpected guest tied to a chair in his workspace, at the back of the Horological Emporium.

It was cold in the workshop. The premises had been closed and unattended for two days, due to the holidays. Harland lit several lamps, and then started a fire to soften the edge of the coldness. His fingers tingled as they gained a hint of warmth to thaw them from the cold outside.

Harland studied his quarry. He was breathing, and seemed to be in a satisfactory state, alive - if not yet fully conscious. Harland searched his pockets, finding a few items of significant interest. He had an air of uneasiness about himself however. It had now occurred to him that this fellow might just be an innocent workman, wandering home from a tavern. *'What if he does not wake up?'*

From the collection of items taken from his captive's pocket, Harland picked up a small well-worn notebook, which had the stub of a pencil pushed into its spine for safekeeping. The cover was dull blue, and embossed upon it was an emblem 'Stafford Shipping Co'. Within it were dates and places – Harland studied them initially without being able to make sense of them, but then he began to see a pattern of familiarity - this was some sort of journal of his own movements over the past few months, perhaps longer. He recognised street names corresponding to Old Barens Yard, The shop, Widow Amshaw's Residence, and much else besides.

He also found a photograph pasted onto a dark green card backing - an old man and a younger women standing in front what he could see was a baker's shop. He could make out the signage above the shop window – it appeared to be written in German. *"Perhaps not so innocent then."* he thought.

By now, the man tied to the chair had begun to come round. He mumbled a few words, "Mein gott..."

"Who the hell is this?" thought Harland – a German seaman following me around the streets of London? Then, a deeper unease hit Harland, the button he found in the hallway! The one he believed was torn from the waistcoat of one of Victoria's vile murders,

the same button he had studied and sought advice upon, only to find it was rather old and of German manufacture. Could this man tied, to his chair, be involved in his wife's murder?

Seized by a fire of anger and suspicion, Harland moved quickly – he would make his captive talk, and know the truth.

The man barely knew what was happening until a surge of pin-sharp pain hit his face, jolting him awake. Harland had taken a handful of snow from the doorway of the workshop and scrubbed it in his face. The cold bit deep into his skin like a thousand needles, and a surge of adrenalin jolted him into consciousness. Though his eyes were still yet a little blurred, and not adjusted to the lamp lights in the room, the man could see upon his wrist a strange object, made of metal, like a tube of some kind. He was also tied by the legs and arms to the chair.

"What is this?" he said, managing to bring himself to a focus at last. He could not see his captor but he was aware of someone standing behind him. Equally, he was not sure where he was – but he could see that it was a room with many tools – had he been brought to a place of torture? His heart pounded, and his head echoed each heartbeat with a pulse of pain in his head, which he guessed had been hit quite hard. It felt wet. Even though he could not touch it, he guessed that this was blood matted into his hair.

"So you speak English, as well as German, then?" Harland spat out his enquiry by way of an introduction. "You seem to know a lot about me, but I know little of you – I think you had better tell me what I want to know."

The captive straightened his head, but could not turn to see who was questioning him. "You are mistaken, I do not know you – who are you, why am I here?"

Harland grabbed his captive's collar. "You know me, don't lie – and do not tell me you were just taking an evening walk when I knocked the sense out of you outside in the street there."

Harland continued. "And do not imagine that I think you to be a singular enterprise – I know you are working with others. I will know who and where they are, if you have any sense of self preservation."

The man responded, "I work for no-one, and my business is my own. What do you know of me? - nothing – what will you know? - nothing - there is nothing to know about a simple man as myself who just goes about his business."

Harland smacked the back of his head, "Do not lie – I know you have killed and no doubt you would kill again if it suited you, perhaps you need to understand your situation a little more clearly."

The man felt a surge of recognition in what was being said – it was true, he *had* killed, but who could know about that?, Who is this holding him captive?

Harland reached forward to the metal object on the wrist of his captive, and pressed a small lever. With a click, the object seemed to come to life.

"Was is Das?" the man spoke in German, forgetting

himself, a certain chill of fear running though him at that moment.

"Shall we see?" said Harland. "This is a little invention of mine, a device I once devised for a client. You see, this cylinder of brass contains inside a powerful mechanical contrivance. It is devised in such a way that with each moment that passes, its internal diameter decreases by one eighth of an inch. Each click represents a contraction that reduces its size. I made this one to cut small logs for my log burner – it is *very* effective. Of course, it will work just as well on flesh and bone. I think you have perhaps thirty seconds before you feel your bones breaking, and soon after that the blades will start to move inward, and then take your hand clean off your arm."

"I tell you I do not know what you are talking about." said the man. In his head he was chilled at the prospect of his arm being mangled by this mechanical devil. But he did not want to tell this stranger anything about his true business – he was loyal to his overseer, and to his purpose.

Harland sensed that the device was now beginning to tighten – the man began to squirm as it clicked. "Just tell me who you work for, and why you were following me tonight, it is not too late to stop this."

"I following you? ... No, that is not right – I was walking behind another – you must believe me."

"So you *were* up to no good then?" Harland interjected.

"Tell me who you are working for, or there is going to

be a mess here. Perhaps you have not realised that once you lose your left hand, I will move on to your right ?"

"Look, I can't tell you anything..."

His words were cut short – the device clicked once again, and the pressure on his wrist had suddenly become more intense. He could feel the two bones in his fore-arm being pushed toward each other – the pain had begun to be excruciating, he gasped between words as he tried to convince Harland to stop.

"I don't know what this is about... maybe something... my master knows someone called Overard – he has something to do with the parliament... I can't tell you more about him, I was sent to watch a man – to look out for his safety – I stopped him being cut to pieces in a back alley only a few days ago... yes I admit I killed one of them but only to protect the man I watched..." His eyes seemed to widen, he shouted incoherently as the device clicked again.

"For gods sake!" Harland shouted aloud, voicing his own thoughts, as he scrambled to grab a small metal tool from the work-table"

"No, please..." said the man, flinching as Harland ran toward him with the sharp bladed screwdriver gripped in his hand. He tensed, expecting cold steel to cut into his heart, or slice his throat, at any moment.

Harland quickly and precisely inserted the tool into a small hole on the side of the device fixed to the man's wrist. In an instant the clicks halted, but the pressure

183

on his bones remained unbearable. Then, with a sharp twist of the tool, all pressure was suddenly released, accompanied by the sound of a tight spring suddenly unwinding all of its tension against the inside of the casing, and with considerable force. Harland pressed another small lever, and the device separated into two hinged parts, and fell away from the man's wrist.

Harland moved into full view of his captor, still tied to the chair. His blonde hair shone in the lamp light from this position, and his blue eyes appeared as wide as those of a cow at a slaughter yard. It was then that Harland also noticed the Star of David worn around the neck of the captive, half exposed by the ripping open of his shirt buttons when he grabbed his collar.

"So you have been paid by Sir Bertram Overard to watch and follow me?" Harland exclaimed disbelievingly. "Why?"

The man looked up and saw Harland clearly for the first time. "You ! ... the watchmaker ! ..." he began to speak, but then started to laugh out loud – a mixture of bewilderment and intense relief.

Harland was taken aback at first, but recovered his control. "For god's sake, you nearly lost a hand, and you can still find humour in this situation?"

"You mean that thing really would have cut off my hand and not just break my bones?, just as well you have had a change of heart then."

"I may have – but that very much depends upon what you are prepared to tell me. If you are indeed in the business of watching over my shoulder, then I am sure it would be easier for both of us if you tell me who you are, what you are up to, and how Sir Bertram Overard fits into all of this."

"Very well Mr Harland, I shall tell you the truth of it, but I hope you will explain yourself too – this creeping about places, walking dangerous alleys in the dark of night, and then there is your unusual overcoat. I am sure that I am as curious of you, as you are of me would you not say? But maybe you untie my hands first at least, and let me at that bottle of brandy you have on the shelf there? I think I am in need of something to soothe my aching joints..."

Chapter 27

Neumann sat in his cabin, aboard the SS Falke, reading the notes he had made earlier at breakfast. The cabin was considerably larger than most onboard, with both a sleeping area with its own small washroom, and what might pass as a day room, with a large opening portal window and plenty of light. The English coastline was now close, and slipping by fairly quickly, as the ship made its way to port.

A knock on the hardwood door announced the arrival of Neumann's visitor. "Komm Herein." answered Neumann.

Geltz entered the cabin, and closed the door. The air had a slight bluish haze, and the familiar smell of cigar smoke was not unpleasant to Geltz. Neumann took his cigar up from the cigarette tray, on the small table by his chair, and puffed on it for a few moments. He then waved it in the direction of the only other chair in the cabin.

"Sit, Geltz! Unless you are thinking of leaving?"

Geltz sat, feeling a little tired. Though sea-sickness was not a problem he suffered from, it was not easy to sleep when travelling in the steerage class, especially with Eichel complaining every ten minutes about his nausea. He said nothing – knowing better than to press his master with any impatience.

"So, Geltz, I am informed we will berth in two hours.

Therefore, we must have our plans rehearsed and laid well. I am relying upon you to keep that dummkopf Eichel on the right side of our business. Remember, he is expendable if he does not prove himself adept when it is required."

Geltz nodded, with a dispassionate detachment. He liked Eichel, indeed he had taken a few risks for him before now, but not enough to put his own neck on the line for him if it came to it.

"Let me reprise what we know, what we expect, and what you will do when we arrive." Neumann continued, "When we make berth, you are to slip ashore with the first crew members, and without Eichel, I might add. You will then wait on the dockside, keeping yourself inconspicuous. You will watch and wait. Remind me, Geltz, what are you waiting for there?"

"Do not worry, I know what is required – You have sent a telegram to someone in London. This someone now believes that they are meeting the idiots we killed in Bremerhaven and Osnabruck. I am to wait and watch. When I see the one I think it is, I am to follow him carefully and write down the places he goes. Then, I will meet Eichel and the others at the rendezvous place we have agreed."

"Good," Neumann replied, "you remember what is to be done, that is a start. But also remember that we only have one chance to do this – do not follow the wrong man, and do not let him get out of your sight."

Neumann puffed his cigar again, and then

187

extinguished it. "Make sure Eichel knows his part equally well. He is to take my letter of instruction to the others, immediately after disembarking with the other steerage passengers. They must begin making my enquiries... I need to know all about the SS Fathom, the passenger list, the crew, the inventories, and all that can be known when the price is right. Now, go and get that Eichel into some sort of state fit to do his work."

Chapter 28

Gemma Amshaw sat nestled in an alcove window, working on a small round-framed embroidery piece. It was an ideal vantage point, looking out over the well-kept gardens toward the main gates of the Amshaw residence. The garden was still swathed with deep snow, though a thaw had begun. Icy jewels of melt water swelled like buds and then fell from the bare tree branches, warmed feebly by the meagre warmth of the afternoon sun.

Gemma kept a watchful eye on the gate, expecting William Harland to arrive within a short while. His reply had been prompt, accepting an invitation, and arranging for afternoon tea with Widow Amshaw and her niece.

Widow Amshaw attended to the arrangements in the day room, where Gemma's alcove window was also situated. She surveyed the array of cakes and sandwiches, and admired the rather unusual tea service, decorated with large pale-yellow sunflowers.

"Aunt Janice, I see Mr Harland is just this moment arriving." Gemma said, with a slight excitement. She laid down her needlework on the alcove seat, and smoothed down her dress, before taking a seat near the mahogany tea table where three chairs were comfortably arranged.

A knock announced the imminent opening of the

solid oak door, and a maid announced the arrival. "Mr Harland, Madam."

"Thank you Charlotte," said Widow Amshaw, "would you be so kind as to bring the tea caddies, and the hot water, in a few minutes."

Widow Amshaw stood, and greeted Harland. "Mr Harland, please – come sit with us." She did not call him William at this point. Given the circumstances it was appropriate to be a little more formal – her duties as a chaperone required a certain etiquette, even though they were formerly acquainted. Whilst Gemma was staying in her guardianship, and her parents were in India, this was an expectation.

Harland looked across to Gemma, who took an innocent somewhat coy demeanour.

"I'm most grateful, Mrs Amshaw, for your invitation so soon after enjoying your hospitality. I must say you are rather accomplished as a hostess. It was a quite charming evening.

"You are most welcome Mr Harland, and I think Gemma found herself rather taken by your charms too."

Harland was momentarily on guard – after all, he had enjoyed a mid-evening liaison with Gemma that was not yet forgotten, though perhaps best kept to themselves for sake of demeanour.

Widow Amshaw continued, "I saw you both dancing, of course. I could see that you were both absorbed in each other's company."

"I must agree, Gemma is quite a lively dancer. I

suspect she would take the lead if allowed to." Harland observed, with an inner smile.

Gemma chose her moment to introduce herself into the conversation. "Well Mr Harland, I must say I am suitably flattered by the interest that you have taken of me. As you might imagine, I was surprised to receive your most welcome correspondence."

"Indeed, I was surprised too..." Harland began, and then remembered himself – after all it was *he* who was supposed to have written the letter according to Gemma's well-laid plan. "That is to say, I was a little surprised to find myself writing it."

Gemma smiled, but subtly so. She knew William was teasing her now, even though Widow Amshaw did not know it.

Widow Amshaw sought to set everyone at ease. "Mr Harland, shall we dispense with formalities? After all, we have been acquainted for a while, and I am sure that first names would be more comfortable for our conversations."

The discourse became a little more relaxed. They talked of the party. Harland commended Widow Amshaw's magnificent array of sweet and savoury fayre, and the choice of wine. Gemma joked about William's dancing.

Before long the maid returned, and brought in the tea caddy and hot water. Widow Amshaw prepared the tea herself.

"I would recommend you try this, William. It is Ceylon Golden Tips, very fashionable at the moment."

Harland agreed, and Widow Amshaw made the tea and then eventually poured it, handing the cups to Gemma and William.

Gemma sipped her tea, and then opened up a new line of conversation, remembering there was more to this visit than simple social entertaining.

"Perhaps it is not my place to ask, William, but My Aunt has told me about your service to our family... how you have been seeking out what you may find about my Uncle's tragic encounter."

William looked to Widow Amshaw, wondering if she was happy to discuss this in front of Gemma.

"Gemma knows all about our enquiries William, so please do feel able to speak freely. I understand that you have some new information. Douglas Barringer has recently informed me that you had made some progress, after he spoke to you during our recent festivities. Tell me, what has transpired?"

Harland began to recount his recent business, in particular the visit to Barens Yard, the fire, and the serendipitous recovery of the watch, which he had brought with him. He kept this in his pocket for the moment, fearing it might upset Widow Amshaw. He then explained how, as he had walked home that evening, he was accosted in the darkened alley by two assailants, there was a fight, and he had then found himself at home, somehow brought to safety by an unseen Samaritan.

Gemma was entranced – a combination of shock at the events, and awe at William's manliness in standing against these mysterious assailants. She felt her pulse racing, and found herself a little aroused, remembering for a moment their previous intimacy.

"Janice, I believe this may be your Husband's watch, do you think it is?" Harland brought the time-piece out of his pocket and passed it to Widow Amshaw.

She studied it for a few moments. "Yes. It is one of the missing watches, of that I am certain. So, you believe this foul arson and murder is connected to my Husband's death? And, indeed, to this poor Mr Barens you spoke of?"

"I fear that must be the case. Of course, the man from whom this watch was acquired may have got it from another – one thief trading to another, but I must suspect strongly that this is not the case. I believe the actions of these men, seen at the yard at the time of the fire, place them directly in the shadow of this damnable business."

Gemma added her own query "My goodness William. Do you think these men were also the same ones that assailed you in the alley-way?"

"I am not sure. I was not aware of being followed from the Yard, but perhaps I was mistaken," Harland replied, "I am minded to think that this was just unfortunate coincidence."

"Well, William," Widow Amshaw began, "I am immensely grateful for your good service to my family in this matter, and thankful that you did not come to serious harm. You have done far more than I had thought possible. I fear I must not expect more of you

193

after this terrible danger you were placed in on my behalf."

William sipped his tea. "I can assure you that I would not wish to give up our enquiries now, indeed I am more deeply intrigued to get to the root of this whole affair."

Gemma could see her Aunt was looking a little paler. The revisiting of the events of her husband's death must be painful for her, she thought. It might be best to shift the conversation a little toward another topic:

"William told me at the party that he is rather impressed with the age of this building, Aunt Janice."

Harland nodded. "Yes, it is an impressive residence, and the different parts dating from centuries past make one think of a great deal of history within these walls."

Gemma once again picked up the conversation. "I have happy memories of childhood visits here, as you might imagine. Especially the secret places."

Harland voiced his curiosity. "Secret places, what do you mean?"

"Well, there are several hidden stairways between floors, once used by servants. They are not easy to find, unless you know which wall panels to go to. And, of course, there is the priest's hole."

Harland now knew where Gemma's conversation was leading. Indeed, that was one reason for his being here taking afternoon tea. He played the bow to her fiddle, and feigned surprise.

"A priest's hole – how exciting. Is it in here?"

Widow Amshaw was content to sit back and allow Gemma and William to talk. After all, that was the purpose of Harland coming to tea – for them to establish a rapport, perhaps to flower into courtship.

"No, William, but I can show you. It is in my uncle's study"

"Then I am most intrigued, I have been there myself with Mr Barringer, when we catalogued your Uncle's collection, yet I had no sight or sound of it."

Gemma turned to her Aunt. "Might I show Mr Harland our antiquity, Aunt Janice?"

Mrs Amshaw agreed, and the three adjourned to Dr Amshaw's study to investigate further.

Chapter 29

Whilst Harland enjoyed tea in the distant warmth of the Amshaw Residence, Geltz stood out of sight alongside a stack of crates at the dockside.

As instructed, he had disembarked discreetly with some crewmembers, suitably bribed to play along with the ploy. Dressed in a fairly lowly attire, he blended in with the crewmen as he and they positioned and secured the gang-planks, and once that work was completed he slipped away a few tens of yards down from the berth, tucking himself into a shadow between stacked crates. There he waited, keeping the cold at bay with a pipe of tobacco and a small bottle of brandy.

As time passed, he watched carefully as passengers gradually disembarked in small groups, and looked for anyone who may be meeting them. Of course, these were exactly the persons of least interest. Those who were arriving and being met by relatives, servants, or carriage drivers, were not of interest. What he wanted to see was someone waiting but not meeting their expected arrival.

Neumann had set a trap. Sending a telegram to the mysterious 'S.B.O' in London, he had been able to give the impression that two travellers would be expected. Of course they would never come. One now lay at the bottom of the river in Bremen, or perhaps pressed up against the ice covering its surface. The other, now dead and dismembered, laid to rest unceremoniously in a disused brick kiln near Osnabruck.

Whomever it was who would come, they would find that there is nobody to meet. Of course, they would wait, and then eventually leave – and Geltz would follow.

Geltz drew on his pipe, and looked over to the berth. He saw Eichel stepping off the gangplank onto the slushy dockside, slipping as he found his footing back on land. Geltz shook his head to himself. Eichel was likeable, but stupid. He certainly was not respected for his subtlety either. He watched him walking away along the dockside, carrying a letter, which he had been instructed by Neumann to deliver. At least he had remembered to take it with him when he left the ship, thought Geltz.

A few minutes later, following Eichel's departure, he saw what he was waiting for. Standing outside a small warehouse, was a man. Tapping his cold feet to keep the blood flowing, he waited. Looking up to the ship at intervals, and then at his pocket watch, he kept an eye on the time as he had been instructed. After all of the passengers appeared to have departed, Geltz made watch for about thirty minutes more. The man then approached one of the crew, and after a short conversation, he began walking away.

Geltz was sure this was his mark. Walking disinterestedly in the same direction, he passed the same crew-men. And addressed them in his broken

197

English. "Hey, you boys – what was he wanting with you?" He passed them a few shillings to aid their interest. One of the men replied.

"He said he was to meet someone and asked if they could still be on-board. I told him all the passengers had gone."

Geltz nodded, and then walked off, continuing to follow the man who had been waiting. Geltz was good at keeping his distance without losing his quarry. He would follow him all the way across London if need be, and as Neumann had requested, he would make careful notes of where he went, and what he did. But, he must not be seen!

Chapter 30

Janice Amshaw stood in her late husband's study, situated at the rear of their large residence. This was a part of the building that was much older than the early Georgian section of the house. That had been built on at a later date, to create a more impressive frontage.

Gemma Amshaw, and William Harland, stood together near the dark wood-panelled walls, and studied them intently.

"I know it is here about," said Gemma, pointing toward a section of the wall, "I'm sure I remember it being here – I think I recall that when a certain panel is pushed, the door opens."

Truthfully, Gemma knew perfectly well the exact location of the priest's hole, for which the three of them were now searching. But, after her potentially scandalous liaison with William a few nights before, she felt that a certain caution was needed.

William took up the challenge, keeping up the appearance of ignorance in the matter, in the vein set by Gemma. He pushed and tapped against several panels, not being as sure as Gemma as to which it was that they were looking for. After a few tries in different places, one panel creaked when pressed.

"I believe you have found it, William!" said Gemma, feigning excitement. "I remember now, you press two corners together."

Harland did as instructed and, suddenly, the wood-panelled wall seemed to split as an invisible joint opened up from floor to ceiling, and the panel began to swivel open.

Janice Amshaw stepped forward, to look further inside, as the door opened. "I haven't seen this opened for quite a few years. My husband stored his papers in here I think, but I have never had a need to go looking there."

"So, William, this is where the friars would hide when the King's men came looking for them, or perhaps they safeguarded their silverware here, safe from thieves." Gemma explained.

In the brightness of daylight, the priest's hole looked a little different. Harland could see many shelves, stuffed with rolled up papers, each tied with string, and labelled. In places, there were boxes of various sizes. Some were of plain brown card, and a few others were old hatboxes. There was also a small wooden crate, and lots of dust.

"These look rather interesting." said Harland as he pointed out one of the boxes. "I do believe they may be part of your late husband's collection, Mrs Amshaw, and certainly they are items we have not catalogued. Perhaps there is something here we should examine, in case it becomes relevant to our pursuit of the truth, and justice."

Widow Amshaw could see the point made by Harland. "Then you must feel free to examine these items in as much detail as you require. If it is not too much to impose upon you?"

"I shall do so. And do not be concerned about my time, I am more than happy to do as you ask. Perhaps Gemma can assist, if I might spend the rest of the afternoon at this task?" Somehow, Harland felt a need to be close to Gemma again. Had she entranced him and brought him under some sort of spell?

Widow Amshaw momentarily looked a little tired. "That would be a good idea. But, please forgive me, I do not like spending too much time in here after what has happened. I will retire into the conservatory in the next room, and take a little rest whilst watching you begin your work."

As Widow Amshaw left the room, and momentarily out of sight, Gemma smiled and slid herself up against William, teasing him with a brief kiss before breaking away. "Well, we have played our little plan out, so let us begin, Mr Harland."

Gemma and William set to work. Each box was brought to the desk in turn, and each roll of papers likewise. Harland had a specific interest in the wooden crate. This was the same container from which he believed the remainder of the parts had been placed, relating to the cog he had removed earlier, the same one which he had used so effectively to knock his mysterious stalker unconscious outside his shop.

The crate appeared to be a moderately sized fruit box. Within it, a coarse packing material nestled an array of parts, clearly some sort of disassembled mechanism. Harland immediately felt that these parts were strangely familiar. Laying them out on the study table, he began to see how they might fit together, and he re-arranged them until their relative positions allowed him to visualise the machine once again assembled in its three dimensions.

At the bottom of the box, he found a note. It read *"machine of polish origin, of no particular function. For disposal as parts, K.Z"* on the other side and in another handwriting it stated *"sold to Dr Amshaw, 18 shillings, 13ᵗʰ of January 1890."* Signed 'Samuel Jensen.'

Harland then looked at the newspaper lining the bottom of the crate. There was no part bearing a date, but it was obviously not English. Various small articles and advertisements were written in a foreign language. it appeared to be something similar to German. "It could be Polish perhaps?" thought Harland to himself. In addition, there were various sheets bearing sketches and drawings. These appeared much more recent, and apparently of the same notepaper as that still on Dr Amshaw's Desk. They were collected together in a leather-bound folio, matching those already in Dr Amshaw's study. It seemed certain that this was the one found to be missing earlier.

"So tell me William, what is so special about this thing that you have such an interest in? What is it that can take your attention away from me for so long?" Gemma Smiled as she spoke, teasing him again.

"I believe it is of great importance, this is the very

device or machine that your Aunt believed to have been stolen from the display case. In truth it was never *in* the case at all, and was not stolen, though I have a feeling that this was what those men were seeking. Why else would they break open the case..."

Harland continued excitedly. "I think your Uncle took the machine apart to clean it, planning to reassemble it, and perhaps he stored its parts in here, to keep it out of the way until he had time to complete the task. I now believe that, whoever sought to steal it, they left empty handed. The damaged and empty display case led us to believe the mechanism had been stolen, but we were mistaken."

Gemma appeared a little in awe. She found Harland's intelligence and enthusiasm something of a fascination.

"We should tell your Aunt about this, I believe it is of great significance."

Gemma leaned over the desk and peered through the window, in front of which it sat, looking over toward the conservatory. "I think my Aunt may have fallen into an afternoon slumber. Perhaps we can let her sleep for a little while? After all, I believe that we have not quite finished the topic of our previous discourse – do you remember? – looking, but not daring to touch?..."

She took Harland by the hand, and led him into the priest's hole, clicking the door gently and quietly closed behind them, as they entered and once again found themselves alone.

Chapter 31

Eichel followed his new associate, Ernst Hausler, through the maze of packing crates, barrels, and coils of rope, some as thick as an arm. They made their way along the cluttered docksides, which were lined by a row of huge warehouses. Halfway down this seemingly endless monument to the British Empire's global trade, sat a building faced with white Portland stone. This was the main registry for this particular dock complex. Within its vast archives, would be the information Hausler had been instructed to find and obtain.

Neumann's letter, delivered to Hausler by Eichel, was quite clear. Hausler was to discover all he could about the SS Fathom, and its cargo inventory, passengers, crew and any association, especially in the late July and early August period, when the ship had arrived from Hamburg.

Hausler knew that his first step would be easy – check the shipping registers under arrivals, and find the SS Fathom arriving on a date that matched their interests.

Inside the building, there were rows of well-worn oak desks, the edges polished by the brushing of countless sleeves over their surfaces. About a third of the desks were occupied, the rest empty.

Hausler approached one of the attendants at the

archives section counter.

"My employer wishes me to make enquiries about an arrival in late Autumn last year. Could you supply me with the ledger please?"

Hausler spoke very good English. Though he had an accent, it was fairly mild after spending nearly two years in London on previous occasions, and during his current stay.

The clerk checked an index book and then a chalkboard, used to keep track of ledgers taken out of the archive. "It seems to be available, one moment please." The clerk then went off into a maze of shelves situated behind the attendant's desks, and returned after a few minutes. He added the volume number to the chalkboard, and then handed the volume to Hausler, taking his name. "The ledger must remain in this hall, please ensure it is returned when you are finished."

Eichel and Hausler took up a position at one of the inspection desks, and Eichel looked on as Hausler began to search through the ledger.

After about ten minutes, Hausler found the entry he wanted. "See here Eichel – the SS Fathom made berth on October sixteenth, arriving from Hamburg. Get out your note book and write that down, then let me read the rest for your notes."

Eichel did as instructed, though he thought this all seemed rather unnecessary. "Why can we not just rip the page out? – who will know?" whispered Eichel. Hausler snapped back at Eichel under his breath, "dumkopf, someone WILL notice, and what if they come looking for some reason relating to our business? Then they will see what has happened, and suspect someone has dubious intentions." Hausler waved his hand impatiently. "Just write what I say now." Eichel got out his pencil and did as he was told.

"So, SS Fathom, Berthed 16th Oct. Cargo shipments totalling 3.2 tons, seven and sixty crates, twelve barrels. Fifteen crewmen registered on arrival. Passengers: *none*. Vessel registered to Stafford Shipping Co. Customs Inventory Index O91-8182d"

Hausler read back Eichels's notes, to make sure they were correct. "Take this ledger back to the clerk, and wait outside." said Hausler. Eichel was turning out to be more of a hindrance than a help.

Hausler mulled over the initial information in his head as he puffed on his cigar. *"No passengers? This means that whoever made it onto the SS Fathom at Hamburg must have been passed off as a crew-member."* Perhaps he could check the previous arrivals of the ship and see who was an extra hand on this visit? - But who is to say the name would be any use? *"False names lead to false trails he thought."* Still, he would follow that up – Neumann liked thoroughness, and he rewarded results as generously as he would deal out punishment to those who he found to be incompetent.

Eventually, Hausler returned to the dockside and approached Eichel, exhaling a large cloud of smoke in his direction as he spoke to him. "Now we will see where our clues lead us. But we will need to 'grease the palms' as they say here. Komm, we will go into the city and see what else we can discover."

Chapter 32

Gemma Amshaw returned to her Uncle's study, with her Aunt, whom she had raised from an unintended sleep in the conservatory. At this time of year, the heat in the house was turned up high, and the conservatory had its own heating system, owing to the exotic plants that filled the space. It was therefore not surprising that Widow Amshaw had fallen into a short sleep, wearied as she was by her emotions.

"My Aunt is returned, Mr Harland." Gemma announced. "I have told her already that you have found something quite unexpected and exciting in the priests hole." Gemma was well aware that this had a double meaning, and she was subtly teasing William once again. However, he seemed quite serious now, in contrast to their earlier demeanour.

"Mrs Amshaw, I can tell you that I have found the missing curiosity, which you had thought stolen from the case here upon your late husband's desk."

Widow Amshaw was indeed surprised. "But how..." she began, but did not know where the question was leading.

Harland explained, "I have looked through the contents of the Priest's Hole, and I can see now that your Husband used this as a sort of storage area. I believe he was in the habit of dismantling the various devices he acquired, and perhaps not so well practiced in reassembling them. I found several such items in the priest's hole, but one of particular note."

Harland gestured toward the desk. There, laid out upon faded newspaper sheets, were the parts he alluded to, along with a hand-written receipt.

"Even though it is in parts now, I am sure that this is the very device that sat in the display case when it was last seen there by you, Mrs Amshaw. The fading of the woodwork in the case matches the layout of the mechanism's base, and its mounting bolts. It seems clear to me now that those vile miscreants did not steal the device after all. Yet, it seems it was the focus of their interest... the case had been broken open, but other items were left untouched. The scene we observed led us to believe the mechanism was taken, but of course it was here all along."

Widow Amshaw thought for a few moments, and looked over the parts laid out on the table.

"And do you suppose we can find out why this device is of such interest, Mr Harland?"

"It is hard to see any obvious path to follow, I cannot see of what interest this mechanism would be to thieves. However, I do have a distinct feeling that this is familiar to me... I need to reassemble the device as soon as possible so I can be certain of that. I feel there may be something extraordinary afoot here..."

Harland seemed to tail off his sentence, as if thinking over a seed of an idea that had just formed in his mind.

Gemma finally broke the silence. "What are you

thinking William?"

"Suppose for a moment that we accept that this device is of great interest to some unknown party – one who would go to the trouble of finding the person who bought it, and then assail its owner in order to obtain it. They fail, and leave empty handed, save for a couple of watches. Then we may suppose they are still pursuing their interest, and perhaps thinking it still to be elsewhere in London."

Harland continued. "The incidents at Barens Yard might well be linked, and indeed I now recollect that I have heard of other watch and clock merchants and jewellers having had burglaries over this past year or more. I thought nothing particular of it, until now."

"So, let us suppose that these men will stop at nothing to get what they want. No doubt, they will become aware of the forthcoming sale of Dr Amshaw's collection, which I have assisted Mr Barringer in arranging. They may well still think that the device is among these items."

Widow Amshaw was intrigued. "Perhaps that is the case, I can see it might very well be so. But how will that help us?"

"Well, let us suppose that we announce the auction in the press, with much more prominent advertisement than we had thought was necessary to dispose of the collection... And we take care to make mention of an unusual, newly reconstructed item to be included in the sale. A Machine of Polish origin, in good working order, an item of unique construction.

Perhaps even include an engraving to accompany the typesetting of the adverts."

Gemma nodded. She understood where William was leading them. "I see, so you think whomever is seeking this machine would surely attend the auction, and do their utmost to purchase it, whatever the cost."

"Exactly," said Harland, "they will attempt to buy the machine, and if they fail in that goal they will most certainly be interested in whoever makes the highest bid and purchases the device. We will observe all who attend the auction, and we will lay our traps. We will have justice for your family Mrs Amshaw. I have some friends who I believe could help us in our endeavour."

Widow Amshaw smiled, not a smile of joyful approval, but a hope of being finally able to look her Husband's killers in the eye, and perhaps see them hang.

"Mr Harland, as always you have exceptional insight. I believe you have looked upon the matter most clearly. We shall do as you say. Let us not waste any time. I will contact Douglas Barringer tomorrow, and set him to preparing the new auction notices."

"Thankyou Mr Harland," said Gemma, "this has turned out to be a most satisfying afternoon."

Chapter 33

On the same evening of his visit to the Amshaw residence, Harland sat in his workshop, at the rear of the Horological Emporium. The workbench was brightly lit by electrical arc lights, powered by a voltaic cell, and they admirably outshone the more subtle gaslights around the room. Harland studied each part intently, matching it to the sketches Dr Amshaw had apparently made when he dismantled the machine before his untimely demise.

Harland was able to make good progress. The machine was fully assembled, and appeared to operate smoothly. What Harland could not ignore, was the great similarity of the mechanism to that of the device Sir Bertram had asked him to reconstruct. They seemed just too similar to be unrelated. Harland would know for sure, when his work for Sir Bertram was complete. But that would take some days, if not weeks, to conclude.

Harland's pondering was broken by a cacophony of bells cascading into the room from the front of shop. The sound of a menagerie of large clocks all chiming the midnight hour was a familiar thing to Harland, but he had not realised it was so late. He looked down at his pocket watch, which he popped open, and saw it was indeed midnight. He then found himself studying the portrait set into the cover – his Victoria. He started to think about recent events once again.

His head had been turned by Gemma. He felt drawn to her, and he did not want to resist. Yet, he still had pangs of guilt – his Victoria, now gone, would she approve? And still another thought stirred in his mind too. In the early months of his grief, he had resolved to devote his every hour and day to finding those responsible for her murder. Had he become distracted by Widow Amshaw's search for justice, and forgotten his own sense of purpose?

Harland turned off the electric lights, now beginning to dim. The voltaic cell would require fresh acid before being used again. He turned to his coat-stand, and turned his leather long-coat inside out. The slash across the sleeve had been made with a very sharp blade, by a blow received on that now distant night in the alleyway. This meant it had been easy to repair. Had there not been a metal object within the sleeve, however, it would have cut his arm to the bone in an instant. No doubt, his throat would have been cut too, had not the mysterious samaritan intervened just as he was rendered unconscious. That person was of course Mayer, the very same man he had held in this same workshop not long ago, and whom he had nearly ended up depriving of a hand.

Harland checked the coat, and adjusted a metal mechanism within the right sleeve. From the coat pocket, he brought out three metal rods, and pressed them into a barrel within the contraption. He then used a small keyed implement to wind something within to a high tension. Harland knew well that the stored energy of a wound spring could be extremely powerful. Turning the coat right side out again, Harland put it on, and then dimmed the gas lights, and left the workshop by the rear door and back yard, locking up as he went. The snow had now all but melted away, the air damp and chilling, but not cold enough to keep the streets of London free of vermin, he thought to himself. The same thought circled in his mind as he walked out into the street and headed toward an area of the city he knew was well populated with all breeds of ill-will and malevolence. Somewhere out there, he was sure to find what he searched for, only time would tell where and when.

Chapter 34

John Stafford paced around the large drawing room of Sir Bertram Overard's Merrington Place residence. Sir Bertram stood at the other side of the fireplace, stroking his lengthy side-burns. Mayer sat by the window, with a small brandy glass in his hand. He nervously tapped a ring, which he wore upon one finger, against the cut crystal. It was just before ten in the morning, and they were each awaiting the arrival of the final piece of this unlikely quartet.

Sir Bertram fidgeted with a telegram card in his hand. "I must say that I am greatly concerned, gentlemen. It seems certain that our friends in Osnabruck have suffered some calamity. We know from the coded telegram that their intention was to arrive on the SS Falke from Bremerhaven, yet Mr Mayer's attempt to meet them at the dockside was a failure."

Mayer sat up straighter in his chair. "That is true, I was there early and waited quite a while. Eventually, I was able to enquire with one of the crew, and there was no one who might fit the description of our friends on-board. If they boarded that ship, then they did not complete the crossing."

"Or perhaps they were never aboard in the first place." Stafford noted. "They may have sent the telegram, and then been impeded before boarding.

And with no word since, we must assume that they have not met with a sympathetic outcome. We are responsible for this."

Sir Bertram looked downcast. "Yes, we have their lives on our consciences. They knew the dangers of course, but it is easy for us to sit here in London and pull the strings, whilst others take the risks. We also have to assume that whomever they have encountered will know that our friends planned to come to London, if not who they were to report to on arrival. That is a problem, and we must be alert to the unexpected."

The room fell silent for a few minutes, whilst each of the group considered the implications, and the fate of the Osnabruck pair.

Their quiet consternation was ended, at last, by the sound of the drawing room doors being opened. Sir Bertram's butler, Masterson stood to one side of the now opened double-doors and announced the arrival of their final guest.

"Gentlemen, Mr William Harland..."

In truth, William was unsure as to the exact purpose of his attendance, though he had of course been summoned by Sir Bertram himself, with a degree of portentousness regarding the possible dangers of dealing with the task he had set to undertake for him. Harland had been left wondering just what this meeting was all about.

The blueprints, provided by Sir Bertram, had proved to be incomplete. However, Harland had managed to construct most of the mechanism as described, and had been near to being able to present the prototype assembly for inspection. Only his encounter in a dark alleyway and his subsequent recuperation had disturbed his progress. Indeed, it was this incident that had ultimately led to the discovery of Mayer's unusual interest in his well-being.

All of these strangely interlinked events would have presented something that would surely demand to be set beyond mere coincidence. However, the addition of Dr Amshaw's unusual curiosity – a mechanism of unique design and apparently of Polish origin, was one happenstance too far. For whatever reason, these parts must fit together – if only it could become clear how, and why.

"Mr Harland, dear fellow. Please come, receive some warmth from the fire, it is yet a little frigid on our streets today in spite of the thaw." Sir Bertram signalled to Masterson to pour another brandy for his latest guest.

Harland of course recognised Mayer, and gave him a nod. He was not acquainted with the other gentleman, however, as their eyes met.

"Allow me to introduce myself. I am John Stafford. A good friend of Sir Bertram, and I should add that our good Herr Mayer is in my employment. I am sure you would like some explanations, I assure you that you shall have them."

Stafford extended his hand and Harland shook it politely. Harland was a little cautious – he had not met this man before, and was not sure how he fitted into the increasingly complicated business he had become immersed in.

Sir Bertram cleared his throat and readied himself to explain his urgent letter, the curious Mr Mayer, and much else besides.

Sir Bertram gestured to Stafford and Harland. "Gentlemen please sit, and make yourselves comfortable. I believe that you all know our ingenious Mr Harland. I have known him for many years to be a highly skilled engineer of minutiae, a master watch-smith indeed."

Overard continued. "I contracted Mr Harland to undertake some work for me, which I considered would need his inestimable talents ... the investigation of a set of blue-prints which were obtained in somewhat dubious circumstances, as I will explain. My intention was, of course, for Mr Harland to understand the contrivance described by these plans, and if possible to build a working model of it. And I understand that he has been working hard upon that task."

Harland nodded. "Certainly. I have made significant progress, and have some rather surprising news to add."

Sir Bertram continued. "I shall be glad to hear of it. Let me enlighten you further however. As you know, Mr Harland, I told you that these plans came into my possession somewhat informally, and my interest was simply an idle curiosity. I fear that may have been a dis-service to you, and may have placed you in possible danger, though the intention of my obfuscation was quite the opposite. You have my deepest apologies, sir."

John Stafford took up the prologue at this point, allowing Sir Bertram a pause. "Although we have not met, I can tell you that I too am involved in this business. Mr Harland, there are dark forces at work in this European continent which we share with our neighbours. It goes unnoticed by most Englishmen that our great empire is at constant peril. Whilst there are those in Europe who plot, plan, and restock their arsenals, the British government has in recent years taken an increasingly isolationist approach to these matters, you might say they have buried their heads in the sand. That is why Sir Bertram, myself, and a few of our good friends of influence, formed the Britannia Club."

Sir Bertram continued, as Harland and Mayer listened intently, some pieces being familiar, yet others completely new to their ears.

"Indeed, the Britannia club has a purpose to protect our great country, to gather information on our would-be enemies, to establish readiness in our industries, and in political circles, in defence of what storms may gather whilst we find ourselves in the political wilderness. And so, we have been busy in many places and in many ways. I dare not tell you all, but I will say that our friend Mr Mayer travelled from Germany with those blueprints, and nearly had his throat cut for his trouble. I then had them copied, courtesy of my friend Mr Stafford, and his engineers at his ship-building offices."

"Of course we tried to be inconspicuous." Stafford added. "I had my draughtsmen redraw the plans as exact copies, but with all words translated into English, such that any references to their original source were disguised. We believed that it would be safer if you did not know where the blueprints had come from, or how we obtained them. And, by erasing the Polish notations from the plans, we hoped that they would simply become an anonymous set of technical drawings, which you, or others, would not associate with anything related to our subterfuge."

Stafford paused for a moment, then looked across to Mayer. "I can assure you that Sir Bertram was most desirous to afford your innocent involvement in the work he set you to carry out for us. I, however, felt it prudent to take measures for your benefit, in the shape of our Mr Mayer. I believe he has explained himself, under a certain amount of duress... You know now, of course, that I engaged him to observe you at a distance, in order to protect you from any unforeseen malevolence. And, it would seem that this was valuable foresight, in spite of its seemingly underhanded nature. I hope you will forgive my intrusions."

Harland broke his dispassionate demeanour, with a slight warmth. "I'm indebted to you Mr Stafford, and to you too Sir Bertram, of course. I wont deny I feel that I have been left a little in the dark as to your true intent, but I also see that your reasons were well intended. I certainly cannot hold Mr Mayer's actions against you on any account, since he most likely preserved my life on one, if not more, occasions. There is undoubtedly more to this whole affair than any of us might individually suppose, so let us not dwell on our own intrigues."

Harland continued. "I believe that you must, of course, be well aware of some of my more uncommon activities, since Mr Mayer has been my ever present and unseen shadow these past few months. That too may deserve an explanation. But first, I have something that I imagine you will not expect to hear, and this is quite extraordinary in itself."

Harland noticed that Stafford had with him, a leather-bound tube, and its displaced end-cap hung by a strap, exposing a set of blueprints rolled up within.

"Are these the original plans?" Asked Harland, pointing to the tube, which stood against a side table where Stafford now reclined.

"Indeed they are, let me show you them in their original state." Stafford rolled out the plans on the carpeted floor, using several objects to weigh down the corners. An ashtray, a poker, and such items as were to hand. "As you can see, they are originally annotated in Polish. The plans also include some alterations and these are all initialled K.Z. We speculate that this may be written by the inventor himself – it is common practice in most drawing offices for plans to be annotated like this and initialled for further action."

Harland studied the plans deeply for a few minutes. The mechanisms were very familiar. He had worked on this for months, studying each drawing, with notation's in English. He had already built a reproduction of this mechanism, and of course, he had observed that the plans were incomplete. One sheet was missing. With a key part of the machine missing, it was not possible to work out how it functioned as a whole, or what it did. But recent events had changed that situation.

"Gentleman, I believe that you will have a great deal of interest in this..." Harland pulled out of his inner jacket pocket several sheets of paper, upon which the drawings of Dr Amshaw were inscribed.

"I obtained these from a source that you might find completely remarkable in its coincidence. Nonetheless, I believe that these drawings are the final part of this machine, and they were drawn by a gentleman by the name of Dr Amshaw. He owned a curious device which some referred to as the 'Polish Machine'. And, being of an eager nature, he dismantled it and drew up plans of its design. I have to say that the similarity of the design of the two sets of plans is exceptional. Both designs are somewhat remarkable, a work of an obscure and insightful mind no doubt, and each have the same nuances and mechanical uniqueness, almost like matching two sets of handwriting you might say. To my eye these are undoubtedly two pieces of work by the same engineer, and almost certainly for the same purpose. Indeed, you might surmise, complimentary parts of the same machine."

Harland paused for a moment, and looked over the plans once again. "I might add that I believe this particular device was owned by a Polish gentleman by the name of Zamolyski, I can imagine perhaps 'Karl Zamolyski' being the K.Z. Of your blue-print annotations. That most certainly adds to the validity of my suppositions. So, you can see now how unexpected this coincidence is. We may now have the only complete set of plans for this device in existence."

"Truly Remarkable!" Sir Bertram expounded. "We may yet have had a turn of luck in this matter."

Harland pointed to the signature on the note of sale. "This is the signature of Samuel Jensen, a clock repairer of whom I know a little, having bought items from him in the past few years. His business was mainly repairs and breaking of old timepieces for parts. However, I have made enquiries, hoping to speak with this fellow, and it seems he was badly beaten during a robbery at his shop last year, and died a few days later. It is possible that this is more than just a coincidence. And I have heard of other incidents involving antiquarians and clocksmiths too."

"Then we must be doubly careful my friends. That is if you intend to remain embroiled in this intrigue, Mr Harland?" Sir Bertram asked the question, hoping that he already knew the answer.

Harland did not disappoint. "There is no cause for me to leave the field now, something deeply troubling is afoot. Indeed, I have an instinctive suspicion that my own misfortune may also be entangled in this affair. If Samuel Jensen was beaten, and Dr Amshaw robbed and murdered, then why not the wife of a well known watchmaker? No!, I will not rest until I have justice for my beloved, and for the other unfortunates who we might surmise have crossed paths with these dark foes of whom we seek."

John Stafford patted Harland on the shoulder. "Bravo Mr Harland. We too are at *your* disposal, and ready to join the chase."

"Quite so." Overard added. "But perhaps we should be candid if we mean to proceed with our plans. I believe Mr Harland, that there are a few other details you wish to share with us? I think that, if we are fully disclosed to one another, it would be easier to proceed. I suggest we take lunch and then complete our frank discussions once we have fortified ourselves."

Chapter 35

Neumann sat at a walnut veneered desk, set in front of a very tall window, with the sun to his back, and shining into the eyes of his rag-tag collection of henchmen. Geltz and Eichel sat alongside Hausler, and another.

Neumann studied his papers, in no hurry to acknowledge anything to his entourage. On one side of his desk there was a set of cards, arranged alphabetically, and housed in a small box, so that any card could be pulled out and inspected at will. Neumann worked through these, reading one, annotating another. Finally, he sat back in the green leather chair and looked his men in the eye.

"So gentlemen, let me recount what you have told me, and go over each and every detail. Nothing should be omitted, or misrepresented. It is essential, as always, that I have certainty of facts and absolute accuracy. If there is any speculation to be made, then that is for me alone to consider."

As usual Neumann had a hard certainty in his voice, things must be done when, where, and exactly how he commanded. He was the conductor, and Geltz, Eichel and the others were mere instrumentalists, playing only their own parts and at the appropriate times.

"Let me start in Bremerhaven. Assuming that our draughtsmen friends gave up all they knew before we helped them on their final journeys, then we know that a telegram, which I sent on our departure, was received here in London before the SS Falke found its berth upon our arrival. We also know that the recipient of this telegram was the somewhat cryptic 'S-B-O', and that whomever this may be, the message would be understood."

Neumann had a certain immoderate egotistical theatricalism to his personality. Geltz was all too familiar with the lengthy monologues that Neumann was given to expounding. Whether this was a valuable way of mentally organising his thoughts, or simply grandstanding, was however lost on Geltz.

"That message, of course, would lead the recipient to believe that two men would travel from Osnabruck, via Bremerhaven, and arrive in London on the SS Falke. I supposed correctly that someone would be expecting to meet them on arrival, and I instructed Herr Geltz to observe this, and follow this person wherever he might go. Now, Geltz has reported to me upon the movements of this man. After waiting for a considerable time, he spoke to several of the crewmen of the SS Falke, and then left the dockside. He subsequently visited the very same telegraph office to which my telegram was communicated, and where we presume 'S.B.O' is known. Geltz informed me that the person enquired if there had been any new telegrams for 'S.B.O', and that there had not been any."

Neumann paused to corroborate his account. "Am I correct insofar as I have progressed Her Geltz?"

Neumann queried.

"Das ist Korrect." Geltz replied. He quickly corrected himself "That is so, Herr Neumann." Geltz remembered that Neumann insisted on English being spoken where possible whilst in London. They were to draw as little attention as possible to themselves. A fellow speaking German in the street would be well remembered, but the same man speaking English, good or bad, would draw less interest. London was full of accents from all over Europe, and they were ten-a-penny.

Neumann continued. "Indeed, I find it certain, then, that the man Geltz followed was indeed connected to our business. Why else would he enquire about S.B.O., at the telegraphic office, if not to find out if the planned arrival of the two draughtsmen had been deviated from, and further information sent ahead to amend their plans for arrival. And then Geltz followed this man, where he came to the Stafford Shipping and Export Company Offices. Here he entered, and regrettably managed to leave some time later without further observation."

Neumann sounded a little irritated at this point, and Geltz felt it necessary to comment. "He must have left, but I think he left by another door – I could not be everywhere at once."

Neumann ignored Geltz.

"Anyway, we also know, thanks to Herr Hausler, that the SS Fathom, the ship which conveyed the mysterious Maierhofer of Hamburg to this city of

London, is registered with the same Stafford Shipping Company. I have no doubt that these things are related, and that the shipment of wines delivered to the residence of Mr Stafford, the owner of this company, was a simple camouflage to disguise the transfer of the Osnabruck plans into his possession."

Neumann stood up, and paced the floor near the window, seeming to raise his sense of self-aggrandisement as he continued.

"And what of this S.B.O.? Well, we have used our skills to reveal the truth here also. Geltz has managed to pick the pearl from the oyster – with suitable bribes. He has obtained for us this information from a telegram office clerk about an unusual ritual. Each day, the chief clerk checks the incompletely addressed telegrams. We know that those addressed to S.B.O. are then despatched immediately by messenger boy to one Bertram Overard, or to be precise, Sir Bertram Overard MP, and received at his residence in Merrington Place."

Neumann now turned back from the window. "So you see, we have made a great deal of progress in just a few days. These high-placed Englishmen are no doubt involved – Stafford, Overard, and others we yet do not know. They must have the plans we sought, and if they do, then we must take them back."

Neumann sat back down, and looked again at the small group assembled. "If this is not absolutely accurate then speak now." No one spoke.

"Then we have much more work to do. I need all the

information you can obtain about this Overard character, and his accomplice Stafford. Find out whom they do business with, who their friends are, where their servants spend their spare time. You will need to be subtle. Geltz, you should ask questions carefully in the taverns near the shipyard. Hausler, you will search the newspapers for the past year for information about them – anything about their business affairs, or even their social engagements. Bring me whatever you find. Meanwhile, I want a list of the places you have visited in your search for the machine. It is a shame you have been so indiscreet –five murders ought to bring much unwanted attention. We can only hope that these English police have wasted any competence they had in this matter, and have lost interest in pursuing it. To work, gentlemen!"

Chapter 36

John Stafford paced back and forth in front of the large fireplace, where he had earlier sat while William Harland recounted his various movements and revelations. Of course, much of this was known to Stafford and his stalwart companion, Sir Bertram, as a result of Mayer's reports. But they now had it in Harland's own words. Now, they met alone to discuss their concerns.

Thanks to Mayer's keen eye, and his light step, Harland had been observed and surveyed almost continually for quite some time. Yet, the full details fell into place only when Harland had made full his confessions, and confirmed what he thought they already suspected.

Stafford stirred. "It still seems incredible to me Bertram, that this apparently mild mannered gentleman has been engaged in such a dark and disturbing business. I really do not know if I should approve of it, or give way to an abundance of caution."

Sir Bertram nodded, pondering Stafford's comments for a moment. "In spite of what you say, I feel I know Mr Harland's nature well, and I cannot in my heart condemn him." He shook his head, as if to emphasise his point. "No, I will cast away my doubts. I have to believe that in each of our own ways, would you and I not find ourselves similarly driven, Stafford? I ask myself, how would I react? To return home from a journey only to find my beloved slaughtered in my own hallway. And then to be imprisoned by incompetents who should have bettered themselves by seeking out the vile assailants who truly caused such bloodshed! Could I retain my calm and composed nature – inconsistent as it may be at times?"

Stafford retreated to his chair – he half hoped to be convinced by Overard's arguments, but he had not yet reached the summit of his acquiescence, he had to convince himself too.

"Quite," Stafford concurred, "I would not be able to carry on my life as if nothing had happened. I agree we cannot judge a man in such circumstances by an everyday morality. But, are we willing to remain silent and allow him to continue this dark engagement?"

Overard nodded. "It may seem that Harland seeks only to wound the world that has wounded him. Yet, I can see a method to his apparent madness. Let us re-examine what he has told us..."

Overard proceeded to remind Stafford of the facts of their earlier conversation. With Harland and Mayer now gone, they could review what had been said and have a frank conversation about the implications.

That morning, Harland had explained the business of searching out those he believed responsible for his wife's murder. The fact that he had not yet found satisfaction in his search, clearly pained him. And, now the possibility that events across the capital could be linked not only to each other, but also to his beloved's brutal slaughter, had renewed his determination. The connection between Sir Bertram's blueprints, and the mechanism believed stolen from the Amshaw residence, was pure serendipity – a turn of luck that could not have been imagined, let alone hoped for. However, Harland had more to explain than his comings and goings at Barens Yard, and the swollen lump on Mayer's crown. Overard returned his mind to the conversation that had recently passed between themselves.

"You may not understand my actions, but nor can I say I regret them." Harland had begun.

"After Victoria's murder, I found myself lost, first of all in grief, and then in despair. Being incarcerated in a prison cell, and wrongly accused of her murder - it made it clear to me that the so-called law of the land, the promise of justice for all, it is nothing but an illusion. How often is it that the difference between justice and the evasion of consequence is little more than chance, and the shortcomings of our London police forces? I wont deny that I wanted recompense – somehow I believed that my pain could be relieved by delivering vengeance on those responsible. But my searches seemed to always be in-vain."

"That is highly regrettable, indeed." Sir Bertram noted before Harland continued.

"Consider the months I spent making enquiries – the button I mentioned earlier, found in the hallway where my Victoria laid dying. I made it my very purpose to exist only to seek out the owner, and obtain my own justice. I discovered that it was pewter, of an old cast-metal type not seen much now, and that it was most certainly crafted on the continent – Germany or Russia perhaps."

As Harland continued to explain himself, Mayer, Overard, and Stafford sat silently, not wishing to interrupt Harland's catharsis of long held secrets.

"I did my best, struggled to keep my business – 'ticking along', you might say... I must be thankful for Frederick, my apprentice. He kept me from falling into total decline, and the Horological Emporium with it. I managed to stumble along day by day. But, by night, I followed my blackened heart. I spent every hour of darkness frequenting taverns. Dressed to blend in, I sat in quiet corners eavesdropping on conversations, played the drunken fool slumped by a bar counter, and engaged other drunkards in carefully disguised conversations. I flirted with whores and bought their services – but not those of the flesh. Rather, they were entreated to observe and report what they would see. If any girl came across a foreigner with an odd button on a green waistcoat, then there was a pretty penny to be earned if I got word of it. Of course, I was as good as sober, drinking enough to become invisible, yet able to gather information piece by piece without arousing attention."

Harland paused for thought, then took up his story again. "At least that was the plan, and yet I could not make headway. Each small step forward which I made only left me two steps further way from those responsible. And so, more often than not, I found myself walking the streets of London late at night, making my way home empty handed. But, it was on one such night that I met my destiny. Perhaps I was blinded on my road of grief, so that I could be made to see the truth?"

"So, I found myself walking along the riverside, returning from several taverns frequented by seamen. I had hoped to garner some information on the seafarers who lodge in the area whilst in port. I wanted to know more of the frequently visiting ships from Germany, but had not gained much insight on this occasion"

"Then, as I made my way along the river embankment, I saw something that I had not noticed before – the utter corruption of our city laid bare. How many times had I walked passed a dark side street, choosing not to see some crime or misdemeanour as I walked past. It was always someone else's problem, and not mine to involve myself with. Choosing to look the other way, out of fear perhaps? I am not sure. But on this occasion I stopped, and did not walk past."

Overard interrupted Harland's monologue, not speaking, but by pouring brandy into his empty glass. He could see that Harland was full of mixed emotions as he gave his unorthodox confessional. A drink would stiffen Harland's resolve to finish his story.

"Something had alerted me to a commotion. I walked into the alleyway, not quite able to see until my eyes accustomed themselves to the darkness beyond the lamplight. I could then see what had drawn my attention – a girl, maybe not even 12 years old. Turned to the streets to pay for her bread and board I imagined, but I could also see a heavy-set man standing over her, one hand on her throat, squeezing the life out of her, the other pressing a knife into her side. I fear it was too late to save her – I could see blood dripping down the knife blade and pouring onto the floor. Somehow, for a moment I saw Victoria standing there and not the girl. I was enraged... consumed by anger, and I called out. The man threw his victim down onto the ground, and then turned full square to face me... I could see that he intended to silence me as he had silenced the girl. At that same moment, he came toward me with a great deal of speed for such a large hulk of a man."

"Damn the man! Damn his eyes!" said Overard, urging Harland to come to the conclusion of the scene of horror he had laid out.

"He came for me, knife in hand. I fancied I saw fire in his eyes as he reached me and lashed out with the blade. But something drew from within me – empowered by my utter rage and a deep well of vengefulness, and perhaps a lack of care for my own soul. I found myself grasping a bottle left on the dank sill of a boarded window, barely visible in the darkness. As his blade slid narrowly past my ribs, slicing my overcoat, I smashed the bottle across his head, and then thrust the broken remnant into his face. He stumbled onto his knees, and I have no doubt that in that hypnotic state of rage I found myself in, I sliced his throat ear to ear with the glass shard that was left in my hand. The girl was beyond help, so I left quickly and quietly – beginning to realise the consequences of the untimely arrival of a constable at this moment. I've had enough of false accusations already."

Stafford looked a little disturbed. Mayer, on the other hand, appeared unaffected – he had seen men slaughtered before now, and most of them deserved it. Overard meanwhile, kept his true feelings guarded.

"And Mayer tells me that this is not a singular occurrence." Overard noted.

"I cannot lie Sir Bertram. Since that first incident, I found a sense of hopelessness being lifted from my shoulders. There was much injustice on our streets and yet, I could in my own way, turn the tables against those who prey on the weak and the vulnerable, whoever they may be. You are right Sir Bertram, and I will not deny either that the newspaper headline you have on your side table relates to my doing – 'Slaughterman' is not a title I would have chosen, but the press have their papers to sell, and their wild speculation is camouflage to my true nature."

"I can assure you that no man has died at my hand, save those who were threatening to take lives themselves. Others have found themselves sorely treated where I have encountered their criminality of a lesser degree. I have become a protector of sorts, a watchman for the vulnerable perhaps? I feel that this purpose found me, rather than me seeking it out."

"And what of the array of contraptions Mayer has spoken of?" Stafford interrupted finally.

"If you mean my armoury, then again, I will not lie. I have a skill for making small and powerful devices. The rod that everyone speaks of as a slaughter-man's bolt is a projectile - a sort of arrow, and it is that which is launched from within the sleeve of my greatcoat by a mechanism of my own design. The band I fixed to Mayer's wrist is simply a larger version of the cigar cutter I once made for Sir Bertram, and the implement I used to concuss Mayer was just bad luck on his part – it was simply a large metal component I had in my pocket at the time."

"Perhaps it seems strange – unorthodox perhaps. After the first incident, I was in a state somewhere between shock and validation. I did not go out at night again for quite a while. Initially I was fearful at my lucky escape – my coat was sliced apart by the murder's blade, and I realised that it was nothing but pure luck that allowed me to find a bottle to hand and to fend off his attack. I spent the next few weeks thinking about how I could defend myself, and gain an advantage should I ever find myself in that position again. I think, perhaps in the back of my mind, the intention was set – had I been more alert I may have saved the girl's life, and I knew there would be other nights and other acts of savagery. Next time I would be ready. And so I set upon constructing an array of defences and weapons, using my skills to achieve my goal."

"I fear now that I have told you all of this, I have put you in an unenviable position – you must feel bound to inform the authorities, and I cannot hold that against you. I realised a long time ago that there must come a time when I am made to reckon for my activities. I am in your hands."

And so, it was that Stafford and Overard had heard Harland's admissions. Now, alone in the drawing room, and by the fire, they faced the question of what to do.

As William Harland walked in the grounds of Sir Bertram's house, with Mayer by his side, Stafford and Overard talked further of these admissions, and tried to decide what should be their response.

Overard shook his head. "I cannot condemn such a man. You know of course he would hang if his confession were to be repeated in a courtroom."

"Undeniably," Stafford replied, "and I am not in the business of hanging a man who has only acted against those most vile in our city, and in the defence of others. Besides which, we have spilled enough blood of our own have we not? We have risked men's lives in our pursuit of the purposes of our Britannia Club, and seen some of them dead at the hands of others. Then of course let us not forget the incident at Tooley Street. A German spy ended up under an underground railway carriage, or perhaps it is more precise to say several parts of him ended up under several carriages. An accident by all accounts, but we know that is not the truth of it – we have our own secrets too."

"Undoubtedly, I agree with you Stafford, we are in no position to judge Mr Harland's actions, and have no reason to. I almost admire his bravado if I am honest in my opinions. And let us not forget that we are close to something of great importance... Those plans, and their mysterious secrets, which seem to attract death and deception at every turn. They must therefore surely be of great value, if only we knew how or why. And there is our Mr Harland, bang in the middle of the whole caboodle as our friend Asner might say. And whose fault is that? It is our own doing, of course."

Stafford felt he had satisfied his moral dilemma. He put forward his solution. "Bertram, my good friend, might I suggest then that we should allow discretion to draw a veil over this business, and all swear silence. Likewise, let us not disclose this to the other Britannia Club members, what they do not know cannot be turned against them if all of this should find itself inconveniently unravelling."

"So be it." Overard concluded. "Let us return Harland to our fireside companionship, and lay the matter to rest."

Chapter 37

A week had now passed since Harland's frank revelations at the Overard residence. Harland had been working night and day toward the plans that had been laid, being careful to keep as much of this business from his apprentice as he could. As he sat working in the back room of the Horological Emporium, Harland reflected to himself that Frederick had been indispensable in the last few weeks, keeping the shop running admirably, as Harland himself had been distracted by one unforeseen event after another.

Harland's concentration was interrupted by Frederick's arrival in the workshop. "Would you like me to make some tea Mr Harland sir?"

"Yes, that would be good. I can see that the shop is quiet today, please make a pot, and come and have a cup of tea with me for a while." Harland suggested.

Harland set down his tools, and poured some warm water from the stove into a washbowl. His fingers were ingrained with the fine grease of the parts he had been working with day and night. He had slept at the shop these past nights, as he had done before, in the small room he once lived in, when old Jeremiah Varey took him in on that cold winter so many years ago. Harland felt sure that he had completed the task in hand, save for a few small adjustments. The cornucopia of disassembled parts, which had been found in the priest's hole at the Amshaw residence with Gemma's subtle assistance, had come together after much experimentation. The blueprints provided by Sir Bertram were useful, they clearly related to the complete device, of which this machine was the final missing component. But the blueprint for this particular part was not available.

Harland had to take clues from those blueprints which he had, and use his knowledge to make educated guesses as to the final assembly. Luckily, the parts had not yet been cleaned. The patina of the metal showed places where certain parts had fitted together – brighter metal contrasting with the tarnished surface of parts exposed to the air, dust, and moisture. It was certain that this 'Polish machine' worked perfectly now, though it was still not clear what it did.

Harland finished scrubbing his fingers, and then dried his hands on a small towel hanging warmly near the stove.

As if on cue, Frederick returned, carrying a small wooden tray with a large teapot and cups.

Harland poured the tea as he began to speak. "Frederick, things have been quite a jumble recently. I can see that my comings and goings must have disrupted the normal routines here in the shop"

"I have stepped into your shoes at times Mr Harland, but I am grateful for the opportunity to take more responsibility."

"Indeed, Frederick. I am very pleased with how you have managed things. You have done more than enough. I have decided that you should have the smaller Champlevé carriage clock that you have worked on so diligently. If you remember, Mr Broadstairs offered this as payment for the restoration of the larger timepiece you have also been working upon. You may keep it if you wish, or enter it alongside our Amshaw auction lots. Either way it is yours, in thanks for keeping things running smoothly here."

Frederick was surprised, and then smiled. "But surely that clock is quite valuable, are you sure?"

"Yes," said Harland, "true, it *is* a rather valuable clock, but only because of your work in restoring it. I think you deserve reward for your hard work. And I am sure you know I have had much to burden me in the past two years. Having you at hand has been invaluable."

"Thank you, said Frederick. I think I may auction it then. I would dearly love to keep it, but I have a young lady in mind who I fancy might accept my proposal of marriage, the return on its sale would allow me to make good my intentions, and assure her parents of her well-founded upkeep."

Harland patted Frederick on the back. "Well, you have been busier than even I thought! I hope I will be able to offer my congratulations in the near future."

Frederick returned to the shop-front with a spring in his step, pausing to admire the Champlevé carriage clock, which was on display in a glass case by the counter.

Harland meanwhile sat down at his desk and began studying a small folio of paperwork entitled 'The Amshaw Collection: Time-pieces and curiosities of European origin.'

After his meetings with Gemma and Widow Amshaw, it had been decided that the planned auction of Dr Amshaw's main collection of time-pieces would take place at *Earnest and Langdon*, the well know London Auctioneers. The opportunity to include the mysterious Polish machine, which he had now rebuilt, was most serendipitous. The idea that the late Dr Amshaw's murderous assailants would stop at nothing to obtain this machine, was a tentative gamble at best. However, the revelation that Sir Bertram and his friends had a set of blue-prints that related directly to this contraption, and that people were willing to kill to get their hands upon them – that had piqued Harland's expectations considerably.

It was now very clear that some dark shadows were being cast across London, perhaps right at this very moment. *"If someone were to be seriously engaged in seeking this device, then they must get to hear of the auction."* thought Harland. Thus, the opportunity to lay a trap had been contemplated, and set in motion.

After the frank discussions a week earlier, with Sir Bertram, he had been reassured by their response. Any business relating to the so-called 'Slaughterman Murders' were of no interest to Sir Bertram, or the

Britannia Club. Besides, here was the perfect opportunity to flush out those responsible for Dr Amshaw's death, and perhaps those of his beloved Victoria, not to mention Sir Bertram's deceased collaborators abroad.

By offering the device at auction, along with 'a variety of sketches and plans believed to be in the hand of the maker himself', they would let it be known to anyone seriously looking for the machine as to its whereabouts.

Of course, the vault at Earnest and Langdon's premises was famed for its high security, and often guarded at night before an auction by men who themselves had no way of unlocking it. Whoever would seek to obtain the Polish machine would know that attempting to steal it would be fruitless. Rather, they must attempt to purchase it at auction, no matter the cost.

Sir Bertram had been very clear on this part of the plan. "We shall of course prevent anyone from purchasing it – members of the Britannia club will outbid anyone who seeks to bid themselves. No genuine collector would pay an extraordinary sum for the machine, but I will wager that the ones we now seek will ride the course neck and neck to our elevating bids, and not be shaken from the chase. Whatever the outcome, the auction sale will not be completed – we shall see to that. The machine will be safe, but the identity of our adversaries will not be so secure once our plan is played out."

Harland had been enthusiastic about this stratagem, and so it was agreed that the Horological Emporium would arrange the programme of the auction and ensure it was widely advertised. Drafting those adverts was now the business that Harland turned his attentions to, as he opened the portfolio and began considering his options. The catalogue of items from the Amshaw collection had to be eclectic enough, such that the Polish Machine appeared no more conspicuous than any of the other items – wood hidden within the trees would be less likely to give any kind of impression of being out of the ordinary. With that in the back of his mind, Harland set to his work.

Chapter 38

Neumann sat at his desk, surrounded by the familiar miscellany of his habitual mode of work. Wherever he travelled, his desk was laid out with the same items. More often than not, these would be packed and unpacked at each new location where he found himself weighing anchor. His travails led him perpetually from one city to another across Europe, and in this case to London once again. It was as if his desk could be wrapped up in a carpetbag and carried with him, though it was his assistants that did the carrying, and bore the responsibility.

Upon the desk were laid bundles of papers. Neumann handled each bundle of notes in turn, as if mentally weighing their content with his hand. These were the pieces of a puzzle he had pursued for some months now. Indeed, the threads of this particular contemplation first began to be unpicked several years ago. And now he found himself in London once again, in pursuit of the mysterious mechanism his employer had set him upon locating. More than twenty-six locations had been broken into, and items of interest taken into his possession. Five deaths, and many other grievous assaults - these were the costs paid for their owner's being in the wrong places at the wrong times. And yet, all of these interventions had proven to be falsely led by incomplete information and supposition.

Guesswork might be too harsh a judgement. None of the actions taken had yielded the desired outcome, but to leave any stone unturned was even more unacceptable to his employer than being empty handed. At this moment, though, his hands were indeed empty, something he must remedy urgently.

Neumann surveyed the information once more. Geltz sat quietly, reluctant to interfere with his master's thoughts, and awaited comment from Neumann.

"So, Herr Geltz, we find ourselves in this great city once again, trying to find the needle in the haystack as they are fond of saying here."

Geltz sat silently, nodding slightly to indicate that he was listening, somewhat reluctantly, to another of Neumann's monologues.

"I think for once we have had some good fortune, however."

Neumann tapped his finger upon a newspaper, folded such that a particular advertisement could be seen. It read 'Earnest and Langdon, Auctioneers and purveyors of fine antiquities'.

"See here – there is an auction in six days time, and if I am not mistaken, there is an item of great interest among these other contraptions and curiosities."

Geltz read the advertisement. His English was good enough to follow the list of items for sale. Among the various carriage clocks, automatons, and timepieces, he noted the item that Neumann most certainly referred to.

"*A machine of Polish Origin, recently refurbished to*

a high standard, purpose unknown."

Geltz looked at Neumann. "So, is this the item you have had us raking over the whole of London to find for two years? It finally turns up in a newspaper advert ... "

"Yes Geltz. The advertisement mentions the sale of the Amshaw Collection. You might remember that name, one of your more recent and less subtle operations. See here – Amshaw – on our list of London collectors – It seems that your visit to Dr Amshaw's residence did not turn over every stone after all. The device was there all along, and now that it has come up for sale, we may obtain it by simply buying it."

Geltz could see the irony – after so much criminality led to no good, an honest transaction would allow them to complete their task. Perhaps then he could soon return to Germany. But there was, as always, a nagging doubt – this business had been so convoluted that anything was to be expected and nothing presumed.

"Herr Neumann, this is a very fortunate occurrence. Yet, I see that there is a problem. If this device is sold at auction how can we be sure to obtain it?"

Neumann nodded, "Geltz, you see the situation as I do, you prove yourself insightful once again. I have obtained an assurance from our overlords, a large sum will be made available on deposit at the bank known as 'Bleasdale and Company', and we will be able to present our guarantees to the auctioneers in good time to participate in the auction. We will have such a sum available that no other buyer might sensibly out-bid our position."

Neumann paused as he toyed with a letter knife, and then looked Geltz in the eye. "But you know my inclination is to consider all eventualities. I will require an insurance against any mishaps, and I think this will be a task that calls for your particular talents once again."

"Very Well." Geltz replied, agreeing to his master's entreaty. "You know I will do whatever is required."

Neumann poured a small glass of brandy for himself and offered the bottle and a glass to Geltz, in an uncustomary act of hospitality.

"Then let us consider our plans Herr Geltz – I will explain exactly what I want you to do, and you will then examine each detail on the ground, and report back to me on the feasibility of our endeavour. Once we have secured our insurance, there will be no doubt about our final acquisition of this troublesome device."

Neumann untied the ribbon from a small bundle of notes, the front sheet of which read 'Observations of the Amshaw residence' and proceeded to pass them to Geltz.

Chapter 39

The air felt heavy with moisture as William Harland stood by a large covered goods carriage, at the rear of the Engineering works of the Stafford Shipping Company. He gave a series of cautious instructions to the four workmen standing by its rear doors.

The Polish machine sat at the edge of the carriage floor, at roughly waist height to the workmen. The driver sat at the front with the brake held fast, and a boy calmed the horses with a bag of oats so that they would stand still during the unloading process.

The road and forecourt of the engineering works entrance were encased in ice. The depths of the preceding frigid January night had been followed by freezing rain at dawn. This had formed a surface like glass everywhere it had fallen. Stafford had however given careful consideration to the arrival of the machine, and had ensured that a pathway was scraped fee of ice and scattered generously with casting sand from the workshops.

Harland's breath turned instantly to thick steam as he spoke. "Carefully now men, two of you at each side – the first pair take the front of the casing... now you two at the back, you need to lift the rear end as it comes to the edge of the carriage bed – slowly now!"

The men each took a firm grip on the rough pine outer box-work that had been built around the device at each end, and secured by struts of planking on each side. This allowed the machine to be moved around with minor knocks against doorways and to keep the actual inner case of waxed hardwood from touching the floor when it was rested.

The men managed to bring the device carefully to the entrance to the main drawing office, where they were met with a flight of stairs. Harland drew in a breath, and hoped that this would not be the undoing of their careful transfer of the device into Stafford's main engineering and drawing office. As the mechanism was carried up the stairs, rocking in step with the raising of the men's feet from one stair-tread to another, Harland was astonished to see that the mechanism appeared to come to life – moving within the case in an unusual manner, almost in rhythm with the men's motions. This was a most curious observation.

Why the machine would behave like this was a mystery. It was true that Harland had studied the machine in great detail, and had spent a great deal of time working out exactly how to reassemble the parts found at the Amshaw residence. The late Dr Amshaw had made copious notes as he had taken the machine apart, and Harland had eventually been able to rebuild the machine in pristine condition, assembled in the only way that Harland could see it being completely functional. However, as to what exactly this mechanism did, Harland remained unenlightened, and the true purpose of the machine still remained a mystery. Today was the final opportunity to study it alongside the full set of plans of the remaining parts, which were to be held by Stafford's engineering office. They were soon to be despatched to the secure vault of Earnest and Langdon Auctioneers for receipt prior to the auction in two days time.

Harland was relieved when the machine was securely placed upon a large inspection table, where large scale plans would normally be unrolled and studied by the engineers.

"It is an outstanding piece of work, Mr Harland" Said Stafford, patting him on the shoulder.

"Undeniably. It was designed by someone of great skill." Harland replied.

"I agree Mr Harland, but I was referring to *your* skill in this instance. The reconstruction and restoration work you have undertaken is exceptional – it looks as if it were made only this morning."

Harland smiled weakly, accepting praise, though perhaps a little embarrassed for his modesty.

Stafford picked up several large rolled up sheets of blued paper. "Let us set out the plans we have for the mechanism, and arrange them around the table so we can see how they relate to this construction. We can then have some refreshments by the fire in my office, whilst we await Sir Bertram's arrival"

Harland and Stafford did as suggested, and then talked for a short while as they waited for Overard, who arrived after a short period of time.

"Gentlemen, please accept my apologies, the

carriageways are like frozen lakes today, my driver made very poor progress in spite of his efforts."

"It is of no concern my dear Bertram." Stafford replied. "We have enjoyed thawing our extremities after the unloading. I am glad to say that everything proceeded without incident, in spite of the weather. As you can see we are ready to inspect what we have acquired for all of our recent troubles."

Harland, Overard, and Stafford, spent an hour studying the device, the blue-prints, and the various scraps of paper and sketches that Harland had collected from the Amshaw residence. There was much discussion and speculation about the purpose of the machine, but little had been concluded.

"Gentlemen, I think we need a fresh pair of eyes to look over this." Stafford announced. After a long pause where no new thoughts had been offered among the group, he felt this was a useful suggestion. "May I bring in two of my senior engineers?"

Harland and Overard agreed to this proposal, and Stafford left the room and returned within a minute, followed by his two best and most senior nautical engineers, announcing their appearance. "I would like to introduce my highly regarded employees, Jonathan Heron and Henry Burbridge."

Harland and Overard introduced themselves in turn, and the newly enlarged group gathered around the table once again.

"Mr Heron and Mr Burbridge are familiar with the plans, they were entrusted with making the duplicates that Mr Harland received." Stafford then turned to his two colleagues.

"Tell me what you think of this. You will know the plans, of course, but the addition of this new mechanical mechanism completes the picture."

Harland briefly summarised the newly enlarged collection of mechanics and blueprints for the benefit of Heron and Burbridge.

"You will no doubt be familiar then with the four blueprints, and you may be able to see that the machine on the table is an exact construction of those designs. I have worked for some months under contract to Sir Bertram to produce the assembly. However, you will also notice that the plans do not include a fifth module of the design, which as you can see, fits perfectly into the mid-section of the machine. Incredibly I was able to bring this fifth component together with Sir Bertram's machine by nothing more than blind luck."

Sir Bertram Responded. "Indeed, the fact that Mr Harland independently came across this final piece, and recognised its significance, is quite extraordinary. It also means that nobody but ourselves have access to the whole machine, or the ability to divine its purpose. That, of course, is something we hope you can assist us with, gentlemen."

Initially there was quiet contemplation. Both Heron and Burbridge were thinking and studying. Eventually, Heron passed a comment, with a soft West Country accent that betrayed his origins.

"I may not have the skill of the man who conceived of this design, but I do think there is something familiar about it. I'm fairly certain that four of the components on the third blueprint are designed to connect to hydraulic actuators, but for what purpose I cannot hazard a guess."

Overard sought to encourage further debate. "Well gentlemen, guesses are all we have at the moment, so by all means offer what you may."

Burbridge took this as a cue to add to the speculation. "I agree with Mr Heron about the hydraulic connections – they remind me of early hydraulic control couplings which I have seen at the Elswick yard as an apprentice, in Newcastle. It is a rather old system now, that was superseded in the 1870s by a more robust design. And I do believe that several other parts of the design are capable of acting as a kind of gearing system, to apply large forces under the control of smaller ones, and that would also make sense if the contraption Mr Harland has assembled were capable of generating those small forces."

Heron nodded in agreement. Overard attempted to summarise the hypothesis, as much for his own benefit as for the others.

"So you seem to be saying that this design perhaps takes some small motions from Mr Harland's additional reconstructed device, and then transmutes them into large forces to drive a hydraulic system of some kind? – have I got that right?"

"Correct," Stafford confirmed, "you have the gist of it

rather well stated."

Harland, who had stood silently, and had been listening intently to the senior engineers thoughts, suddenly stirred. He brought his hand to his mouth, as if to prepare to make his point. But, he said nothing. Instead, he walked away from the table, toward the fireplace. He paced back and forth, for what seemed like five minutes, but it was undoubtedly less in reality.

Harland suddenly came to a halt where he stood. "Gods Grace – I believe I have it!"

Harland stepped briskly over to the table. "Gentlemen, please indulge me for a few moments. Each of you stand at a corner of the table, and be ready to lift that corner which you have chosen, upon my instruction."

There were a few looks of slight perplexity at this request. Nonetheless, each of the four fellows did as requested.

Sir Bertram made a half-hearted attempt to make light of the situation. "This table is rather large and heavy, somewhat like myself – but I cannot imagine we will move it far from the window Mr Harland, if that is your intention?"

"You may be relieved to hear, Sir Bertram, that I do not wish you to take upon yourself the role of a furniture mover! Rather, we shall gently rock the table in a certain way, if we can coordinate ourselves correctly."

Harland then proceeded to explain what it was that

he required of them. "Heron and Burbridge, you will lift first, perhaps three or four inches, slowly up and down. Then I would like you, Mr Stafford, and you, Sir Bertram, to lift your corners in the same manner, but out of step with your colleagues – imagine the table is a boat and you gentlemen are akin to waves lapping around its hull – please try it, and we shall see what will happen."

The four colleagues did as asked. For a few moments, perhaps tens of seconds, they acted their parts, and there seemed to be no noticeable consequence. However, with Harland's continued encouragement, they persisted. Then in amazement they looked upon the reassembled device set at the centre of the table – it seemed to have almost come alive!"

Harland could not help breaking into a smile, as his colleagues at last rested the table back on its four feet, with a certain relief from its weight.

"Perrelet! gentlemen. Abraham-Louis Perrelet!"

Chapter 40

The Britannia Club had once again convened, at Sir Bertram Overard's London Residence. Belford Smythe, Jerome Asner, Lord Marcus Ainscough, and John Stafford sat around the large dining table, with Sir Bertram Overard maintaining his reputation as a good host, as was always the case.

"More Brandy Gentlemen?"

"Indeed, my dear Bertram, I for one shall not refuse another glass of such a fine cognac. But, perhaps whilst I savour it, you can tell us exactly who this fellow *Abraham-Louis Perrelet* is, and why your extraordinary Mr Harland should think he is at the centre of all of our recent affairs?"

Sir Bertram nodded in acquiescence to Belford Smythe's request, and resumed his explanation of the day's events.

"Well, gentlemen, I have explained how we have come to be in possession of that inscrutable machine, which we now know was the work of a Pole of some undoubted genius. And I have also recounted the peculiar way in which Mr Harland validated his inspired theory of the purpose of that mechanism. But you are correct, dear Belford, in so much as I have not explained exactly what it was that we have discovered as a result."

Sir Bertram paused to pass around an ornate silver

box, containing a selection of his best cigars, before continuing.

"So, let us recall that Stafford and I were in the draughting room of Stafford's shipping company office. Our Mr Harland had demonstrated the behaviour of the mechanism most effectively through his rather unorthodox methods, and we were amazed at the result."

Sir Bertram began to replay the events to his compatriots exactly as he remembered them some hours earlier that day...

"Mr Harland, what on earth has just occurred? I saw the very same thing as we all did, but I must confess I cannot divine its meaning."

Harland walked over to the table. "Well Sir Bertram, I believe I can tell you exactly what this device does, and indeed what makes it so important to those who appear prepared to kill for its secrets."

"Its behaviour was most peculiar." Heron noted, awaiting Harland's explanation.

"Not so much *peculiar*, indeed the machine behaved in a very *particular* manner, as you no doubt observed. You will of course have noted the way in which the table was rocked under my direction. It was very much akin to the rolling of waves in open sea, the swell of the ocean, upon which the smaller ebbs and flows of waves are superimposed. We imagine these to be of a random nature, but they are not. Quite the contrary – the waves of the sea are not random, but appear so because they are simply too complex to be conceived of as a simple expression of a mathematical nature. And yet, when you moved the table, the machine appeared to capture the very motions which we created. Not only capturing it, but seemingly to actually *anticipate* it."

"To anticipate it? What exactly do you mean?" Stafford enquired.

"There is a rhythm and repetition in the sea, that we cannot easily define, but this machine seems in some sense to 'learn' the patterns of motion and to capture their repetitiveness, in such a way that it can operate the control rods you mentioned earlier, such that they oppose any motion experienced."

Heron nodded. "Yes, I see it now, I did notice that the rods appeared to behave chaotically at first, but they soon became synchronised in some odd way to our table movements – almost as if it knew what we would do."

"Exactly!" Harland stated excitedly. "The machine captures the essence of individual motions, and somehow repeats them in concert, like players conducted in an orchestra. When several of these captured motions are combined they conspire to produce a force on each controlling rod that contradicts that motion – you might say it compensates for anticipated motions of the waves."

"My god Mr Harland – I see what you are getting at now..." Stafford interjected. "Imagine if this device were aboard a ship... It would create forces through the additional parts in the blueprints, and could perhaps then drive more powerful hydraulic pumps, perhaps in the way Burbridge suspected with his reminiscence of those Elswick Yard hydraulics. Suppose that these forces were used to control an artillery piece... The gunner would then be able to sit inside a gun turret that appeared to him to be on a calm sea, no matter how fiercely the sea conditions would toss and roll the ship itself..."

"Yes," agreed Harland, "and anyone who has this machinery and knowledge of its principles would be able to aim and deliver artillery with unprecedented precision, even in a rough swell, and whilst moving at speed. They could hit targets in such seas even with the first shot, and at distances which any unfortunate enemy would find impossible to return with equal accuracy."

Sir Bertram shook his head in incredulity. "Gods Eyes, Mr Harland, how on earth did you see this as if it were as plain as day, when it was as clear as mud to the rest of us in our ignorance?"

"Well Sir Bertram, I must confess some luck and a little flash of inspiration. Earlier today, I encountered the element of luck: when the men were carrying the machine up the stairs, I could not help noticing its odd behaviour – their coordinated movements upon the steps created a rhythmic motion, and the machine appeared to dance in time with their efforts. I could not quite see what this meant at the time of it. But just then, as I was pacing back and forth here by the fire I received a flash of insight. I remembered *Abraham-*

Louis Perrelet!"

Stafford was the next to urge Harland on with his explanation. "This Perrelet fellow, you mention him again – just who is he, and what has he to do with this machine?"

Sir Bertram continued with Harland's exposition. "Abraham Louis Perrelet was a watchmaker of great inventiveness. Indeed, it was more than 120 years ago that he contrived a mechanism that allowed a watch to wind itself up, simply by capturing the motion of the watch whilst sitting in the pocket of its owner as they walked about in their daily business. Indeed, it would be wound in any place it encountered such perturbations – even in a carpet-bag rocking side-to-side in a carriage perhaps. So you see, it was then that I realised why some parts of this design were so familiar. They reproduced the self-winding principle, but in a somewhat new and clever way. Rather than simply winding up a spring, to power a small timepiece, the Polish machine uses this self-winding concept to power repetitive motions that seek to oppose the very same movements that drive it. The machine is arranged in such a way that each component of motion may be captured individually – up to five of them – it may be considered a sort of embodiment of a kind of mathematics known as polynomials – a sort of 'difference engine' as that great mind Babbage might once have expressed it."

Marcus Ainscough put down his cigar, and tapped his hand upon the table, almost in semi-applause for his recognition of Harland's brilliance, and bringing Overard's focus back to his present company. "Utterly Incredible Bertram – and may I say your account of the day cannot be faulted... It has the makings of some sort of novella I would wager. However, we must keep this story to ourselves. Your Mr Harland is an extraordinary fellow – and he has done the nation a great service. If we can indeed translate this knowledge into a naval advantage then it could give the Empire a bulwark against its enemies. Even if they have superiority in tonnage and numbers of ships, that is no match for an artillery piece with an almost supernatural accuracy."

Belford Smythe nodded and took the opportunity to speak. "Indeed, this is most incredible and fortuitous. But what of the machine – where is it now Bertram?"

"As you know, with Widow Amshaw's consent, we intend to use the final part of the machine to flush out those rogues who have wreaked so much slaughter and sorrow across London this past year or two in their pursuit. Now we know exactly why it is so important, we must also ensure that those who seek it are exposed and sorely afflicted for their criminality. That part of the machine is now in the vaults of Earnest and Langford, and will not be going anywhere. The rest of the machine is currently held in a strong room at Stafford's Offices. In two days, the complete device will go to the auction floor and we shall see what quarry may show itself in the bidding."

Overard put out the stub of his cigar, and sat forward

in his chair. "So Gentlemen, let us adjourn our Club business, and return to our good ladies in the drawing room. We shall see what may arise come auction day."

Chapter 41

Janice Amshaw stepped slowly along the pathway, her progress made much easier by the fact that this path had been scraped clear of ice earlier that morning by the park-keepers.

Gemma, walked beside her Aunt, with her hands slipped inside a fur muff. Widow Amshaw's two small dogs, well-bred west-highland terriers, scurried back and forth between them and the maid. Violet, who was responsible for managing the two excited dogs, *Whiskey* and *Brandy*, called them to heel when they got out of hand.

"It is refreshing to be out of our house for a while. The fresh air will do us both some good, don't you think, Gemma?"

"Yes, I do like the freshness of the winter air. On such a clear day the air is so much better than the usual London veil of chimney smoke and smog."

The park was busy, various ladies, gentlemen, and nannies with perambulators, were coming and going. Several barrow-stalls were set up in the park and the smell of hot chestnuts could be caught on the air.

One man walked around the park carrying a board on his back, repeating an announcement in a fairly monotone delivery. His demeanour betrayed the fact that his endeavour was primarily out of a desire to earn his rent rather than conviction for a cause. *"The*

Labour Party. Meetings this week in Spitalfields – hear Kier Hardy speak about the working man's rights to representation in parliament."

Widow Amshaw and Gemma gradually slowed to a halt. Violet had allowed Whiskey and Brandy to run off towards the lakeside, and she walked briskly to return them to the route they were taking around Baldwick Park.

"Tell me, truthfully Gemma, how is your courtship with Mr Harland? Are his intentions honourable?"

Gemma blushed a little, though hoping it would not show. She had not expected her Aunt to ask such a direct question.

"Aunt Janice ..." Gemma paused, blushing slightly. "Mr Harland... William... if I am true to my own sentiments then I must say that my heart is his. I do believe I love him most dearly. I hope and pray he loves me also."

"I suspected as much." Widow Amshaw replied. "You look at him like those dogs look at our cook when she is trimming the Sunday roast. Of course, I have noticed your wide eyed adoration every time he calls upon us for afternoon tea."

"Why do you ask, Aunt Janice?"

"Oh, no reason really... although... well, I have received a letter from your parents today from India, and they have mentioned the possibility of you joining them in Jaipur. Apparently, there are many eligible gentlemen there, and you are already of marriageable age. They feel it is unseemly for you to remain unmarried. After all you are now twenty-one years of age, and a singleton in my wardship."

"No!" Gemma gave an exclamation that might have sounded like she had been mortally wounded in other circumstances. "Please don't make me go to India – not now, what about William..."

Gemma's eyes began to well up. Her breath billowed out as steam, as she breathed heavily with emotion.

"Well, it is up to your parents of course. However I had intended to write to them to say that having you here has been a great comfort to me since ... well, we know what I'm talking about ... and that you would be welcome to stay as long as you wish."

"Please tell them to let me stay here in London, Aunt Janice."

"I think I must be diplomatic, but your emotions have told me all I need to know. My conscience tells me that life is too short and too fragile to be bound by old-fashioned traditions. I have learned that we must all grasp the love we have, and keep it close by. I cannot insist upon anything, but I shall do my best to convince them that you are thriving here in London, and that a highly eligible suitor is at hand. I must say that, a year ago, I would have agreed with their thoughts wholeheartedly. In any case it will take weeks for our correspondences to be exchanged, given the delays involved for postage to India and back again."

Gemma was very quiet, as they walked on and back toward Old Friary Lane, the dogs having being retrieved by Violet and now held by their leather leads to prevent further excursions. Her head was swimming with thoughts.

How could she go to India now? There had been suitors of course, and her time in Paris was certainly not spent learning to paint, in spite of that having been the expectation of her parents. She had dallied with men, and enjoyed their attentions, but none had been so immediate in their impact as William. She could still remember how their eyes had met that first night, when her Aunt had introduced them at the party. She cannot, must not, go to India. William was the one she had set her heart upon.

She was certain that William felt the same, if only she could overcome his sense of loyalty to his late wife Victoria. But that would need much more time than a few weeks. She could only hope that her Aunt's persuasiveness would be able to convince her parents that she would be best off remaining here in London for the time-being.

Chapter 42

Victoria Jane Harland stepped lightly across the ballroom floor, following William's lead. Her smile was radiant and her crisp white wedding dress was dazzling in the sunlight streaming through the large windows. The ballroom floor was busy with other guests, dancing alongside the happy couple. It was summer, the very day of William's marriage to Victoria.

William had no desire to dance with anyone but his beloved Victoria, but a hiatus in the music marked the point at which dance partners would exchange with the couple alongside them. As William stepped away from Victoria, and to the lady on his right, he was startled. Her red hair and green eyes were unmistakeably familiar.

"Hello William, do you not remember me? I'm Gemma..." Suddenly, the dark green velvet dress which Gemma was wearing, appeared to fade to white, and it too became a wedding dress.

"Shall we dance, my Husband?" Gemma said with a smile, as the music picked up pace again.

William felt the dance floor spinning, or rather it was his head which was spinning and the floor that was standing still. He could see Victoria held by another man, struggling to get away, still in her beautiful white wedding gown.

Suddenly, the man with whom Victoria was entangled drew a knife and stabbed her. Bright red blood seeped out over the white dress in moments, as she slid onto her knees. Guests ran forward to hold her, and William rushed to her side, as the man slipped away.

"Victoria, for god's sake, please hold on, we will get a doctor, here let me hold you. Someone, get a doctor!"

Victoria pushed William away with one hand, as the other clutched her wound.

"William, it's time."

"Time for what?"

"It's time to let me go now, time to let me go... time to let me go..."

Then her blood began to flow from the wound like a stream cascading over a small waterfall. But as each drop of blood hit the hard polished wooden floor, it became transformed into a metal button, cascading across the polished surface, each one with the face of a wolf upon it.

Harland, awakened in a wash of perspiration, his heart pounding like a distant artillery gun, his bedclothes tangled and tossed aside. He suddenly felt the cold of the morning air around him. The fire he set the night before had burned out, and the curtains allowed in enough light to see that it was already past daybreak.

This was not the first nightmare he had had since Victoria Jane's murder. But this was the first time Gemma had been there, in his dreams. What did it mean? As Harland washed himself, he thought about it. "How can I let her go? Not without justice for my love, so her soul may rest. Then perhaps I can rest too … he stopped washing for a moment, what did he mean by rest? he had once thought of his own death as a release, but perhaps it was his heart that now needed to be set free?"

This was auction day. Perhaps the very day that Harland may indeed have the justice he sought. The mysterious Polish machine had seemed to have left so much destruction in its wake. So, it would be fitting if it finally led to the destruction of those who had been the actors in that savagery. The auction should, by all accounts, flush out their quarry. Whoever had made it their business to go about London seeking this machine, they must now surely be aware of its existence and sale at Earnest and Langdons's today at 11am.

The disposal of the Amshaw collection had been widely advertised. Deliberately so, in order to attract as much notice as possible. Those, as yet unseen, must surely seek to out-bid any buyer in order to lay their hands upon the device, no matter at what price. And that would be the means of their exposure.

Sir Bertram and his colleagues had hatched a plan to raise the bidding far beyond that of any legitimate collector, of which there would no doubt be a few. The genuine bidders would surely fall by the wayside, leaving only those who knew the true value of the machine. Then Harland would be able to look upon those who had destroyed his life, murdered his beautiful Victoria, Widow Amshaw's Husband, and God knows what else. Then there would be a reckoning ...

Harland finished dressing and then put on his dark leather long coat. His arms slipped into two mechanisms within the sleeves as he put it on, and he secured them with hidden straps. He was not intending to face his foes empty handed, not today.

Chapter 43

Sir Bertram Overard picked up the auction brochure, which he found placed on his chair. Indeed, there was one copy neatly placed on each empty seat in the auction room.

'Messrs Earnest and Langdon, auctioneers to the discerning of London.' read the embossed cover of the rather fine looking catalogue, which was bound in red card, and with smooth pages of high quality paper within. No expense had been spared.

The auction room was a large vaulted hall, with glass portals set into the roof, allowing copious daylight into the room, in spite of the winter-grey pallor of the sky outside. The room bustled with new arrivals, as well as a jumble of conversations from those already seated in anticipation.

Belford Smythe sat to Sir Bertram's left, about six seats away. They acknowledged each other with a discreet nod, but did not seek to openly advertise their familiarity of acquaintance. Overard, Smythe, and Stafford, were all present, and each seated apart from the others. Their intentions were well rehearsed.

The auction had been heavily promoted. The usual channels for auction announcements were awash with advertising. Cecil Fowlhurst had also made good play of the event in an article in one of his several London news-sheets. He had been running an article about a great sale of collectible items resulting from the late Dr Amshaw *'a reputed collector, with special interest in continental devices and curiosities.'* This was of course a deliberate exaggeration, intended to ensure that no-one who mattered would be unaware of the forthcoming sale.

Overard, and his compatriots, would be bidding heavily on the Polish machine, in order to draw out the singular elusive bidder who would value it highly enough to pay any price, no matter how exceptional. The plans were more carefully laid than this, however. Several of Belford Smythe's personal staff had been pressed into service, to create a buzz in the auction room. Certain items had been earmarked for heavier bidding, with the prices to be pushed up by these colleagues. The impression would be given that a few serious collectors were bent on obtaining the best of Dr Amshaw's collection. That way the bidding on the Polish machine would not seem too irregular at first – it would just be one of several surprises at a well-attended auction. What would happen, once the mystery bidder was known, was another matter.

After ten minutes, the auction room was full. Indeed, many additional people stood at the back, even spilling around to the sides a little. Overard noted William Harland's arrival. Mayer would be here also, but Overard could not observe him from where he sat. Harland sat with Douglas Barringer, who held a sheaf of papers in a leather folio. He would be recording the sales on behalf of Widow Amshaw, keeping up the appearances of a normal sale.

At precisely one minute to 11am, an usher rang a hand-bell and called out an announcement. "Ladies and Gentlemen, please be seated now, the sale is about to commence."

As the last few people took their seats, and the hubbub began to fade toward silence, Overard surveyed the room, looking for likely candidates to fall under his suspicion. Belford Smythe, Harland, and the others were doing the same thing, with as much subtlety as they could manage. Between them, they were able to cover the whole auction room with their collective gazes. The chief auctioneer tapped his gavel upon the podium, and began to speak.

"Ladies and Gentlemen, good morning, and welcome to Earnest and Langdon. I am John Teesdale, your auctioneer at today's sale. I am pleased to say that we have a superb collection of curiosities, automata, and mechanical miscellany – the major part of the late Dr Amshaw's personal collection. We have thirty-two lots today, as itemised in the catalogue. So, let us begin with a series of automata. Please bring lot number one to the front, gentlemen."

The auctioneer turned to his stewards and gestured to them to bring up the first item. All of the auction lots were stored in a large fireproof vault built into the back of the wall, situated at the end of the hall, and behind the auctioneers podium and desks. The vault was hidden from view behind a set of screens, such that any lot could be brought forward as and when required, to be shown to the audience as the bidding commenced, but allowing the items to be kept out of sight, and secured easily in the event of unexpected occurrences.

Overard continued to look about, taking the excuse to look in whichever direction the latest bid came from. Nobody stood out to a degree that might deserve any suspicion. Overard wondered if their carefully laid plan had fallen at the first hurdle. Then Overard saw something! He began to exclaim, forgetting himself ...

"By God ... er ... I ...."

Overard realised his indiscretion almost immediately. He had not spoken particularly loudly, but a number of heads had now turned in his direction. The whole damned game could be up if he did not think quickly...

"By God I will have that piece – fifteen pounds!"

Overard may just have covered his mistake, a few heads shook mockingly at the man who had taken the bidding from £5 pounds to £15 in one leap, but he had managed to distract attention from his initial outburst sufficiently to avoid consequences. No doubt, they assumed he was just an inexperienced and over-excited bidder.

"Do I hear more than an admirable £15 pounds, ladies and gentlemen... I am asking for the last time ... going ... going ... gone! Sold, to the gentleman with the silver topped cane, in row eight."

The auctioneer nodded to the clerk to note down the details, then moved on to the next lot.

Overard waited a few minutes to allow the dust to settle on his indiscretion. Then, he carefully glanced back in the direction he had been looking earlier. At the near end of the row, in which he himself was seated, he could see those at the front of a small group of people standing, slightly squashed, down the side of the over-full auction room. He looked carefully, and observed one man, wearing a green waistcoat with buttons of silver-grey. As he had thought, one button seemed out of place from the others, and he could see that the rest of the buttons looked familiar – were they the very same design as the button Harland had shown him some time ago? Was this the murderous rogue who had killed William Harland's beloved? And, he wondered, perhaps the murderer of Widow Amshaw's husband too?

Overard noted that Harland would not be able to see the villain from where he was seated. Perhaps just as well, thought Sir Bertram. After all, who would blame Harland for taking a knife to the vile animal if he came face to face with him? But caution was needed too. He could not be certain of what he could see without getting a closer look, something that would not be wise just at this moment. In any case, he was corralled on either side by other seated auction attendees, and he had other parts to play yet. For the moment, he simply studied the man himself, and kept him discreetly in view as the auction proceeded.

A number of lots were offered over the next hour and more. There was a buzz in the auction room, and the bidding was fluid. Evidently, the advertising had brought a gaggle of well-heeled collectors forward to vie for the best items.

Belford Smythe remembered his role – to bid extravagantly on certain items to give the impression of their being plenty of money around the auction hall. His staff, whom were strategically spread around the hall, helped the process by counter-bidding, and raising the prices further. Overard's apparently eccentric earlier bid now seemed less exuberant, as several lots had now gone for twice any sensible collector's price range. He felt a little more comfortable to be able to blend in amongst these other spendthrifts.

Finally, the sale moved to lot number twenty-three, and Overard sat up in expectation of what would occur next.

"Ladies and Gentlemen, that concludes lots sixteen to twenty-two, in the category of *'various pocket watches'*. We now come to *'curiosities and miscellany'*. We start with lot twenty-three, which our stewards will bring to the table in a moment."

The stewards brought the Polish machine, now fully assembled and back in its display case. They carefully placed it on a large table at the front of the auctioneers staging, opened the glazed case frontage, and then stepped away to allow it to be viewed clearly.

"Lot twenty-three... a mechanism of unknown purpose. Described by the Late Dr Amshaw as 'the Polish machine'. Believed, with good reason, to be originally from Poland, and constructed by a Mr Zamolyski of Utska. The mechanism has no understood function, but appears to be in full working order, and complete. There are various drawings, some believed to be in the hand of Zamolyski himself. The lot may be of particular interest to collectors of calculating machines and other mathematical curios. May I open the bidding at ten pounds?"

There was an initial pause – Overard, Smythe and Harland had laid out a careful plan for the bidding on the Polish machine. They would wait to see who started the bidding, with a rather high opening price. Perhaps it would be the mysterious individuals who had pursued it across the continent and through the streets of London. However, there was apparently no-one willing to start the bidding. Whomever they were waiting upon to show their hand, they must be holding back too. Overard decided to break open the logjam.

"Ten pounds sir."

"I have ten pounds, from our friend with the silver topped cane in row eight. Do I hear twelve pounds..."

Now the plan was able to start to unfold. One of Smythe's staff, Bartholomew Johnson, picked up the bidding – jumping back and forth between Overard and himself ...

(Johnson) 'Twelve pounds here."
(Overard) "Fifteen pounds."
(Johnson) "Eighteen pounds."
Then, a new voice entered the fray. "Twenty five

pounds!"

The bidder was determined and confident. He spoke as if twenty-five pounds would be merely loose change to him.

Harland now knew that they had made headway. He turned to see who had placed the latest bid, and kept a close eye upon him.

Overard gradually escalated the bidding, with help from Belford Smythe's two trusted staff, and soon the price had exceed any sensible value. There was a cacophony of surprised comments in the auction room with each new bid.

"Ladies and Gentlemen, please try to be calm, let me have your indulgence so we can hear the bidders clearly. So ... we now have a bid of one-hundred pounds from the gentleman with the small gold-rimmed glasses. Is there perhaps an appetite for one hundred and twenty pounds?"

Harland knew the game was up now, as did Overard and Smythe. If they kept bidding, then so would their opponent. Then, he would undoubtedly see through their subterfuge. They could hardly go on toward two hundred pounds without losing any semblance of genuine bidding. They had already anticipated this – they knew that there was no way they would allow themselves to be out-bid, yet they could not simply keep raising the stakes without showing they knew the true value of the machine, and in so doing so they would alert their quarry to the hunt.

Now it was Mayer's turn to play his unorthodox part

in the scheme they had constructed. As the bidding had steadily crept upward, Mayer had been listening carefully in a service corridor, behind a side doorway. This led off from the main auction room, and there was one pair of doors on each side of the hall, concealing two identical corridors. Their main purpose was to allow gatherings to leave quickly at the end of sales without all being funnelled uncomfortably into the main doors at the entrance to the hall.

Mayer stood at one of these doors, pushed very slightly open so he could observe proceedings, and listen. He had his instructions well rehearsed. And so, as the bidding began to approach one hundred pounds, he followed his part of the plan.

He pulled a bundle of damp straw, wood-shavings, and paper scraps from his coat, setting it on the floor by the door. He then quickly lit it with a candle he had earlier set alight and placed out of sight. No-one had come down the corridor, and he had been undisturbed the whole time he had been there waiting. He could hear the auctioneer calling out the latest bids.

"Ninety pounds, I hear from the gentleman in row eight, dare we go higher ladies and gentlemen? "

As the bid for one hundred pounds was called and the audience became animated at the new heights of the bidding, Mayer readied himself and then burst through the door loudly. As he did so, he made sure that the billows of smoke from his bundle were drawn into the auction room as he swung both doors open, and then closed them quickly to hide the true source of the fumes.

"FIRE – FIRE!"

He slammed the doors closed and pretended to hold them in place, as if holding back a calamity ...

"FIRE! – gentlemen, please take your ladies to safety, we must leave whilst we can – save yourselves!"

Mayer's accent was unmistakably Germanic, but he spoke good English, and those assembled in the hall had no difficulty understanding his warnings.

Teesdale, looked shocked for a moment, but then remembered the protocol for such events.

"Ladies and gentlemen, please be calm, there are several other exits. Please move to them without panic and we shall all be well. Ushers – attend to the rear doors, quickly now..."

At the same time as Teesdale spoke, his stewards came forward to the table, where they had stood away to the sides previously, in order to allow a good view of the lot.

"Stewards - take the artefact to the fire vault, and lock it immediately. Then assist our guests to the exits."

There was surprisingly little panic. Everyone moved toward the exits as requested, and Mayer stood by his own door, deliberately wafting a fresh billow of smoke into the room now and then for effect. Then he turned his attention to Harland and Overard, who were moving toward their unusually interested counter-bidder. They did not know his name, but it was none other than Neumann himself.

Chapter 44

Mayer moved toward Harland, as did Overard. Meanwhile, several men moved toward Neumann, including the man whom Overard had observed earlier. Their movements, coming together in their two distinct groups, and against the direction of the evacuating people, made it obvious to themselves that they were squaring up for a confrontation.

Within a few moments, the room suddenly seemed abandoned, and fell silent. The worried conversations of those leaving the hall had subsided, they had all left. But now there were two groups left standing. Neumann and his men had been unable to leave, as Overard's group had effectively blocked their way. It was now obvious to each side that their opponents were here because of the Polish Machine.

Not quite knowing what to do next, Overard could not stay silent. His contempt got the better of him.

"So you *gentlemen* are here for the Polish Machine – It could hardly be plainer than it is, so do not deny it. Do you really think we will let you have it, after all the blood you have spilled trying to get your hands upon it?"

As if to underline his determination, Overard drew his silver-topped cane up, and pulled out a long and very sharp steel blade from its hollow shaft. At the same moment, Belford Smythe slipped a small revolver from his pocket, and Mayer pulled a blade from his boot.

But, Harland stood motionless and silent. He was glaring at the waistcoat of Geltz. Dark green, with eight silver-grey buttons, each with a wolf's head emblem. But one button did not match, it was a different hue and size, and it too had a wolf's head, not of the same character as the others. Harland knew immediately that these buttons were the same as the one he found in the hallway, days after his beautiful Victoria's brutal murder. In that moment of realisation, his blood seemed to surge like hot lead through his whole body. His rage made him blind to anything except that one vile disgusting animal. He looked him straight in the eye, and spoke slowly with pure hatred in his soul.

"You ...... I know who you are ... you were there when my Victoria was cut to pieces like some animal in an abattoir!"

Harland paused for a few seconds, his lip trembling with emotion. "She lay there alive for twelve hours, unable to call out in her feeble state, her body ripped open. She bled slowly, and died in agony ... like you will now ..."

Overard felt a surge of anger too. He had not known just how brutal the murder of Harland's wife had been. But then, suddenly, Harland lurched forward, and in an instant, he raised his right arm and fired a metal bolt out of the mechanism hidden in the sleeve. He aimed straight for Geltz – right into his face. But at the same moment, Eichel, who had stood alongside Geltz, slammed his fist against Harland's extended arm, and deflected his aim. The bolt shot out and smashed into the ornate glass light fittings on the distant wall behind.

Geltz made a grab for Belford Smythe's revolver, but was slid aside by Belford's quick footwork. In the same moment, Eichel drew a blade and lunged at Harland. But just as he did so, Harland raised his other arm, and activated another hidden mechanism. A flurry of powdered metal, fine brass filings from Harland's workshop, flew into Eichel's face – thousands of tiny needle sharp particles piercing into his eyes like ground glass. Eichel recoiled in agony – blinded and crippled in one moment. Disoriented, he fell onto his knees.

Neumann drew his revolver and fired a deafening shot into the ceiling, bringing down shards of plaster.

"HALT!" he shouted.

Everyone stood motionless, wherever they were, pausing in their respective struggles to take stock of the situation.

"Gentlemen please, we should not come to blows like this. Indeed, if you do not listen very carefully to what I have to say, then very much more harm will be done than your blinding of my poor Herr Eichel."

Neumann spoke in a detached, self-assured, and arrogant way. Like he was in charge, and had known it all along. He barely cared about Eichel, who was now rolling on the floor, every blink of his bloodied eyes adding a new searing pain to his misfortune.

"Do you really think I am so stupid? Do you really believe I have come all this way just to be caught like a mouse in a trap, and with such little effort on your part? Please, do not underestimate me so…"

Harland, Overard, and the others were silent – anticipating that this was not the end of Neumann's diatribe.

"No, No!" Neumann added, shaking his head with a certain smugness. "Of course, I did not expect to be able to simply walk out of here with the machine – how foolish an assumption you have made. You see, I considered the fact that this machine just happened to turn up, and was being sold by idiots who had no idea of its value … but I also considered the opposite – that I was dealing with calculating individuals who were bent on putting an end to my little business."

Belford Smyth, still holding his revolver, interrupted. "So what of it? You say you knew we had laid a trap for you, then you seem to have been caught old man. And there is a crowd outside that will come to our aid if it comes to it."

"Quite so, *old boy*." said Neumann, mocking Belford Smythe's stereotypical Englishness.

"But consider my ingenuity if you will. To walk out of here I must have assured myself of a plan of my own. An insurance policy you might say … Tell me, which of you is called Barringer? "

"That is myself, Douglas Barringer, Mr Barringer to you though if you would be so good sir."

"Well then, *Herr Barringer*, you can confirm what I am about to say. Am I right in saying that you received a telegram from the widow, Janice Amshaw, via the office here this morning, whilst you were preparing for the sales?"

"yes, that is true – but how ..."

"How is not important. But I also assume that you will confirm that this Widow woman has decided not to come to the auction today. It was *'too painful for her to attend the sale of her husband's collection'* ... am I correct? "

"Well, yes as it happens. So you have read my messages then? And what possible relevance does that have, apart from showing your ill mannered insolence?"

"Dumkopf! I did not read that message – I wrote it! Do you still not see ... I paid a visit to the Amshaw residence this morning, and I helped them despatch a little telegram on my behalf. That was the very same message, which you think I have been skulking around and reading behind your back. Ha! You fool."

Harland suddenly felt a deep sense of foreboding – a sinking feeling and a sting of fear wrapped together in an uncomfortable embrace that seemed to draw around him.

"What the hell have you done?" Harland exclaimed.

"I have done nothing, my dear Mr Harland. Yes, I know who you are too ... and I know much of your business, and of your friends activities here too."

Neumann paused for a moment, pacing theatrically

287

to underline his perception of having the upper hand.

"So, Let me tell you that your much-beloved Widow Amshaw is safe at home. And her servants will be unharmed – if they keep to their senses, and do not cause trouble. Four of my men have very clear instructions to remain there and keep them captive, until one-pm, when the sale should have been concluded."

Neumann took out a pocket watch and checked the time. He held up the watch for all to see.

"Look how well my plans have been laid." Neumann said, gloating at the fact that the watch showed the time was now be barely two minutes to one.

Harland was outraged, but Overard held his arm, silently encouraging him to hold himself steady.

Neumann continued. "But of course you must be wondering why Mrs Amshaw would be held captive and then released? …. come, gentlemen, you must keep up with me if we are to resolve this business as gentlemen."

Overard, growing impatient, pressed Neumann to proceed. "Well I'm sure you are about to tell us, even if we do not see it for ourselves. So why not just put an end to this theatre play-act and give us the *coup de gras*."

"I shall. I know you too, by the by. The over indulgent member of her majesty's parliament who looks like he eats for two – eh? You may know that your Amshaw Widow has a young ward – Mr Harland certainly will know of her, he has spent enough time walking with her in the park has he not? So, you see, the reason we held the Amshaw woman was to make sure she could not send word to you that we have taken the girl. Had the sale proceeded sensibly, then she would have been released unharmed of course. But since that is not the case, she offers me the bargaining power I require to ensure I can rely upon your cooperation."

"You evil bastard." Harland blurted out. He was ready to strangle Neumann with his bare hands. However, a calm fell over him, as he realised that there was no room for mistakes now. Not with Gemma held captive, and god knows what else.

"Gentlemen, you should know I am a very responsible host. This girl of yours will be held somewhere safe, and she will not be harmed. My men know what will happen if they disobey my instructions in any way. She is my property now and I will only trade her for the machine. If you do not agree, then of course she ceases to be useful to me, and she shall be killed. I do not like bad debts. But, should it come to that, my men will be free to do what they will before they cut her throat."

"You will be sent instructions forthwith. You will bring the machine to a location of my choosing, and we shall exchange our respective goods, and we will all live happily ever after my friends – I do hope you will deal well with me, if not then this little story will end rather badly."

Overard had weighed up the situation, and realised,

as Harland too had concluded, that this stand-off was intractable. They must lose the infernal machine, and save Widow Amshaw's niece. It was Harland that finally broke the stalemate, and acceded to Neumann's demands.

"Very well, since you know us then you will know the residence of Sir Bertram Overard. You can send your correspondence there. But you must understand that the machine now lies secure in the fireproof vault, here in the hall. Once locked, it has a time delay. We will not be able to get the machine for you until two days hence."

Neumann nodded. "Very well, we will arrange for an exchange in two days. BUT - DO NOT UNDERESTIMATE ME!" Neumann spoke these last words slowly and firmly, then turned to walk away, his men assembling to leave with him.

"What about Eichel?" Geltz prompted, moving to approach him to get him off the floor.

Neumann turned back to face them. "I have no use for a blind cripple. But blind or not he can still talk, and that will not do either."

Neumann raised his pistol, and fired a shot straight into Eichel's head. Blinded by Harland's earlier assault with metal powder, he did not even see the gun raised to his face. Blood and brains spilled from his head, as his lifeless body was thrown back by the force of the bullet exiting from the back of his skull, taking much of it away in the process.

Neumann walked away, and slipped out of an exit to

disappear into the crowd outside, with his men quickly merging in behind him. Evidently, the gun-shots were not heard clearly, due to the chaotic congregation in the street, and the group quickly dissolved into anonymity.

"I think it is best we leave too, Mr Harland," said Overard, "I don't want to have to explain this to the police any more than you would."

They quickly followed Neumann's example, and left surreptitiously by merging into the crowd gathered outside the building. In their haste, none of them noticed the metal rod embedded in the wall, near a smashed glass light fitting. But, considering how far their plans had already gone astray, this was the least of their concerns.

Chapter 45

Janice Amshaw sat quiet, impassive, unmoving. She could be mistaken for a statue, if not for the traces of tears still visible upon her cheeks.

Harland and Barringer sat on nearby chairs, not quite knowing how to break the silence that had fallen over those assembled in the day room of the Amshaw residence.

After slipping into the crowds gathered outside the Auction Rooms, Harland, Overard, and Barringer had taken Sir Bertram's carriage directly to the Amshaw home, making haste as quickly as they could. The men Neumann had sent to 'visit' Widow Amshaw had gone, but they had left a chaotic and disturbing situation in their wake.

Overard, Harland, and Barringer, had arrived to find the house looking quiet from the outside, as if nothing had happened. Was the whole thing a trick constructed by Neumann to allow him to escape from them? Had they been stupid enough to be fooled so easily by imaginative misdirection?

Harland knocked on the door impatiently and then rang the bell aggressively. He needed to know the truth, needed to get inside, to see Gemma standing there, wondering what on earth had come over him. But Harland's heart sank when the door finally opened.

At the Amshaw residence, it was usual for one of the maids to attend to callers and welcome them into the hallway, to be received by their mistress. Instead, an older servant boy answered the door, and a younger boy stood next to him looking terrified. Both looked ragged – their clothes untidy, their hair uncombed. The younger boy had a poker from the fireplace, and the older of the too held a large kitchen knife.

Harland could see that they were more scared than threatening – he knew immediately something had happened, and perhaps Neumann was telling the truth.

"Thank god! Mr Barringer has come, the older one called out toward the back of the house."

"Mr Barringer, thank god you are here – we have been attacked and beaten by villains."

Harland now saw the red marks on both boy's faces and arms, and the hint of bruising beginning to flourish on their pale skins.

"We tried to stop them, but there were too many of them, they have taken Mistress Gemma."

Harland and Barringer quickly entered and closed the door behind.

"I don't think anyone is coming back, but keep the door bolted and watched." Harland said to the boys.

"The two stable boys." Barringer noted to Harland, as they walked quickly down the hallway into the main day room. There they found Widow Amshaw, distraught and sobbing, and two of her maids trying to comfort her.

"Oh thank God, William, Douglas ... "

Widow Amshaw's voice tailed off, she was too upset to speak. One of the maids took the initiative.

"Oh Sirs, they came upon us – two came to the kitchens by the back doorway, and others forced themselves in when I answered the front-door – I couldn't stop them. The stable boys came running from their rooms at the top of the house, but they were beaten down, and cowed. They were so vicious sir, they threw me against the china cabinet and slapped the kitchen maid, and made her have a feinting fit."

Widow Amshaw managed to grasp some composure, and then took over the explanation.

"Thank you Mary. She is correct in what she says – those men – those beasts – they beat my servants, they grabbed me and threatened me with knives. We barely had time to react. Gemma ran to the priest's hole and hid. But they demanded to know where she was. They knew all about Mr Harland, the auction, everything."

"My God!" Harland exclaimed. "And did they find her?"

"They searched the house top to bottom, and could not find her. They knew she was hiding somewhere downstairs. They shouted out that if Gemma did not come out they were going to slice someone's throat, and I am sure they meant it. She was so brave – she came out and faced them. Then they held us all in the day room, and when they heard the clock chiming the quarter hour before one, they spoke to us once again."

Widow Amshaw paused and dabbed her eyes with a handkerchief. Barringer prompted Mrs Amshaw to continue.

"They said that they were taking Gemma, and that if we contacted the police or called out to neighbours, then they would kill her without thinking twice about it. They said that we had what they wanted, and if a trade could be arranged, then we would get her back unharmed. But, if we tried to cross them, she would be cut up like... like meat at a butcher's shop!"

No-one spoke for a few minutes after this, no-one was sure what to say. Finally, Harland began to explain what had happened at the auction and what they knew of Gemma's abduction. Finally, widow Amshaw replied to Harland's explanations.

"So this is all because of our stupid plotting, and my selfish desire for justice, isn't it! What am I to tell her mother and father if she is harmed? Tell me that..." Widow Amshaw sounded angry – with her self and perhaps with Harland and Barringer. She had been holding a glass of brandy to steady her nerves, but she threw it down onto the wooden floor, smashing the cut-crystal glass.

"Please don't blame yourself." Harland said. "This was not your doing – there is much more at play here than a simple theft and murder. The men we are dealing with are evil, there is no doubt of that, but they have a purpose, and that is to obtain your late husband's Polish machine. It is of great value to them, and I am sure they would not harm Gemma as long as they believe they can trade the machine for her freedom. That may be our only advantage in this whole situation. If anyone is to blame it must surely be me – we should never have considered such a reckless plan – this is my fault."

Finally, Widow Amshaw recovered her demeanour, almost like a storm that had passed. Her mind had become clear, her composure calm.

"We have nothing to do, there is nothing we *can* do. We must wait for the instructions from these evil braggarts and do whatever they say. Please, just get Gemma back here safely, Mr Harland."

"I will, I promise my life upon it. Whatever it takes to assure her safety, consider it done."

Chapter 46

After arriving at the chaotic Amshaw residence and leaving Harland and Barringer, Sir Bertram Overard returned to his small town house in Westminster as quickly as his driver could manage. They paused only to establish that the Amshaw girl had indeed been taken by Neumann. Mayer and Belford Smythe accompanied him, and they now found themselves sat in his study.

The room was rather cold. Overard had not expected to be here for several days, and his servants had not expected to need to keep the fires alive in his absence.

"My apologies, it is rather chilling in here gentlemen. I shall have a fire lit shortly."

Belford Smythe slumped into a leather chair by the as yet redundant fireplace. Mayer stood by the window, seemingly looking out in contemplation.

Belford Smythe began to speak. "I'm dumb-founded Sir Bertram. I cannot understand how they were so well prepared for the situation. All of our plans and machinations were to no avail, and we may speculate that we have in fact achieved nothing but to lay a trap for ourselves, and one in which we have surely been caught."

"I agree Belford. This was entirely unexpected to us. Perhaps we have not been alert enough to the consequences of what we have done. And, furthermore, I fear that we have allowed our disdain for the brutality of these soulless malevolents to lead us to think we were entrapping common thieves and murderers. We have overlooked too much about the sort of people we are dealing with here, in our haste to wreak justice upon them. And now we have put that poor girl into harms way because of it. I promise you, if they harm her, I will never rest until every one of those vermin are hung, drawn and quartered. And I will curse our foolhardy Brittania Club endeavours every day until we do."

Belford began to slip out of his dark mood, spurred by Sir Bertram's bravado.

"I agree Bertram. Damn them to blazes. But undirected anger will achieve nothing good for us. We must seek to regroup our thinking and not merely sit here in a fog of frustration"

"What shall we do then?" Mayer queried, ready as ever to take instructions.

Belford carried on, acknowledging the prompt. "We must use our most familiar resources as well as we can. My newspapers provide valuable opportunities. I will have my best journalists go out and seek out information – facts, gossip – whatever we can gather, that may relate to this mysterious group. They have a multitude of contacts to call upon – the eyes and ears of London will be at our disposal. Someone must have seen something, or known something – we will find out if they do."

Sir Bertram nodded. And then added to the thoughts

Belford Smythe had put forward.

"And perhaps you Mr Mayer can use your knowledge of the German and Jewish community to ask questions too? We would be most grateful if you would do so. I will give you a substantial sum from my cash box before you leave. Use whatever inducements you need to get something, anything at all, that could give us an idea as to the fate of this poor Amshaw girl."

"Very Well Sir, I will do as you ask. I will go directly to Mr Stafford's offices and brief him on what has taken place, then I will turn all my strength to this assignment"

Belford Smythe concurred. "We shall do these things, and anything else that is within our gift. But I must say, gentlemen, that we may have a slim chance of it. Even if we find out where this girl is being held, can we dare attempt to release her without risking a tragic outcome? We have seen how their leader behaves. He will kill without conscience."

"You are right Belford. And I cannot help but think that to try to use force to overwhelm them, during the exchange of the girl and the machine, would end in a similar tragedy. We have to consider the glaringly obvious – we may have been checkmated before we even realised we were engaged in this damned game of chess."

Belford Smythe tapped his fingers on the chair arm, and thought for a moment.

"We must release the young lady safely. Yes, indeed. Keeping the machine is a minor concern. Let us think outside our boundaries for a moment. We have copies of *all* of the plans now. I can only speculate upon who wants this machine, and who it is that employs these foes. They surely do not act on their own behalf. We shall know soon enough, if warships begin to appear with this new artillery compensator. But we shall also have our own device rebuilt from the plans we hold. We can be thankful that the best they can achieve now against the British navy is parity and not superiority."

"Of course you are correct Belford, but it would offer them a significant advantage against any *other* naval power they sought to confront, for whatever martial purpose they have in mind – expansionism, control of trade routes such as the proposed Panama Canal – one can only speculate on the damage that could be wreaked."

Belford Smythe nodded in agreement.

"Nonetheless, our plan must be to give them the machine, and retrieve the Amshaw girl. Perhaps we will discover enough about them to bring a sore reckoning upon them as they try to leave London?"

"Belford, as usual, your analysis is pragmatic and soundly thought through. We can only hope that our enquiries will dredge up something valuable enough in the next twenty four hours or more. Something that may allow us to grasp the upper hand, and change the game. Let us get to work immediately and let there be no rest until all avenues, and all men, are exhausted."

Chapter 47

The morning sun was not yet above the horizon as Sir Bertram Overard's large carriage pulled to a halt at Old Wapping Stairs.

Overard disembarked, followed by Harland, and Belford Smythe. It was barely daylight, the Thames was at high water, and the fog drifted from its filthy expanse into the ice-cold air. In the distance, the sky seemed to be lightening. Inside the carriage, Stafford sat watching the machine, which was strapped down on the floor. Harland leant in and checked it was secure, then spoke to the driver. "Keep the brake on hard. Do not allow the carriage to move any further."

Harland whistled, and soon Mayer came into view, having spent the night in a room in the *'Town Of Ramsgate'*, an inn overlooking the staithes.

"What news do you have?" asked Harland as Mayer approached.

"I have seen nothing all night. I have been over these staithes and the waterfront ten times, and surveyed the streets around about the same number of times. I have seen nothing. If they are coming then they are not here yet, and I can see no-one hiding around here that we would not already know about."

"Then we have nothing to our advantage." Overard stated, sounding downhearted.

"I had hoped our enquiries would have thrown up

some useful information, yet all we know is that our adversaries may have arrived from Bremen after Christmas, and, in spite of our investigations, we know nothing about where they have located themselves."

Belford Smythe tried to reassure Overard.

"We have done all we can Sir Bertram, do not blame yourself. We have what they want, and we can trade that for the safe return of the young lady. That *is* why we are here after all. Their instructions were quite clear."

"Yes, of course. It just galls me to see them play us for fools, Belford, my good friend."

Harland tried to maintain a calm detachment, and reprised the expectations for what was to come next.

"So we know, from the instructions sent to us, that we were to be here at no later than six am, and to bring the machine with us. We are to wait here until we are met, and the exchange will take place without bloodshed if we act entirely as directed. Those were the instructions, and we seem to have no option now but to wait and play out the script."

"We could still use our revolvers." Smythe noted.

"No," Overard barked. "We cannot risk the girl, even after the exchange is made, there could be blood spilled on both sides. I feel the same way, believe me, but we shall not use our weapons unless Mr Harland calls upon us to do so. Unless they make some drastic miscalculation, then we cannot assume anything we might attempt to do has not already been anticipated by them. They have already proven themselves to be adepts in that respect"

The group stood quietly for a few minutes. Up river, peaking above the banks of fog, they could see the silhouette of the new Tower Bridge, not yet fully constructed. Muffled sounds carried across the river, of boats firing up their boilers and sounding their horns. There was a pale illumination to the sky now, and it was beginning to become lighter.

Mayer interrupted the silence. "I believe I can hear a carriage. Listen ..."

Mayer was correct. The distant sound of carriage wheels on a cobbled street broke the relative silence of the early morning. It grew closer as they listened.

"I think this is it." said Overard.

Smythe returned to their own carriage, drew his revolver, and sat within, joining Stafford to guard the Polish machine. Stafford had a 12-bore shotgun, his favourite grouse-shooting firearm. He also had an army service revolver.

"Be ready for any trickery Belford. If there is any foul-play, it is up to us to protect the machine. The girl's life depends upon it." Belford nodded, and sat back so he could look out of the window without being seen too easily.

The carriage drew up alongside Pier Head, where the group had been instructed to wait. Four men climbed down out of the carriage, followed by their master. As they moved toward Harland's party, he could see that they were mostly of the same group from the auction house confrontation.

No-one spoke for a few moments. Instead, they sized each other up, observing the potential for serious miscalculation. They could see that Overard had a revolver, and Mayer held his usual large bladed knife, which he had sharpened carefully during the night whilst sitting watch.

Harland, Overard, and Mayer could see that their visitors also had an array of weaponry. The one in charge had a gun. One of his men had a shotgun with a sawn-down barrel, the others had various knives, and some wore knuckle-dusters.

"Gentlemen, I am glad to see you have followed my instructions. I am sure you wish to see your young lady returned without harm. So I hope we can proceed as gentlemen and not have cause to let any more blood flow?"

Neumann was uncommonly restrained on this occasion. He would happily slit the girl's throat and shoot down the whole group. However, he feared that any mishap now would prevent him from retrieving the machine. He had spent too long pursuing the damned contraption, halfway across Europe and back again. Now he finally had it almost in his possession. He would play his cards carefully for now – he was holding all the aces after all.

"We want to see the girl. Is she in the carriage?" Overard demanded, trying to take some control of the situation...

"She is not sir. I would not make it so easy for you to make a grab to release her. The carriage is empty – go see for yourself."

Mayer quickly ran over to the carriage and checked the truth of the matter. The carriage was indeed empty.

"It is empty – the girl is not here."

"Then what in hell-fire are you playing at sir?" Overard became angry, and his hand twitched at his revolver.

Neumann did not flinch, but spoke in his usual slow and patronising way, which he had a habit of falling into whenever he knew he had the upper hand.

"Please, please... You English gentlemen are so quick to make presumptions. The girl *is* here, she is just not in the carriage. Now, you will allow one of my men to check the device is here and you shall see that I speak truly."

"Very Well, said Harland, but our men are well armed."

Harland called out to Stafford and Smythe in their carriage.

"Let their man see the machine."

After a short while, the man returned to the group. As he approached, Harland now observed that he was the same man from the auction house with the buttons that matched the one he found after his Victoria's murder. He despised him, but held his emotions in check. There was more at stake than his own hatred for this one man.

Neumann, meanwhile, was becoming impatient.

"Well Geltz, what did you see..."

"It is there sir, and it looks exactly like the sale catalogue pictures."

"Good. Then we are in a position to make a trade my friends."

Neumann took from his pocket a brass whistle, similar to those used by the train guards at most stations. He blew it hard three times, directing the sound out toward the water.

A distant whistle sounded back twice in return. It came from within the bank of fog on the river. And presently, the sound of oars could be heard pushing through the water. The river was just past high tide, and the current was now weakly beginning to turn and flow again toward the estuary and to the sea beyond. Soon a boat came into view, rowed by two men. And then two further boats emerged, side by side, from the fog, tied to the first by a long rope that hugged the water as it traversed between their hulls. A small lamp was lit on one of the second boats. In the dim glow, Harland could see Gemma's face. He could also see a further boatman in the adjacent vessel. He was holding the two other boats together with his hands, as if ready to push away and leave Gemma alone at the assigned moment.

Harland could see that Gemma was tied up and also tied to the boat itself. It bobbed side to side as it was towed by the first vessel.

"So you see gentlemen, I have kept my side of the bargain – there is the girl, I assure you she is unharmed."

"Thank God." said Overard.

Neumann whistled once more, and the first boat stopped at the foot of a steep set of stairs running down to the waterline. The first pair of oarsmen disembarked, trailing the long rope behind them, still attached to the last two boats at the other end. They pushed their own boat away and it drifted into the staithes wall, pinned there by the current against a timber post. Harland and his friends assumed that the oarsman was readying to tie the remaining boats to a mooring ring. But their relief at receiving their part of the bargain soon turned to horror.

Suddenly, the remaining oarsman, still out on the river, smashed a boat hook down into the planking of the boat Gemma was in – the one which she was tied to, and unable to leave. He pushed her boat away from his and rowed quickly into the fog, disappearing across the river. Water began to flow into Gemma's boat. The disembarked oarsmen ran away from the staithes and threw the end of the rope down the stone steps. It began to slowly slip, from one step to another, down toward the waterline.

"Now we will exchange goods gentlemen- and I suggest we make haste. That boat will sink within minutes. Your men will leave the carriage and we shall take it, if you don't mind. Then you can save your dear lady from drowning. Or we can stand here pointing guns at each others heads whilst she sinks to the bottom of the Thames."

There was no choice. Neumann and his group had

guns on them, and they would surely use them if they had too – then who would save Gemma?

"Do as they say," shouted Overard, "leave the carriage and step away. Driver – dismount and stand aside."

Overard could see that they had been played once again. Who could have expected this? He could see that the boat was sinking fast, and they must act quickly together – there was no time to salvage any last minute recovery of the machine, or start a gun fight with their adversaries.

Stafford and Smythe stood back as Neumann's rabble mounted the carriage and prepared to depart, guns ready in case of any last minute violent assault.

Harland ran down the steep stone stairway, grabbed the end of the rope just before it slipped out of reach, and then began to pull in the rope as quickly as he could. It was much longer than he had expected, and heavy too. The current in the river was now beginning to gather strength, the rope was slipping in spite of his grip, as he pulled it hand over hand, seemingly bringing Gemma closer to safety with each moment, yet far too slowly.

"She is sinking fast Mr Harland!" Mayer shouted, as he ran down the stairs behind him. He jumped into the now empty first boat and grasped the oars.

"Keep pulling her in, I will row to meet her and try to untie her." Mayer rowed hard and fast. He was strong, and fired up with adrenalin as his oars cut through the water repeatedly.

"The boat is nearly swamped Mr Mayer, row faster!" Overard shouted.

Mayer pushed himself beyond his limits, rowing to meet the sinking boat as Harland, and now Overard too, pulled on the rope, bringing the two vessels closer and closer to each other mid-stream. Finally, Mayer reached the sinking boat, and he wrapped the trailing rope around an oar, using it to lever one end of the fast sinking boat up against his own. Gemma was now half underwater, screaming in pure fear. She would surely slip under the water within seconds, and still tied to the boat – she would sink with it.

Mayer jumped across to the flooded boat just as its hull slipped under the water. There was nothing left now to stop it sinking under its own weight. But Mayer had managed to grab the rope with which Gemma was tied to the mid-seat, and if the boat went down then he would go with it too.

Water washed around Gemma's shoulders and she gasped to take a breath before sinking below the waves.

"William..." she shouted.

Harland and Overard had almost pulled the boat to the staithe now. But the water was deep here and the boat, including Gemma and Mayer, was now completely underwater. The hull was now immersed too deeply and was too heavy to resurface, no matter how hard they pulled the rope. It was being pressed against the staithes downstream of the stone staircase by the gathering current. Harland and Overard could not let go, for fear of losing the boat all together.

In the dark and dirty water, Mayer could see nothing. However, he could feel the rope around Gemma's wrists, binding here to the mid-seat. He grabbed at his boot for his knife, blindly trying to locate it in the darkness. He thanked god he found it still there, and in moments the newly sharpened blade sliced at the rope. Finally it severed, and he could feel Gemma moving freely. Their heads were now several feet under the water. He pushed Gemma upwards to the surface, toward what little daylight was guiding them, and then struggled to swim toward it himself.

Stafford threw a rope out to Mayer, who had now been carried some feet down stream, and pressed along the stone wall, running past the steps, by the flow of the turning tide. Luckily, he gripped the rope tightly and was quickly hauled back to the steps and up to safety.

Harland grabbed Gemma, and pulled her onto the lowest step above the water. She coughed out mouthfuls of water then spluttered as she began to breathe again. She was safe now. Gemma could not speak. She was too cold and shocked at her ordeal. They brought her up the steps and sat her in the carriage left behind by Neumann, readying it to depart as soon as it could.

Overard spoke. "Thank god Mr Harland, we have her."

"And we must thank god for Mr Mayer too, I think." Harland replied.

"But they have beaten us Mr Harland – I don't even care now, this whole business has made me sicken of intrigue. Let them run away with their spoils, like rats."

Harland said nothing for a few moments. Instead, he took out his pocket watch, and stared at the picture of his Victoria set into the lid.

Overard saw what Harland was looking at. He was suddenly embarrassed.

"Mr Harland, how foolish- I apologise for my insensitivity. That Geltz fellow – he killed your beloved Victoria. No doubt, he had a hand in the Amshaw murder, and the others - the whole lot of them are brutal killers, and yet now they are free. And worst of all you have no justice and no peace of mind – it is outrageous misfortune. Come, we must regroup ourselves and pursue them..."

Harland did not react. Instead, he closed his watch and placed it in his pocket. In the distance, they could now see their requisitioned carriage speeding away along the waterfront road, the fog now having begun to lift away in the early sun.

"Time is a great healer Sir Bertram. And all good things come to he who waits..."

Overard seemed puzzled by Harland's apparent dispassionate demeanour in view of Neumann's escape.

But at that very moment, as he watched the carriage shrinking into the distance, Sir Bertram heard a tremendous cacophony. It was like a splitting of wood, but not just one sound. Rather, it was akin to a whole fusillade of violent impacts. He stood incredulous as the carriage appeared to be torn apart – turned inside out – fragments of wood and metal flying in every direction, the sound of pieces of glass shattering and cascading onto stonework. Metal sounded against metal, and metal pieces rang out as they scattered across stonework and cobbles. The driver appeared to be thrown off and fell badly, not getting up. Overard fancied he could hear shouts of pain too. But they were short lived. And then, nothing but the sound of horses clattering to a halt, followed by silence. Without a driver, they had run themselves into a dead end, and now stood skittishly, unsure what to do without direction. Sir Bertram was astounded.

"My God Mr Harland, have you been busy again?"

Chapter 48

It was some days later that Sir Bertram met Harland again, at the Old Wapping Stairs. Only then could he come to fully understand what had happened that earlier morning. After the shocking events of a few days earlier, Harland had rushed Gemma away in the remaining carriage, with Mayer's assistance. Overard, Stafford, and Smythe found their own means to get away to the refuge of Sir Bertram's town house, and they had been left only to speculate about what had happened.

"Mr Harland. I am pleased to see you in good health. I trust the young lady is well?"

"She has been rather ill with the river water, Sir Bertram, but I am assured that she is recovering, thankfully. I have no doubt you want to know exactly what occurred here a few days ago?"

"Indeed, I would Mr Harland, though you may choose to keep your secrets, and I will not press you upon it, if that is your preference."

Harland sat at the top of the steps, and Overard joined him, resting his sliver-topped cane on the third step down. The sun warmed their faces as they looked out across the river.

"Once I realised that the one they called Geltz was the very same villain to have killed my Victoria, I was bent on his destruction. I would have killed him with my bare hands had they not brought Gemma into all of this. I wanted to save her, but I could also not bear to think of them getting away with all that they have done."

"Of course, I can imagine how you felt. But what happened in that carriage on that morning – it was like some sort of cannonade, yet there was no smoke or fire, and from where did the fusillade come?"

"I think you may have guessed that those events were my doing Sir Bertram. Once I realised that we had been out-manoeuvred, I saw a way forward, I worked day and night from the moment we left the auction house. Initially I thought to duplicate the machine and give them a copy. That is why I told them that the vault would be locked for two days. But then I realised the opportunity to make all things right in one grand deception. You might say I decided to build a Trojan horse."

"I begin to see now Mr Harland... So the machine they took away was not the machine at all, it just looked identical to it..."

"Yes, it certainly looked identical from the outside, but what they did not know, or suspect, was that they had carried away a rather more interesting mechanism than the one we thankfully still have in our possession. Do you remember how the machine was able to react to motions? How it could somehow recognise rocking actions, and then react to them?"

"I do remember, most clearly Mr Harland..."

"I copied that part of the machine, and adjusted it so

that when it was activated, it would recognise the motions of a carriage, and then trigger a timing mechanism with an allowance of a few minutes. When the timer expired, it released the springs to the other part of the mechanism."

"And what was this other part, Mr Harland?"

"Within the casing of the machine, I placed eight spring-loaded devices – wound to an immense point of stress – practically to the breaking point of the steel itself. Each of these was arranged so that it could eject eight steel rods in one moment, metal bolts honed to a fine point and sharpened on their edges like rapiers. A spring can hold tremendous energy, almost like a cannon or rifle shot. You have seen how my coat sleeve can project a metal arrow, this is the same, but even more powerful, perhaps by ten-fold or more. When the movement of their carriage, speeding away, set in motion the timer, their fate was sealed. It had occurred to me that they might make an escape with the machine without returning Gemma to us, or after attacking us perhaps. This was my way of ensuring that they would not escape justice, no matter what their strategy."

"Ingenious." Overard said. "So as they sped away in their carriage, they must have begun to wonder why the machine was making sounds as it prepared itself for retribution?"

"That would most certainly be the case Sir Bertram. And so, when the time ran out, the metal rods exploded out of the machine, cutting through anything in their path, and sending shards of the wooden casement, and its glazing, everywhere in the process, multiplying the fusillade of projectiles within the confined space of the carriage."

"So they died in a hail of razor sharp splinters and cold steel – launched by the very machine they have sought to kill so many to retrieve... Therein lies a certain sweet irony for their reversal of fate. And so, your Victoria, Widow Amshaw, and many others have restitution. I hope it gives you some comfort to know that those responsible for such evil are finally ended."

"A little, Sir Bertram. A little ..."

Sir Bertram stood up once again, and walked a few paces away from the top of the stone flight of stairs.

"I have seen many things in my life Mr Harland. Our great country has become the grandest of man's achievements. Who knows what advantage that machine may have given to our enemies had they succeeded. This Empire of ours ... it is too precious to give away, or to fall at the feet of such men as those. We should guard it well, or else we are destined to become subordinate subsidiaries to some future European imperialists. You have done a great service to your country."

Sir Bertram paused for a moment. He felt he should perhaps leave Harland to his own thoughts now.

"And what will you do now Mr Harland, now that you have the justice you have been seeking? Will you return to your clocks, make a new life with the young Gemma Perhaps?"

"That is something I cannot say... This city! It has so much evil, and I cannot rest in my bed knowing there is work to be done – wrongs to be righted. Perhaps my true purpose is not to make watches, but to 'make watch'. And so that is what I shall do, until I feel my work is done."

Harland Opened his pocket watched once again, and looked at his beloved Victoria, forgetting his company. Overard turned and began to walk away, but as he did so he spoke once more. "You are an extraordinary fellow, Mr Harland. I am sure we will be meeting again."

Harland nodded. "Indeed, Sir Bertram, perhaps it is only a matter of time..."

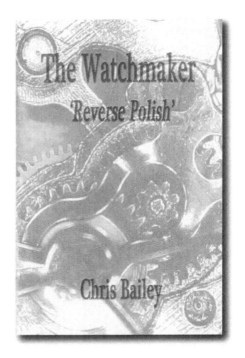

A first Novel, by Chris Bailey.